Hang the Men STACKS High

Hang the Men High

Noel Loomis
and
Paul Leslie Peil

Thorndike Press • Waterville, Maine

Published in 2003 by arrangement with
Golden West Literary Agency.

Thorndike Press Large Print Paperback Series.

The tree indicium is a trademark of Thorndike Press.

The text of this Large Print edition is unabridged.
Other aspects of the book may vary from the original edition.

Set in 16 pt. Plantin by Al Chase.

Printed in the United States on permanent paper.

Library of Congress Cataloging-in-Publication Data

Loomis, Noel M., 1905–
    Hang the men high / by Noel Loomis and Paul Leslie Peil.
      p. cm.
    ISBN 0-7862-5045-3 (lg. print : sc : alk. paper)
    1. Executions and executioners — Fiction.   2. Large type
books.   I. Peil, Paul Leslie.   II. Title.
    PS3523.O554 H36 2003
    813'.54—dc21
                                             2002072894

to HOMER CROY, *a listener*

Introduction

In April of 1875, Fort Smith was a case-hardened, frontier town. Straight west from town, across the "Arkansa" River not much farther than a man with a good arm could throw an Arkansas toothpick, was the Indian Territory, which had had no law for forty years. The Territory — or the Nations, as it would soon be called — was a sanctuary for the cast-offs of all North America. Men on the scout, men with prices on their heads, the depraved and degenerate, rapists, perverts, killers — all these swarmed into the Indian Territory and proceeded to create a veritable hell in the blackjack.

The year 1875 was only ten years after the Civil War, and most of the rebel states were still in the "reconstruction" period. The panic of 1875 and the grasshopper plagues of '73 and '74 had slowed their economy from a crawl to a dead stop, and there were times when it seemed nobody really gave a damn about anything.

What kind of man would it take to bring law to this country? Heavyhandedness alone would not put the fear of God into the Territory. Something more was needed —

something beyond even iron will. There was required a man with a fierce single-mindedness of purpose and an unwavering belief in the absolute rightness of his course — plus an unswerving determination to impose it on others. Some might have said, and many did say, that such a man was a fanatic.

This is the story of that man — the man who whipped the Indian Territory into submission, and of why and how he did it, and of what it did to him.

Chapter 1

Isaac Parker stood back from the rail of the *Indian Maiden*, his silk hat pulled squarely down on his head. The boat eased into the Fort Smith dock, and Parker, scanning the shambling town, held his big Bible more tightly under his arm. He stole a glance at his wife, a little anxious as to how she would react.

She was a large woman but she carried herself well. Mary had always been conscious of her position. She wore a stylish red velvet dress that had taken fifteen yards of material; it had a bustle and a vast hemline, and great loops of material draped from front to back. Over it but only partly subduing it was a brown cloak, and he knew from the way it hung that she was standing stiff and straight. He glanced at her brown hat and then at her face. "What do you think of it, Mary?" he asked hopefully.

"It's terrible," she said without hesitation. "It's an awful letdown after Washington. It's dirty, littered, uncouth."

He took a slow, deep breath. "It will improve."

He wondered if it would. It certainly didn't show much promise: a tiny dock crowded with slatternly women, unshaved men in shapeless hats, blanket Indians; a muddy street which, under the heat of the sun, gave off eddying swirls of vapor.

"I like it," said Charlie, four years old. "It has Indians."

Parker was sweating in his heavy wool suit and double-breasted black coat with its square-cut bottom. "It's hotter here than in St. Louis," he said.

The second mate, somewhere on the Texas deck above them, shouted an order. Two boathands threw a big rope over the side; it was grabbed by half a dozen men on the dock, and they made a turn around a capstan.

At the end of the dock, their huge iron tires deep in the mud, stood three freight wagons, each with four yoke of oxen lying comfortably in the mud alongside the lead chain. At the nearest wagon a bearded teamster, wading the mud in knee-high leather boots, began to kick the bulls to their feet while two Negroes brought a big oaken ox-yoke from the wagon and laid it across the necks of the leading pair.

The *Indian Maiden* hit the end of the rope, and the rope creaked. Mary moved forward to steady herself at the rail, still staring at the unappetizing crowd on the dock. The stern began to swing out, but brought up against a second rope, then began to settle back as the men on the dock pulled her in closer.

Parker, watching with interest, heard a step behind him. The first mate looked down. "Good trip," he said.

"Yes. Very good." Parker indicated the wagons. "What are they here for?"

The mate studied him. Parker was six feet tall, broad-shouldered and a little spare. He was thirty-seven years old, with brown hair, blue eyes, a very natty brown moustache and an imperial goatee. The mate said finally, "Those wagons belong to Garth's Freight Lines. They say Bentley Garth is making a right smart piece of money out of them, for nobody else could ever haul stuff to the Indians without heavy losses."

"What are they hauling?" asked Parker.

"These here are going to take sixteen thousand pounds of winter clothes to We-wo-ka for the Seminoles and down to Doaksville for the Choctaws."

Parker considered. "It's early for winter, isn't it?"

The mate laughed shortly. "This stuff is for *last* winter."

Parker frowned, puzzled. "What good will it do now?"

The mate shrugged. "Who cares? They're nothin' but Injuns."

Parker said stiffly, "It is my understanding the government made a contract with the Indians."

The mate looked at him. "They understand a lot of things in Washington," he said. "Out here we have to live with 'em."

Parker said hotly, "A man's word is his word, no matter where he gives it."

"All right, mister, all right. Nobody out here kept the Injuns from getting their winter clothes last fall. The entire shipment is below decks here, and we picked it up from some Philadelphia freighters. It's not our doing. Maybe you better take another look in Washington. Nobody there gives a damn what happens to *anybody* out here — white *or* Indian."

"I assure you," Parker said spiritedly, "that is not true. President Grant himself is very concerned over affairs in this country."

The mate snorted. He glanced at Mary, who was eyeing him with some scorn, and touched his worn seaman's cap. "Pardon me, ma'am. I didn't mean to let a bad word slip out where you could hear it." She didn't answer, and he went to the stern of the boat.

The boat was tight against the cotton-bale bumpers now, and had settled down. Parker

12

turned to look west across the river. Over there, he realized, was the notorious Indian Territory — Parker's special charge from now on. "Order must be established," the President had said. "The entire Territory is a place of murder and rape. Nor do I want any advantage taken of the Indians or Negroes. Many of the criminals are whites, and they must be apprehended and punished all alike."

So that was the Territory — a flat, dry-looking area of grass scattered with clumps of trees. He turned back as two Negroes brought up the gangplank. Southeast stretched Fort Smith's only real street — Garrison Avenue, he had heard it called by Banks, the drummer from Cincinnati who played poker all night and slept all day.

From his travels in Missouri Parker recognized it as a typical frontier town. He heard the bell-like clang of a hammer on an anvil from somewhere not far away. Saddled horses stood before saloons, and two empty spring wagons splattered through the mud as their drivers came down to watch the unloading. Four girls stood in a cluster on the wharf — girls very colorfully and fashionably dressed, wearing small hats and holding parasols.

Mary sniffed. "*That* kind of woman ap-

13

parently is the best Fort Smith can boast."

"Now, Mary," he said placatingly.

"You will have to admit, Isaac Parker, that it will be a terrible place after living in Washington all these years."

He took refuge in his duty. "You must remember, Mary, that the President said there is a great need here for justice, and he sent me here to bring order out of chaos because he had implicit trust in my ability and my honesty."

She could not very well answer that without impugning his honesty. Nor did she try. "You have had no experience as a judge," she said more mildly.

"I practiced law before I went to Congress," he reminded her. "I expect to learn as I go."

They went down the gangplank, Charlie, big-eyed and scared, backed against his mother. Three dirty little boys in overalls spotted him in his fine coat and knee-pants, his be-ribboned hat and white-collared shirt. "Yah, lookit the damn Yankee!" they cried in unison. One took a few steps forward and swung his arm.

Charlie broke and ran. He was only four years old, and, although he was big for his age, Parker saw that he was terrified by this unexpected hostility. Parker took a step after him but Charlie darted along the edge of the dock, all three of the boys after him now. There was a swirl of fancy dresses and long black curls, and one of the painted ladies ran forward, shrieking at the boys in an unidentifiable tongue. She tripped the first one and batted the second one on the side of the head; the third one swung back out of reach.

Charlie ran to the woman and clung to her skirts.

Parker reached them. "I'll take care of him now," he said. "We are very grateful to you."

"You're welcome, mister," she said coolly, and he looked at her face in some astonishment. Here was no painted woman but a very pretty Indian girl, slender, but round and full, with olive-colored skin and black eyes. Parker nodded and backed away.

"I like the lady," said Charlie. "She chased those boys away."

Parker nodded absently; Mrs. Parker said nothing.

They had to move on. Behind them, other passengers were coming down the gangplank. Some were greeted carelessly; some were embraced; others apparently knew where they were going and hurried by.

Parker took Mary's arm. "Here's the hack," he said gently, and steered her toward it.

A man hurried out of the crowd to confront them. He was not as tall as Parker but he was equally spare. He was shaven but he had a fringe of reddish whiskers under his chin from ear to ear. "You're Judge Parker?" he demanded. "Judge Isaac C. Parker?"

"Yes."

"I'm Weaver, editor of the *Western Independent* in Fort Smith." He glanced at Mary.

Parker bowed briefly. "Mary, may I present Mr. Weaver?"

She smiled perfunctorily.

Weaver swept off his broad-brimmed gray felt hat. "Madam, it is a pleasure." Abruptly he replaced the hat and turned back to Parker. "Now, as an editor, may I ask your honor's opinion of conditions in the Indian Territory?"

"Bad," Parker said. "Very bad. The President is very much concerned. He insists that the Territory be made a law-abiding portion of the United States."

Weaver's stare seemed somewhat sardonic. "Do you think you can do that, sir?"

Parker rather liked Weaver's soft drawl, but he wasn't sure about the man's manner.

16

He gripped the big Bible more tightly. "I expect to," he said.

"How?"

Parker cleared his throat. "By punishing the guilty," he said, and looked over Weaver's head. "It is not the severity of the punishment but its certainty that checks crime."

Weaver stared at him. "You may change your mind about that, Judge. Hangin's too good for a lot of our citizens."

Parker didn't answer. He wasn't quite ready to take up this phase of the matter.

"Well," said Weaver, "I must be off. Press day is coming. Thank you, judge."

"You're quite welcome," Parker said formally.

Weaver started away, but he stopped to touch his hat brim. "Afternoon, Si. Afternoon, Miz Hampton."

"Afternoon, Gil."

Parker saw a pleasant-faced man of about thirty, dressed in overalls and driving a light wagon with a span of mules. Beside him was a very comely woman dressed in gingham with sun-bonnet to match.

"Thought we'd get here in time to see the *Maiden* come in," said the man called Si, "but I guess we didn't make it."

"Nothing special," said Weaver.

"Only thing ever happens in *this* country that isn't trouble."

"How are the children?"

"The three oldest ones are home. The little one we brung with us."

Weaver said pleasantly, "Well, so long, Si. So long, Miz Hampton."

Hampton slapped the reins on the mules' rumps. "I planted some pertaters," he called to Weaver. "If they make a crop I'll bring in a bushel on my subscription."

Weaver waved. "Be very welcome," he said. "My family eats too."

It *was* different from Washington, Parker thought as he helped Mary up into the hack. Very different.

"Well, well, judge. You made it, I see," said the wheezy voice of Banks, the drummer from Cincinnati. He climbed into the hack, puffing a little, and looked at Charlie. "Kinda big for four years old," he guffawed, "but not too big to make friends."

Out of the corner of his eye Parker saw Mary's back stiffen. Banks' voice subsided. "That there girl was Indian Rose. She runs a house down on the Row." He looked up and saw Mrs. Parker's indignant glance. "Beg your pardon, ma'am. No offense."

Mrs. Parker said haughtily, "Such women should be kept off the streets when decent

18

women are in town."

"Beggin' your pardon, ma'am, there *are* decent women in town. But Indian Rose and her girls have to have *some* recreation. Anyway, it's local custom. Long as they stay out of the saloons and get off the streets by nine o'clock, nobody bothers 'em. And I'll say they mind their business, ma'am. You won't see any better-behaved girls west of the Mississippi."

Parker moistened his lips uncomfortably. He said soothingly, "All this will be taken care of in good time, Mary."

"You'll find more important things, judge, I'll give you odds."

The driver climbed into the front seat. "All aboard fer the *ho*-tel!" he sang out, and cracked his buggy whip over the mules' backs.

They started off with a lurch as the wheels broke away from the sucking mud. They went half a block down the middle of Garrison Avenue, and the driver turned around. "All comfortable back there?"

"As comfortable as can be expected," Mary said stonily.

"I'll get your baggage off the boat in a couple of hours," the driver said. "Hey, what's that up ahead?"

On one side, not a hundred feet from the hack, a burst of hoarse curses came from the swinging blue doors of the House of Lords Saloon. The driver of the hack hauled back on the reins. Si Hampton and his wife were just passing the saloon.

A dark-skinned man with uncut, straight black hair staggered out backward, a pistol in his hand, shouting at somebody inside. He floundered an instant, turned around, saw Hampton, and shouted:

"Get down outa that wagon!"

Hampton stared at him.

"Down, you —"

Hampton rose slowly, dropping the reins over the dashboard. With his eyes on the man with the pistol and seemingly hypnotized, he stepped over the side of the wagon-box, found the wheel-hub with one foot, and stepped down into the mud.

The black-haired man pushed him in the chest and knocked him flat on his back in the mud. Then he vaulted into the seat, snatched up the reins, and cracked the whip over the mules.

The wife was on her feet. The man took one contemptuous look at her, planted his foot in her stomach, and shoved her backward into the street. Shouting at the top of his voice, he lashed the mules into a soggy gallop. The woman, getting up, began to scream, and started after the wagon, floundering in the mud. Hampton was standing now, white-faced and apparently petrified. The woman ran after the wagon and caught it at the cross street. There she hung onto the tail-gate and ran as long as she could, until she dropped exhausted and lay sobbing in the mud.

Parker was down, running heavily. He was the first to reach the woman. She was moaning something about her baby when Parker helped her to her feet. Her starched and ironed dress was covered with mud.

Parker wheeled. A saddled horse stood tied to a hitching iron, and Parker put his hands on the reins.

"Whose horse you takin', mister?"

Parker hesitated, then straightened slowly. A squatly built, swarthy-faced man with cold black eyes was pointing a rifle at him.

Parker said, "I'm going after that man in the wagon," and bent over again to untie the reins.

"You got the wrong horse," said the cold voice, and Parker jerked as he felt something in his side. This time he straightened carefully. He looked at the man, who had heavy eyebrows and very little forehead. "That —" For a moment he was too wrought up with indignation to speak co-

21

herently. He gesticulated toward the wagon.

"You got the wrong horse," the cold voice said again.

At last Parker saw the man was deadly serious, and he turned away slowly, aghast at the realization that in Fort Smith a man with a rifle was able to overrule all the laws of decency and justice.

Chapter 2

For a moment Parker was too shaken to speak. Hampton was still standing there, white-faced. "Why did you let him do it?" Parker demanded.

"I can't —" The farmer shook his head, seeming to search for words. "I can't stand up to the Kiamichi Kid," he said finally. "There's no law in the Territory, and the Kid takes what he wants. Anybody who gets in his way gets killed."

Parker looked around at the crowd that had collected. "Is nobody going to the rescue of that baby?" he demanded.

They looked at him blankly. Nobody answered.

"I —" Parker looked back. The low-browed man still held the rifle. "I'll see you're put in prison for this!" Parker shouted, almost beside himself.

"It's my horse," the man said flatly.

Parker jumped back in the hack. "Get us to the hotel as fast as possible!" he ordered the driver.

Another man made a leap at the iron step. His foot hit it. He grabbed the seat-iron and climbed in. "Your honor," he said, "what are you going to do now?"

Parker glared at Weaver. Then he gathered his wits with an effort. "First, I am going to find out where the law enforcement officials are."

The hack lurched forward.

Weaver said, "What law enforcement officials?"

"The U.S. marshal, of course."

Weaver looked at him coolly. "In the first place, the town of Fort Smith is not in the Indian Territory and the U.S. marshal has no jurisdiction here. In the second place, a marshal is no good without a court to back him up."

Parker's jaws tightened. "Who was the man with the rifle?"

"John Duck, one of the Kid's men. That's why nobody would chase the Kid."

Parker shook his head. "It's incredible."

"Not so incredible. The Kid has killed several men already. He's only nineteen years old and afraid of nothing. He takes what he wants, including wives. Hampton was lucky to get off as easy as he did."

"What will happen to the baby?"

Weaver shrugged. "Who knows that? Nobody can read the Kiamichi Kid's mind. Nothing he *does* makes any sense."

The hack was drawing up in front of the

hotel, and Parker, still finding it unbelievable, demanded, "Do you mean to say that this kind of thing goes on right in sight of everybody?"

"There's nothing to stop it," said Weaver, getting out. He helped Mrs. Parker down. "What are your plans now, your honor?"

Parker sensed something unpleasant in the way Weaver kept saying "your honor," but he let it pass. "I'm going to get a deputy and go after him," he said uncompromisingly.

Weaver followed him to the wooden porch of the hotel. "Remember one thing, your honor. Most of us in Fort Smith want law and order as much as you claim to."

Parker turned in anger, but Weaver was stalking away. Parker stood there for a moment, pondering. Why was everyone in Fort Smith so hostile toward him?

Perhaps it resulted from his political affiliation. Naturally the people of Arkansas, being violently Democratic, would resent the appointment of a Republican. Parker resolved, as he stood there looking down at the muddy town, that he would show them how impartial a Republican judge could be. He would have only two guides: the law of the land and the Word of God. And of those two, his mother had always said, the Word

25

of God was the more important. The Word of God he knew quite well; the law of the land he would learn. In the meantime, he had the fortification of common sense.

The way was plain. He would apply his good sense and mature judgment to every criminal brought before him, and he would see to it that justice was meted out accordingly. The way was clear: if a man should be innocent, he must be freed; if he should be guilty, he must pay the penalty.

The sun was low across the Arkansas River. Over there was the Indian Territory, where a man's property was his own only as long as he could protect it, where his life might be destroyed on a whim, where even his wife's honor was safe only as long as he could defend her with a rifle. Parker's jaw hardened. That would be ended; the Territory would become a place where any man could travel or settle down without fear for his life. Standing there on the hotel porch, Parker made that silent promise, and, having made it, felt a great satisfaction descend on him. He was impatient to begin his work.

He turned, his head high, and went inside. He mounted the stairs and doubled back to reach their room. He knocked, and Mary called, "Who is it?"

"Judge Parker," he said with a surge of pride.

She opened the door. "I've been lonesome without you."

He looked at Charlie sitting quietly in a chair. "I take it you had to punish him."

"He couldn't go out in the mud, of course," said Mary, "and he was too rowdy for one little room."

He nodded gravely, and turned to other matters. "What did you think when I answered, 'Judge Parker'?"

She smiled. "For a moment I didn't know what to think, but then of course I realized that really is your title." She held him at arm's length, her blue eyes taking him in. "A very fine judge you should make, too."

"I will do my best. Now —" Abruptly he was businesslike. "I have work to do."

"Tonight?" She looked disappointed. "I thought we'd have a glass of wine to celebrate our arrival."

"I'm sorry, Mary. It's impossible. I might as well start tonight showing them what law and order is like."

She went to the window. "Do you think you can do it, Isaac?"

"Certainly," he said. "I *will* do it. And Mary —" He went to her and tenderly put his arms around her. "Don't worry about what you have seen today. Remember, it is a great opportunity and that is why we are here. We shall make Fort Smith both safe and attractive."

She turned in his arms. "I hope it won't take too long, Isaac," she said, and her voice was on the verge of breaking.

He patted her softly. "You've had a terribly hard trip, and everything looks much worse than it really is."

"Isaac," she said, holding his coat lapels, "it *couldn't* be any worse than it is."

He looked down at her and knew that she was close to hysteria. "You'd better have a glass of wine," he said. "I'm going over to the marshal's office."

He got directions from the hotel clerk. "You go right down Garrison Avenue here back to the river. The old fort is on the left, and the buildings are used for the courthouse and jail. Just walk in and make yourself at home. There's nothing to prevent it."

"It would appear," Parker said thoughtfully, "that the federal court is something of a haphazard institution in Fort Smith."

From under the worn and unpainted desk the clerk took a pair of black sateen sleeve guards. "Since it moved here from Van Buren," he said, pulling on one of the sleeve guards and carefully adjusting the elastic

28

above his elbow, "it's been the same: bring criminals in here and turn 'em loose. What happens? Men like the Kiamichi Kid go up the street to celebrate. That's why we got eleven saloons in Fort Smith." He pulled on the other sleeve guard. "Sometimes I think the judge was in cahoots with the saloon keepers — brought in the outlaws just so the saloons would have some business — along with Indian Rose and her outfits along the Row."

"What about Indian Rose?" asked Parker. "I saw her today — and she looked like a very pretty and decent girl."

"She's pretty, all right. Men go crazy over her. But I wouldn't trust her." He leaned over and spoke in a whisper. "She's a twin sister of the Kiamichi Kid."

Parker drew back, biting his lip. "I didn't know that."

"Sure. Some say she runs a house here to make money to bail the Kid out whenever he's brought in."

"Do you mean she buys his freedom?" Parker asked harshly.

"Hard to say. She's here, she makes money. The former judge used to be at her place every night." He shrugged. "Who's to say — money or charms — or both. I'll say one thing for Rose; she does the best she can. I can't think of any other way an Indian woman can make a plugged nickel in this country. And Rose don't do no beggin'."

Parker went out, his long strides quickening as he descended the steps two at a time. A narrow path, fairly firm, wound among the woods of the vacant lot next to the hotel and Parker followed it at a fast walk. He picked his way through two cross streets, passing the saloons and the blacksmith shop. On a cross street at his right were three forlorn-looking buildings, each with a red-shaded lamp in the window. Two men staggered in their direction. Parker's eyes narrowed but he did not hesitate.

On his left now loomed the huge dark buildings that apparently marked the fort. The nearest one had a feeble light in one of its windows, and he crossed the gravel and went in the door.

A man sat on a high stool sharpening a knife on a whetstone. He spit on the stone, spread it carefully with the blade, and then honed the blade in one direction, raised it and reversed it, and honed it carefully in the other direction. He looked up, his gray eyes taking in Parker both ways from the chin. Then he tilted his head back a little and looked at Parker's silk hat. At last his head resumed a normal position and he said,

"Something, mister?"

He wasn't very old — perhaps the son of the jailer, Parker thought, though it was hard to tell. With his big dove-colored hat and his shaggy black hair, plus the ease and self-reliance in his manner, he might have been older than he seemed at first glance. Parker observed his ragged red cotton shirt, his oversize, worn denim pants, his Indian moccasins in place of boots. He observed the lack of a beard and he thought it was high time the boy's mother took him in hand and dressed him a little better. "Where's the marshal?" Parker asked.

"St. Louie," the boy said tersely.

"Then where's a deputy?"

The boy's face did not alter. "I'm the only one around right now. My name's Brett Malone."

Parker looked hard at him. Maybe the boy *was* older than he looked. "I was witness to a criminal act that occurred just after I got off the boat from Little Rock."

"On the dock or in town?"

"Why — in town, I'd say."

"Not our jurisdiction," said Malone. "There's a little piece of land around and above the dock, here, that's in Indian Territory even though it's on this side of the river. The line cuts through the fort here. But anything happens in the town is in Arkansas."

Parker thought fast. "The man who did it probably went back to Indian Territory."

Malone laid the whetstone on the high bookkeeper's table, above which hundreds of "wanted" circulars were pinned to the wall. "Violence is nothing unusual here, mister."

In spite of Malone's lack of enthusiasm, Parker did not resent his manner. Probably Malone was constantly confronted with this kind of thing. "A man called the Kiamichi Kid," said Parker, "forcibly ejected a farmer and his wife from their wagon, and took over the wagon and team and drove off."

"The Kid won't drive a team far," said Malone. "He probably just took a notion to do it."

"You know the Kid?"

Malone got down from the stool. He was long-legged and almost as tall as Parker. "We had him here last night waiting trial, but he broke out."

"Broke out?" Parker frowned. "Why aren't you out after him?"

"I can't be everywhere."

"You must have known he would stay in town last night."

"I figgered he would."

Parker pushed his hat back on his head.

"Do you mean you knew that or suspected it and yet you just sat here sharpening your knife?"

"It's a good knife," said Malone. "It ain't like a pistol; it never misfires. Likewise, it don't cost money to use."

He made a quick movement and the knife was in his hand, point forward. It was a very long, slender blade with a wicked-looking point, and showed the shiny marks of much honing.

"That's a Bowie knife, I take it," said Parker.

"No, sir, we don't favor the Bowie knife up here." He looked fondly at the weapon. "A Bowie knife is a sort of a sword, made for swingin' and hackin'." He put the knife back in a sheath under his belt. "This here toothpick," he said, "is made for cuttin'. It ain't no good for a meat cleaver but it sure is fast."

"Very well — but what about this man, the Kiamichi Kid?"

Malone looked at the ceiling. "A bad egg. Been in jail fourteen times — once for rape, twice for murder, eleven times for robbery." He paused. "No convictions."

"Why no convictions?"

Malone looked at him squarely. "Hard to say. I'm not a lawyer."

"Wasn't he guilty?"

Malone nodded. "Stinkin' guilty."

"But —"

"Sit down, mister. You act nervous."

"I *am* growing impatient," Parker said, "but I won't sit, thank you."

Malone said, "I will, if you don't mind."

Parker demanded, "Am I to understand that you do not wish to have anything to do with the Kiamichi Kid?"

"There's two answers to that," Malone said judiciously. "First off, nobody does. Second off, there's no use riskin' my neck when I know it isn't going to do any good."

"That's a strange remark."

"Anyhow," said Malone, "the other deputy went after him — Jim Wilkerson."

Parker said coldly, "He couldn't have looked very hard."

Malone studied Parker. "He wouldn't have looked in town," he said. "It would take an army to arrest him there. Jim's probably waiting for him across the river — in the Territory."

Parker pulled himself up to his greatest height. "I demand that you go with me to save that baby."

Malone's eyes narrowed. "I didn't know there was a baby."

"There was a baby in the wagon."

Malone pursed his lips. "You'll have to say what you're thinking, mister, when you're dealing with the federal law. How'd it happen?"

Parker told him, and ended, "I demand that you go with me to save that baby."

Malone got up, took a well-worn gun-and-cartridge belt from a nail, put it around his waist and buckled it. "That's some different from a team and wagon," he observed. He pulled his hat down and stepped to the door. "With a headstart like that, we'll never catch him from behind; that's for sure. About all we can do is pick up the pieces, and probably by now somebody else is doing that."

Parker took a step after him. "It's incredible," he said, "that this kind of thing can happen and nobody tries to stop it."

They went into a shed, and Parker smelled horses.

Malone's voice came out of the near darkness. "Did *you* stop it, mister?"

"No — but I tried."

"So have others tried before. Can you ride a horse?"

"Yes."

"I'll saddle up the bay gelding for you. He isn't any flash but he'll go all night and never miss a lick."

Parker heard the clink of bridle-irons, and Malone said, "Nobody wants to stop a man who's going to get loose no matter what he did."

"Meaning what?"

"Here, take the reins."

Parker felt the leather strips in his hand and the pull of a horse at the other end.

"The Kid can't be convicted," Malone went on.

"Why?"

"Cut that out, you!"

Parker heard a rapid shifting of hoofs on hard dirt, the shuffling of moccasins, and then, "Damn!" He heard movements in the dark, and the horse squealed. The bridle-irons clinked, and a moment later came Malone's voice: "Bite me, will you!" He led the second horse toward Parker. "I bit his damn ear half off," he said with satisfaction.

Parker stared.

"The judge won't let a jury convict him," Malone said. "No deputy is going to risk his life to bring in a man who's going to be turned loose. We bring him in only when he wants to be brought in — when he gets tired of the hills and wants to see some bright lights." He led the horse past Parker. "Follow me — and look out for them heels."

Parker kept a respectable distance between himself and Malone's horse.

"What about the other deputies?" he asked.

"What other deputies? We've only got three."

Parker exclaimed, "Three! For all of Indian Territory?"

"That's right. We go plumb to the Colorado state line and we take in everything between Texas and Kansas. Would take a man a month to ride across it."

It was practically dark. Malone said, "Pull up your horse alongside the fence and we'll throw on the saddles. Ought to go up and see how George is coming — but he'll be all right. Doc DuVal is sitting up with him."

"Who's George?"

"George Isha-harjo, the other deputy."

"An Indian?"

"Why not? Ain't Indians as good as anybody?"

"Yes, of course, but —"

"Out here," said Malone, "we take anybody for a deputy who can shoot and is willin' to get shot at for twenty-five a month — Indians, Mex, niggers, white. Sometimes an Indian makes a good deputy. An awful lot of this work is trackin' a man down."

Malone cinched up the saddle girth and said, "There you are, mister. Now, I figure like this. If the Kid took a team, he'd head up or down river. He might drive to a ferry or he might try to ford. In that case it would be south toward the Poteau."

Parker heard the creak of leather. Malone's voice came from above. "We'll head for the Poteau ferry. Water's high now. He'd have to go pretty far to find a ford."

Parker mounted. He was not a skilled rider, but he had ridden considerable in his younger days in Vinegar Valley in Ohio.

They went back up Garrison, walking the horses in the mud. Malone pointed to the three buildings with the red-shaded lamps. "That's the Row. Got about sixty girls down there, and they don't bother anybody — especially Indian Rose's girls. She bats their brains out if they don't behave."

They passed an unpainted saloon with a big sign that Parker could read in the reflected light of the coal-oil lamps: "Two Brothers Saloon." From inside came the sound of two mechanical fiddles sawing on *Only a Flower That He Gave Me*.

Parker remembered something with a shock. "You said George Isha-harjo was shot in a jailbreak?"

"Yes. It was George's own fault." They passed the Last Chance and turned right into utter blackness. "Jim and me both

38

warned him to get out of the way. We figgered the Kid was due for a break. But George is a stubborn Creek Indian. He allowed he was paid to keep men in jail and that's what he was gonna do. Us old-timers know better than that, but George —" He didn't finish, and the sound of the horses' hoofs for a moment was loud in the night.

"You said 'old-timers'," Parker noted. "How old are you, Malone?"

There was a barely perceptible pause. "Going on seventeen."

Parker thought for a moment that he had heard wrong. Then he asked, "How long have you been a deputy United States marshal?"

"Almost five months," said Malone.

Sixteen years old — but going on seventeen. A year made a difference at that age. Parker stared at the vague form ahead. The boy had looked young, but Parker hadn't dreamed —

A voice came out of the blackness. "That you, Brett?"

"Sure, Hank," Malone said easily. "What are you doin' down here?"

"Little business," said the voice.

Malone did not bother to answer, and in a moment they passed the place from which had come the sound of the voice. When they were out of earshot Malone said in a low voice, "That's Hank Fillmore. The Kid hamstrung him."

"That's mayhem," Parker said harshly.

"Yup."

"How did it happen?"

"The Kid and John Duck and Blue Snake come onto an old man about eighty who was supposed to have a lot of gold hidden away from a train robbery. They put his feet in the fire to make him tell, but I guess he never did. Anyway, they found his body in the creek about a month later. That was over in the Arbuckle Mountain — Chickasaw country. We found out Hank Fillmore had been over there cuttin' fence posts, and we ast him some questions. It come out that he had watched them the night they mighty near burned the old man's feet off, and Clayton persuaded him to testify. Everybody warned him to skip the country, but he told his story anyhow. There wasn't any doubt about the Kid, but never the nohow the judge instructed the jury to bring in a verdict of not guilty; they never even left the jury box. And a week later the Kid and his men paid Hank a visit out on his farm. First they strung him upside down and took turns raping his wife, and then they cut the leaders in Hank's heels." There was a pause. "It's the things like that that kept

Hampton from running after the wagon. He knew what would happen."

"My God!" Parker's exclamation was a cry for strength.

Chapter 3

"But that — that's a capital offense itself," Parker said incredulously.

"Yup. They brung 'em back and tried 'em, but Hank's wife was in an insane asylum and couldn't testify, and Hank had disappeared. Now there's some say Rose bought him off and keeps him in eatin' money now." He paused for a moment. "Rose is a good girl."

This was an interesting comment on a woman who was openly a madam, but Parker remembered the honesty in her face, and he thought he could understand.

"And so Fillmore is a handy man for the girls in the Row."

"You mean a procurer?"

Malone's voice sounded different, as if he had turned around. "It doesn't have a nice sound, that word — but it keeps him from begging for a living. How else could he support himself, with them feet?"

"What about his wife?" Parker asked presently.

"She died a while back."

"Were there any children?"

"Five. They went to her sister's back in Georgia."

Parker drew a deep breath. This was a nightmare country and this was a nightmare he was living. If he had seen it in print he would not have believed a word of it. It seemed unreal now, but he had seen a part of it with his own eyes. He stared into the dark, trying to overcome the revulsion that threatened to engulf him. "This is an awful country!" he burst out finally.

There was silence for a moment. The horses climbed out on dry ground and began to jog.

Brett Malone said from alongside, "I reckon you come from the East, mister, and you ain't acquainted with what things are like out here."

"I didn't expect it to be such a *savage* country," Parker said.

"Well, we got Indians —"

"I have worked with Indians, and I have nothing against them."

"That's good," said Brett. "Because they're no different from other people. Some are bad, some are good."

"But the Territory," said Parker, "is like nothing I ever heard of."

After a moment Malone said, "Wait up a minute. We'll head for the ferry."

"You could have tracked the wagon," Parker pointed out, "if you had brought a lantern."

Malone said, "Uh-huh — but we don't want the wagon. We want the baby. And it might take us two-three days to track that wagon down. Now I figure the baby will be all right until the Kid gets across the river and slows down. Then the baby's crying will make him mad."

"And then —"

"We'll wait and see."

Malone turned to the right, and Parker's horse followed. They rode for two hours in almost complete silence save for the horses' hoofs, their heavy breathing, the creak of leather, the chorus of crickets, and the distant booming of bullfrogs. Then Parker saw a yellow light.

"That's the ferry," said Malone. "Old man Conkling runs it."

They rode up to the light, which was a lantern hanging outside of a tiny one-room shack. Brett shouted, without dismounting, "Hello!" He called again, but there was no answer. "Oh, hell," said the sixteen-year-old deputy, "the old man's prob'ly drunk."

He got down and hammered on the door with his fist. It was made of driftwood planks, and when Malone hit it the second

44

time it flew open. Malone took the lantern off its nail and held it high. "Hey, Conkling, you got customers!"

The old man lay on his back on a wolfskin flung over a pile of rushes. He struggled awake, shaking his head and blinking his eyes. "Whatta you want? Oh!" he said as he focused his eyes on Malone. "Marshal. Need somethin'?"

"Come on out so we can talk to you," said Malone.

"All right. Lemme slip my pants on."

Malone hung the lantern back on its nail. Conkling came out, a shriveled old man, bent-shouldered, with a huge, ugly scar on the right side of his ribs.

"Old Bill was in Andersonville for a year," said Malone. "It left him a little touched."

"That scar — was that from Andersonville?"

"No. He got that with Lee. He jumped on a Union cannon just when they blew it up, and got a chunk of it in the ribs."

Parker scrutinized him. "He's too old to have been in the war."

Malone squinted at Parker in the lantern light. "It ain't very long since you thought I was too young to be a deputy," he pointed out.

Parker had no answer.

Malone turned back to Conkling, who was beginning to look alert. "You been here all day?" asked Malone.

Conkling nodded, looking up. He wore no shirt and he was bare-footed. His only garment was a shapeless pair of brown pants, held up by suspenders that had long since lost all their elasticity.

"Anybody cross late this afternoon?"

Conkling nodded eagerly. "Zeke Johnson, from up the river; wife and eight younguns. Lousy MacDonald by hisself. A couple fellers goin' back to Texas by wagon; reckon they come from Memphis."

"The Kid," Malone said impatiently. "What about the Kid?"

Conkling looked reproachful. "Thought you might like to know about these two fellers. They had money and they talked loud."

Malone nodded. "I'll try to remember. What did you say their names were?"

"Didn't get the names, but one had a knife scar along the side of his neck. I told 'em not to cut across Choctaw country but they laughed at me."

"They'll prob'ly turn up later — when it's too late for us to help 'em." Malone's voice turned suddenly sharp. "What about the Kid? Did he come this way?"

The old man shivered in the night air. He looked around him in the dark. "He went across," he said in a low voice.

"In a wagon?"

"Wagon and a span of mules."

"Baby crying in the back?"

Conkling nodded slowly, his eyes filled with fear. "Whose was it?"

"Hampton's."

The old man shook his head sadly. "I couldn't do a thing. You know what's likely to happen to us ex-Confederates if they ketch us with a shootin' iron."

"I know that," Malone said impatiently, "and I'm not layin' into you."

"If we had a federal judge we could trust —" The old man looked sharply at Parker, still on his horse, wearing a silk hat, and did not finish.

"We've got to get across," said Malone. "Wind her up."

Conkling nodded and shambled down the river bank in his bare feet. "You can ride right on," he said.

Malone led the way. The ferry was a flat-bottom, home-made barge. "You might as well leave her on the other side for a while," Malone said. "We'll probably be back this way with the wagon."

The old man went behind his shack, and

presently reappeared, leading a white mule. He put a collar on the mule and fastened a strap to a cross-bar that ran over the mule's head. Parker saw that one end of the bar was attached to a windlass, around which had been thrown several coils of rope. One end of the rope was fastened to the ferry, the other disappeared in the brown water.

"We'll take the lantern," said Malone.

"It's mighty dark tonight," the old man said in a quavering voice.

"No man who rode with Mosby is skeered of the dark." Malone chuckled. "Besides, you got eyes like a cat. You can see a bottle of rye whisky farther than a buzzard can spot a dead rabbit."

The old man began to swear at the mule, and the rickety windlass began to turn, shrieking on its axle for lack of oil. The ferry began to move slowly out into the stream.

Malone got down. "Might as well stretch your legs, mister. It'll take twenty minutes."

Parker dismounted, already a little stiff from the saddle. The ferry gradually moved out toward the center of the black water.

"Somebody said the Kid is a crossbreed. What mixture?"

"Part Sioux," said Malone, "part Cherokee, part Mexican, part nigger, part white — with the worst of all of them in him."

"Hasn't anybody ever told you not to call them 'niggers'?"

Malone stared at him. "Not in this country. It don't mean anything. We got some mighty nice niggers around. We also got some bad ones — but we call 'em all the same. 'Damn' nigger is something else, just like 'damn' Yankee."

"All right, all right. About the Kid."

"Nineteen years old, runs a gang in the hills out from Bidding Springs up to the Cherokee Country. That's where he'll head soon as he gets a horse."

"Do you think some of his gang will meet him?"

"It won't be necessary. He'll take the first horse he comes to."

"I can't understand his hold — so young and all."

"Twenty-five is old in the Territory. A good many outlaws are under twenty."

"You started to tell me —"

"Yeah." Malone set the lantern on the floor of the ferry and watched the opposite shore. "He's a sort of symbol, you might say. He does what he wants and gets by with it, and the rest of them figger if the Kid can do it, they can too. But he's as deadly as a water moccasin. There'll never be law in the Territory until the Kid is put behind bars for good."

They rode off the ferry on the other side, and Malone picked up tracks. "That'll be Zeke Johnson and his eight younguns. See how deep the wheel marks are? And that'll be Lousy MacDonald ridin' a light wagon off to the left with two unshod horses. That only leaves one that goes straight out. The hoof tracks are small — a span of mules. That's the one we're huntin'."

Malone pulled a short-barreled carbine out of a scabbard on the saddle and balanced it across his thighs. He kicked the horse forward. "We may be close; we may not. He might have gotten across the river and laid down for a nap. You never can tell. He might have whipped the horses until they fell — but my guess is he didn't go too far. The Kid wants to fight when he first gets drunk; then all he wants is to sleep."

They rode for an hour in silence, Malone occasionally checking the tracks with the lantern. "There really ain't but one way he can go, but, like I said, he's crazy. He *might* do anything."

"What's the Kid's real name?" asked Parker.

Malone looked at him sidewise. "Fauntleroy Butterfield," he said. "Some census man hung it on him. That's the way most of the Indians got their — Stop!"

It was a sharp command, and both horses stopped dead still. Parker looked and listened.

"Crying," said Malone. "A baby crying a long way off."

He turned his head to one side, then to the other. Finally he kicked the horse into a gallop straight ahead. The crying became louder. Parker hung onto the saddlehorn and followed Malone.

When they seemed almost upon the sound, Malone stopped his horse and began to circle, holding the lantern high. "Right in here somewhere," he said.

"Over there," said Parker suddenly. "To the right."

Malone jumped down and threw the reins over the horse's head, then went forward with the rifle in his right hand, the lantern high in his left.

Parker felt a physical shock when he saw the baby in a bed of prickly pears. Malone swore. He gave the rifle and lantern to Parker and went into the thicket in his moccasins. He picked up the baby gently and brought it to the light. "Might' near cried its lungs out," said Malone.

"Is it — hurt?"

Malone said with sarcasm, "Sure it's hurt.

There was so many stickers in it that it was hard to lift. Them stickers don't pull out easy. That's why he started yellin' harder. But its eyes are all right," he noted. "It'll be swole up tomorrow and probably festered from the fuzzy stickers for a couple of weeks, but it'll be all right."

Parker said harshly, almost afraid to trust his voice, "I'd like to see the fiend who did that. I'd ride all the way to Colorado and back just to —"

"Too far," said a guttural voice. "Too far."

Parker and Malone swung around together, Malone holding the baby, Parker holding the lantern by its bail and the rifle by its barrel. He knew without being told that he did not dare try to get the rifle in firing position.

The Kid was just within the circle of yellow light cast by the lantern. He was hatless and wore a buckskin shirt and a pair of old blue army pants. A rifle was cradled in his arms. He was short and squat of stature; his hair, uncombed, was like a shock of black straw; his swarthy face was broad and expressionless, his cheekbones high. His eyes, under heavy brows that met across the bridge of his nose, were cold and hard and without feeling, but not without alertness.

"You look me over, damn Yankee. You like what you see?"

Parker knew enough not to talk back. He saw the cold eyes turn on Malone, and glanced at the boy. Malone did not look scared, only watchful.

"You damn fine deputy," said the Kid. "No follow too close. I damn sure get tired waiting."

"Look here," said Parker indignantly, "this outrageous conduct will not be tolerated. You cannot run loose and kill like a mad dog and not suffer the consequences. Eventually you will come before the bar of justice and you will have punishment meted out according to your sins. The Word of God —"

"You talk like preacher," the Kid said. "Too much."

But Parker had not quite finished. "I will talk again," he said, coldly and clearly, "and you will listen. You will hear every word I say, and you will not answer back."

The Kid took half a dozen steps toward him. There was no indication in his eyes of what might happen until the last instant, when he raised the rifle and brought it down on top of Parker's skull.

Parker's knees buckled. He closed his eyes and felt himself falling. His head was filled with a ringing noise. He felt the rifle jerked out of his hand. "You — talk — too — much," the Kid said in his deadly voice.

Parker shook his head to clear his brain. He opened his eyes and saw Malone standing motionless. The Kid, with both rifles, went to their horses. He got into the saddle of one and caught up the reins of the other. With the rifles across his arms, he galloped into the black night of Indian Territory.

Malone said, "Follow the tracks with the lantern. We'll probably find the wagon close by."

It was less than a hundred yards away, undamaged. The mules were grazing on the new grass. Malone said, "You get up in the seat and I'll give you the baby. I'll drive."

The baby was still screaming piteously, but now its cries were turning into long, choking sobs.

Parker was trembling with rage. "Why did he have to be so brutal?"

"So we'd get off our horses and give him a chance to hold us up while we were busy getting the kid out of the cactus. I never thought of that," Malone said morosely. He looked at Parker sidewise. "For a judge," he said, "you got a lot of nerve."

Parker said, "How did you know I was a judge?"

"Nobody else," said Malone, "would wear one of them hats in Fort Smith — nobody but a Republican judge. But I still like your nerve. You knew he might kill you."

"I knew it," said Parker grimly, "and now we're even — because I'm going to *hang him*."

Chapter 4

It was three o'clock in the morning and pitch black when they drove the wagon into Fort Smith. The baby finally had quieted and slept fitfully. Parker had held it all the way, distressed because there was nothing he could do for it except smear some dirty axle grease from the wagon wheels on the punctures made by the beargrass. They had left the lantern with old man Conkling and finished the trip without a light.

A great resolve had hardened within Parker that night. He had known before that crime reigned in the Territory, but that knowledge had been abstract. After this long, weary night of horror and compassion, the Indian Territory was as real to him as his mother's Bible, and he knew now that his previously expressed intention of bringing order had been implemented by this night's experiences. It would be a crusade, a modern crusade against the forces of evil and terror. *Vengeance is mine: I will repay, saith the Lord.*

And as he sat on the hard, bumping seat, Isaac Charles Parker heard the call and accepted it. If it was the will of Divine Providence that he smite down murderers and rapists, then there would be no weakness on his part. If Justice needed a strong hand, then his would be strong.

Having reached that understanding with himself, Isaac Parker felt a great relaxation come over him, and somewhere on the dark road between the Poteau Ferry and Fort Smith he recovered from his earlier turmoil of bewilderment and horror and began to rock the baby gently in his arms, crooning a few wordless sounds now and then, and wondering when day would break over Fort Smith.

Malone crossed Garrison and stopped at a small, frame, box-like house where he said Mrs. Hampton's sister lived. He drew the wagon up before the house and called, "Hello!"

The door opened a crack, and a woman's voice said, "What do you want?"

Malone answered. "We've brought Miz Hampton's baby."

There was a shriek from inside. The woman said, "Show your face."

Malone struck a match and held it up in front of him. The door slammed shut, and Malone sat quietly. There was talk inside, and then a light showed in the single window.

"I reckon we passed the test."

The door opened again. The woman appeared, with a lamp in one hand and a rifle in the other. She held the lamp high. "If that's you, Brett Malone, come on in. If it ain't you, git out of here before I blow you to kingdom come."

Malone wrapped the reins around the iron. "It's me, Miz Miller."

He got down slowly, and spoke to Parker. "Come on, Judge, but don't make no sudden movements."

The woman held the door wider. Behind her were three children — two tall, skinny boys in nightshirts, and a small girl in a flowered flannel nightgown. She herself wore a faded silk wrapper and a boudoir cap made from the same material.

"How's Miz Hampton?"

"Out of her head most of the night, but we got her to sleep a while ago. She keeps moanin' but she hasn't woke up."

Parker came into the circle of light thrown by the lamp. "We brought the baby," he said.

The woman looked at him suspiciously. "Pretty fancy rig you got for riding around the country, ain't you?"

"Perhaps," said Parker. "Do you want the baby?"

She had not reached for it. "Is it alive?" she asked suspiciously.

"It's in some pain," said Parker, "but it's very much alive, and it will be all right in a few days."

"Take the brat, Katy," the woman said.

The girl, about seven years old, came forward, her face alight, and took the baby into her arms, making cooing noises.

"She can handle him," Mrs. Miller said. "She's a right smart hand with younguns. She ought to be; she mighty near raised my last three herself. You men want some coffee?"

"We'd be obliged," said Malone. He dropped into a ragged, overstuffed leather chair. The springs must have been broken, for the seat gave way and he ended up sitting almost on the floor.

"Katy, put a dry didy on him, and see he's warm. Wash them sticker-holes with soap an' water. B.J., fetch in some sticks and build up the fire. The poor thing must be freezin' after all night outside."

"No, ma'am," said Malone wearily. "It hasn't been cold tonight. Where's Ben?"

The oldest boy went outside in his night-shirt and bare feet. Katy laid the baby on a blanket on the bare floor and began to undress it. Mrs. Miller set the rifle in a corner near the door and put the lamp down on an ancient, massive black walnut table, "Him and Si went out to old man Lamar's to git his bloodhounds."

"They won't be needed now," Parker said. "May I have a drink of water?"

"The dipper's hangin' right there. Help yourself, mister. We got the hardest water in Arkansas, but drinks good."

Parker paused only momentarily at the tin dipper and the open water bucket when he noted a spider on top of the water. Then resolutely he scooped up a dipperful and drank it down without stopping. He hung the dipper back on its nail.

Mrs. Miller was examining the punctures in the baby's skin. "Dirty skunk! If I ever git my hands on him — Owen, go out to the cooler and bring in a pail of milk. We'll rub them places with cream and he'll feel better."

The second boy disappeared through the back door. The black sky was beginning to lighten. Mrs. Miller filled the coffee pot with water from the pail, poured in a cupful of coffee and set it on the big kitchen stove. "It'll be ready in half an hour," she said cheerfully.

But Brett Malone was asleep.

"He snores tol'able," said Mrs. Miller.

Parker nodded. He wished he could do the same.

Back at the hotel he found Mary awake, red-eyed and tearstained. She held him close. "I thought you'd never come back, Isaac. I thought you had been killed. I thought they had kidnaped you. I thought — What *were* you doing?"

He patted her shoulder. "Just getting a good look at my jurisdiction," he said. "I like to know the kind of people I'm dealing with. Now, you'd better get some sleep. I need a catnap or two myself."

"It will soon be time for Mass," she said. "I may as well stay up. I'll have to ask forgiveness for doubting."

He nodded tolerantly. Though he was a staunch Methodist and Mary was a Catholic, religion never had been an issue between them. Nor would it ever be.

Mary O'Toole her name had been, daughter of a devout Roman Catholic family. She would never change — nor did he expect or want her to. He had been raised by a militant mother who relied on the Bible as the cornerstone of all decisions. With that Rock-of-Gibraltar foundation he would never hesitate in his own faith. They had understood this before they married, and it

61

was not a problem.

"Very well," he said. "You go, and I'll get a couple of hours' rest."

He did not awaken until he heard her back at the door. His heavy silver watch said it was ten minutes to eight, and he got up at once.

"You should sleep a while longer," she told him. "You look haggard."

He pulled on his pants under his night-shirt. "There is work to do," he said. "More work than I ever dreamed of. You are the one who needs rest. It doesn't matter if I look haggard, but a woman must always look beautiful."

"You're a flatterer," she said, trying not to appear too pleased.

He smiled. It was easy to flatter Mary, for she was handsome and usually pleasant. Her unhappy mood on the riverboat up from New Orleans was the longest difficult spell she had ever had.

He whipped up a lather in his shaving mug, stropped his razor one hundred licks both ways, and went to work on his whiskers. He *was* haggard, he saw. Naturally a spare man with somewhat prominent bones and heavy lines in his face, last night had not helped his looks. But it didn't bother him; a good night's sleep would take care of everything.

"Where will you eat, dear?" asked Mary.

He knew from her voice that she was drowsy, so he said soothingly, "There's a café down the street. Don't worry. I'll be all right." In a town like this there would be many of them.

She didn't answer. When he finished shaving he put on his brocaded vest and his suit and was astonished to find that somehow she had brushed the mud from it when he wasn't looking. That was like Mary. He got his silk hat and tiptoed to the bed and kissed her on the forehead. She stirred a little and her arms went around his neck. She murmured something he could not distinguish, and then her arms went slack and dropped away, and he left the room as quietly as possible.

The mud from the day before was drying up pretty well, and he had no trouble keeping his shoes free of it. He went into the "Fort Smith Oyster Saloon" and sat down in a mighty uncomfortable straight-backed chair. He asked for coffee and breakfast, and got fried potatoes and round steak. He emptied the glass of water. "It's good," he said, and the waiter nodded approvingly.

"Comes from our own well. Hardest water west of the Mississippi."

Parker glanced at him but said nothing. He ate his breakfast and paid for it — thirty cents in silver or fifty cents in paper. He paid in silver and went on down Garrison.

The street looked different this morning. There was not a single wagon in sight. The saloons were closed except for the swampers emptying the spittoons in the street just off of the wooden sidewalks. A small, bald-headed man with purple sleeve garters was sweeping the walk in front of a small brick building labeled "Bank." The bald-headed man looked up as Parker's firm tread reached his ears. He watched Parker, shading his eyes against the morning sun.

"Nice morning, mister."

"Very nice," said Parker.

"Don't recollect seeing you before."

"No." Parker smiled. "And you would remember these Eastern clothes, wouldn't you?"

"I'm a banker," the man said. "It's my business to remember people."

Parker stopped. "I'm Isaac C. Parker, judge for the federal district court of Western Arkansas. Just got in yesterday."

The man shook his hand. "I'm Hoffman — C. C. Hoffman. Glad to make your acquaintance."

"The pleasure is mine."

"You brung a family, I take it."

"Wife and small son about four years old."

Hoffman smiled. "We've got a good, safe bank and we'll be happy to handle your accounts."

"Thanks." Parker went on. He saw a light in the marshal's office and opened the door. Malone was sitting in a cane-bottom chair with his feet up on the rolltop desk. He was asleep.

Parker said sharply, "Malone!" and the deputy opened his eyes, looked groggily at Parker, shook his head, and yawned. "Judge," he said, "you're up early." His feet hit the floor.

"So are you," said Parker.

"It's nothin' for me. I sleep here half the time. Anyway, I figgered you'd be here this morning, and I thought I'd show you around."

"Very good."

Malone got to his feet and stretched. He hadn't begun to fill out yet, but he looked as tough as a piece of bois d'arc.

"I'd like to see George first," Parker said.

"Come this way." Malone took him up an inside stair and into a room that smelled of medicine. A man of very dark skin was asleep on an iron bed. A second man, fully

65

dressed, was asleep on a pallet on the floor.

"Doc DuVal," said Malone without raising his voice. "We got company."

The man on the pallet opened his eyes, automatically rolled to one side and began to pull on his boots. Then he looked up. He was a medium-sized man with a well-shaped face, a neat black beard, and quick brown eyes. "Oh, sorry," he said. "Forgot my manners."

"This here's the new judge," said Malone.

DuVal shook hands with Parker, then sat down again to pull on his other boot. "We had a doubtful patient last night," he said, "but I think he got over the hump this morning. He had a bullet in his hip, but missed the bladder. I dug it out this morning and gave him some morphine. He's been sleeping ever since — but it was a close call."

Parker turned to look at George, and found the deputy staring back at him, his black eyes inscrutable. Parker took in the broad, reddish-brown face, the high cheekbones, the straight black hair. "Does he speak English?" he asked Malone.

"Oh, sure. Ask him something."

"Does it hurt?" asked Parker.

The black eyes did not change and the

man did not answer immediately. Then he said, "No hurt now. Doc make good medicine."

Parker nodded. "I'm glad," he said.

He went to the office of the court clerk, who was a woman with a huge bust, dressed in striped calico. "I'm Mrs. O'Rourke," she said in a bird-like voice. "My husband was clerk before me, and when he passed on from consumption last winter they gave the job to me."

"Uh-huh." Parker looked around and nodded. The office was very neat. "May I see your calendar for the May term of court?"

"You mean the important cases?"

He hesitated, then said, "Yes. Yes, I suppose those *are* what I want to see."

"I can tell you something about them," she offered.

"Please do." He put his silk hat on the table.

"There's one man in Murderers' Row, waiting to be hanged."

"That implies the jail, I presume."

"Yes. We call it Murderers' Row when they're convicted of a capital crime. Name is McClish Impson — half-Cherokee, convicted of murder, sentenced to die by Judge Caldwell a year ago."

"And not hanged yet?"

"Colonel Bert DuVal, his attorney, got a stay of execution so he could try to get the President to commute his sentence."

"With what result?"

"Turned down. But by that time Judge Caldwell wasn't here any more, and Judge Story didn't set a new date, so McClish Impson is still there."

Parker looked up. "Did you say DuVal?"

"Yes, sir. He's the court doctor too."

"Oh," said Parker. "I'll want to see Impson's file later. How about the important trials?"

"Here they are. Daniel Evans, accused of killing his partner for a pair of boots. John Whittington cut an old man's throat for a hundred dollars. Edmund Campbell killed a colored man and woman for insulting him. James Moore robbed a crippled man and killed one of the posse that was hunting him. Smoker Man-Killer is an Indian from Flint District, Cherokee Nation; he killed a neighbor without warning. Samuel Fooy is a complete no-good, a drunkard and carouser; he killed a white school teacher. When he was arrested he bragged that he had broken all of the Ten Commandments."

Parker took a deep breath. "That's a terrible thing to say."

"And him with a wife and three children," she said indignantly.

Parker looked at the papers before him. "You talk as if you assume that they are all guilty, but these men haven't been tried yet."

"From a legal point of view, I reckon they're still innocent," she admitted, "but from a practical point of view I think you'll agree with me that every last one of them ought to meet his Maker."

Parker smiled wryly. "Ours must be the legal point of view, Mrs. O'Rourke. A man is innocent until we prove him guilty."

"It may be, but you take one look at that bunch and you'll agree with me; the only question is how high they should be hung."

There were steps at the door, and Parker turned. A small, slender man came in. He had an imperial goatee like Parker's except that it was black; his face was triangular and his eyes gave an impression of intelligence.

Mrs. O'Rourke seemed flustered. "Oh, judge — your honor — Judge Parker, Mr. Clayton, your prosecuting attorney."

Clayton smiled and stepped forward. "Judge, this is indeed a pleasure."

"Thank you. I was just looking over the calendar."

"After the night I have heard about, I should think you would be home in bed."

Parker sobered. "Mr. Clayton, there is much work to be done in this district. I expect to waste no time getting on with it."

Clayton nodded. "My sentiments exactly." But he seemed dubious as he looked at Parker. "What do you think of our country at first glance, your honor?"

Parker looked at him coldly. "Frankly, Mr. Clayton, I think too many men have gone unhanged."

Clayton's eyes were watchful. "Do you expect to remedy that, sir?"

"I will remedy it," said Parker, "or know the reason why."

"You will have my full cooperation, sir," Clayton declared.

Parker said, "I'd like to see your office."

"This way, your honor."

"Will you excuse us, Mrs. O'Rourke?"

"Sure will, ju— your honor."

Parker followed Clayton down the hall, which was bare and floored with badly warped, unpainted boards. Clayton's office was not much better. He had some bookcases of assorted sizes: rows of statutes, a wall filled with U.S. court decisions, and a shelf of legal textbooks. His desk was a battered rolltop. His swivel chair had broken its springs, and the back leaned toward the rear at an angle of forty-five degrees. He had a small homemade table and straight-backed chair. Parker sat down. "The government does not provide very much in the way of luxury for you," he observed.

Clayton sat down too. "Have a cigar?"

"I don't smoke."

Clayton hastily put the cigar back in his pocket.

"However," Parker said, "I have no objection to your doing so."

Somewhat slowly Clayton took out the cigar again. He bit off the end, licked the wrapper, put it back in place, and lighted it with a match.

"I would like a straight answer," said Parker.

Clayton looked at him over the match, his eyes questioning.

"I have heard many rumors or implications that this court is corrupt. Are they true?"

Clayton coughed suddenly. He took the cigar out of his mouth and observed it for a moment. "Let's say it has not been the most efficient or reliable court in the world."

Parker got up. "Thank you. From now on the situation will be different."

"I'm glad to hear that, your honor."

"I know about the six capital cases on the calendar, and I suppose there are many lesser ones."

"Yes."

"We shall neglect nothing." Parker stared at him. "Every offender will be called to answer for his sins. But especially, Mr. Clayton, the murderers and rapists. Especially those. I have seen enough deeds of violence in eighteen hours to disgrace any civilized community in the world."

"Yes, your honor."

"These murderers in jail now — I want them brought to justice and I want them convicted. If you can't convict them, I will. That is" — his voice lowered — "provided, of course, that I believe them to be guilty."

Chapter 5

"Court will be called on May tenth. I want you to be ready to prosecute these men at that time — not the next day, sir. May tenth!"

"Yes, your honor." Clayton looked pleased. "You can count on me, sir."

"Now," said Parker, "I'm going to visit the jail. I want to familiarize myself with the premises."

Clayton got up. "I'll take you to George Maledon. He's a special deputy in charge of the prisoners and he's also the hangman. A good man at his trade, according to those who know something of the trade."

"By all means, let's get acquainted with Mr. Maledon."

Maledon was a small, slight, unsmiling man with eyes that stared without seeming to see. He had a long, wavy brown beard, and wore two six-shooters stuck under a wide leather belt fastened on the outside of his coat.

"I understand you are the hangman," said Parker.

"Yes."

"I'll be going back," said Clayton. "Have to get ready for the next session."

"Drop into my office any time," said Parker.

"Thank you."

"I understand," said Parker to Maledon, "that there have not been many hangings."

"Not many," said Maledon.

"But you have had some experience?"

"At Van Buren and here also. I've hanged seven men on this gallows."

"How did you come by such a trade?"

"I saw a man bungling a hanging at Van Buren, and offered my services."

"Without previous experience?"

"I know ropes," said George Maledon emotionlessly.

Parker nodded. It was not comfortable to be around the slight man, but that did not concern Parker. "I would like to see the gallows," he said.

The first hint of cordiality came into Maledon's voice. "I'll be glad to show you. It's just outside. You can see it from the courtroom windows. This way, your honor."

Parker followed Maledon down the stairs. In the hall a long-legged girl in pigtails and an ankle-length gingham dress was going into the marshal's office.

They went down the steps outside, facing the river on the southwest. The great gallows of Fort Smith stood not over a hundred yards from the courthouse.

"I whitewashed it last week," said Maledon.

Parker nodded. The huge structure gleamed in the mid-morning sun. There was a shed with a sloping roof, open on the side, facing the courthouse, with a stone wall at the back.

"That bench against the stones is where they sit while the sentence is read," said Maledon.

The roof was twenty feet high in front and sloped down in the back. The platform was made of three-inch planks, and twelve steps led up to it. A huge beam, at least twenty feet long, ran the length of the roof.

"That's where I tie the ends of the ropes," Maledon said. "The trap is thirty inches wide and runs the length of the platform — twenty feet. They stand on that. Then I pull the bolt out of the staple and they drop."

"It looks efficient," Parker said grimly.

"It is — if you know your ropes."

"I'd like to see the ropes."

He thought Maledon almost smiled. "The rope room is in the courthouse, your honor."

He followed Maledon back. The rope room was a dusty, gloomy place, with big ropes hanging from rafters and some coiled on a bench.

"Ropes are very important," Maledon said. "I don't use sisal, only real hemp. I buy inch-and-an-eighth rope and oil it carefully with linseed oil, then drop it a few times with sandbags to take the stretch out. That brings it down to one inch."

"By how long?" asked Parker.

"Twenty-seven feet."

"And this is a storage room, I take it."

"It's more than a storage room," said Maledon, picking up one of the heavy coils and running his slender fingers over the strands. "The ropes have to be moved around to keep from getting a set or a kink. Every day I change them. I move them from the rafters to the table and back the next day. When there is a hanging, I select the ropes to be used and take them home a week or so before, so there will be no tampering with them. I bring them back the day of the hanging and test them with sandbags. That way there's no slip-up."

They went back outside. Parker walked to a position in front of the platform and stared at the massive structure for a long time. Finally he asked, "How many can be hanged at once?"

"Twelve," said Maledon.

Parker continued to stare at the gallows. "Has it ever hanged twelve?"

Parker moistened his lips. He said absently, "Twelve men hanged at one time would have a deterring effect on criminals in the Territory, don't you think?"

"It would not encourage them," Maledon agreed.

"This country needs something like that — something to shock them." He looked at Maledon. "Do you think you could hang twelve at one time?"

Maledon's face did not change. "I can hang them," he said quietly. "And when I hang them, they never come back for more."

"Well —" Parker cleared his throat. "You'd better oil up your ropes; there will be work."

"I'll do that, your honor." The man's voice almost had a touch of warmth in it.

Parker went to the marshal's office, to find Malone leaning back in the chair with his feet on the table, and the pigtailed girl sitting on the edge of the high stool.

"Howdy, judge," said Malone. His feet came down off the table. "You better run along," he said to the girl.

She turned big brown eyes on Parker, then slowly and with apparent reluctance got down from the stool and went out with her head high.

"That's Ann Garth," Malone explained. "She's sorta stuck on me."

"She's a nice girl to be stuck on a man."

"Too young," said Malone.

Parker started to say Malone was too young himself, but then he remembered how the deputy had handled things the night before. What did a man's age in years have to do with his manliness? Not a great deal, it seemed. Perhaps boys grew up fast on the frontier. For that matter, perhaps girls did too. Ann Garth, for some reason, did not give the impression of being girlish.

"You might be wrong," Parker said. "She's mighty close to being a woman."

Malone nodded. "When she gets independent and quits coming here to see me, then I'll know she's growed up — and then I reckon I'll have to go after her. I like her, all right. I'm just waitin'."

Parker sat down in an empty chair.

"Brett, how did you get to be a deputy?"

"My pappy came home from the war all shot up," said Malone. "He lost an eye at Shiloh and got a twelve-penny nail through his guts at Champion's Hill, and when he came home he took to his bed and I had to look out for him."

"Where was your mother?"

"There wasn't no quinine during the war. She died of chills in 'sixty-four."

"Of course your father had a pension, being disabled."

"Pension!" Malone looked bitter for an instant. "There's no pension for Confederates. That's only for damn Yankees."

Parker took off his silk hat and wiped his forehead with his handkerchief.

"Then pappy died and the panic of 'seventy-three was on, and they gave me this job so's I could eat. They told me to sit tight and draw my pay and not get in no gun fights."

"Who told you that?"

"The marshal — Art Stoddard."

"And you've done that, I take it."

"Yeah." Malone stared at the floor. "Sometimes it gets a little tiresome — running back and forth and never really doing anything. Like with the Kiamichi Kid, for instance. The Kid *needed* to be locked up, but we knew he wouldn't stay locked up — and it isn't always easy to be off somewhere else when somebody like the Kid is getting ready to break out."

"You knew ahead of time, then?"

"We knew," said Malone disgustedly.

"You could have done your job anyway."

"A deputy like that would last as long as a snowball in hell around here. There's no use riskin' your neck anyway. You know the man is going to be turned loose one way or another. That's what George Isha-harjo couldn't get through his head. That's why he's up there now with a bullet hole in his hip. He tried to keep the Kid from getting away."

"How about Jim Wilkerson?"

"He's like me. He'd *like* to do his job but he's got better sense."

"Have you seen him today?"

Malone nodded. "Sure. He came in early this morning. He picked up the Kid's trail a couple hours after you and me got caught with our hands down, but by that time the Kid had joined up with John Duck and Blue Snake, and Jim showed some sense and came on back."

"Where is he now?"

Malone turned his head. "In there sleeping."

"I'm awake now," said a voice.

Parker turned. In an inner doorway stood a tall man in his stocking feet. He was three inches taller than Parker, and still thinner, but he had a pleasant face that Parker liked instinctively. Here was a man without subterfuge — an honest man, one who could be counted on.

"This here's the new judge, Jim," said Malone.

"Oh, howdy, judge." Wilkerson stifled a yawn with the back of his hand. "Pleased to meet you."

"He's like an older brother to me," said Malone. "He give us food and stuff before pappy died, and then he took me under his wing and give me my raisin'."

Parker asked, "Do you have any children of your own, Wilkerson?"

"Five," said Wilkerson, "and another comin'. But there's always room for one more, and I knowed Brett a long time. I seen he was worth raisin' and I done my best by him."

"How old are you, Wilkerson?"

"Twenty-eight."

"Do you have any opinions on law enforcement in the Territory?"

Wilkerson said without hesitation, "Give the Kid what's coming to him and you won't have any trouble. As long as he's loose, everybody else who wants to kill will do it."

Parker looked at Malone. "You indicated to me, Brett, that you were not entirely happy with the way things are going. Would you go over into Indian Territory and bring outlaws back to Fort Smith if you knew you had the court behind you?"

Brett looked at him. "Sounds interesting."

"How about you, Wilkerson?"

Wilkerson nodded. "I don't like this pussyfootin' around. I'd rather earn my money honestly — if I knowed I wouldn't get shot in the back for it."

Parker studied him intently. "How'd you like to be chief deputy, Wilkerson, at ten dollars a month more than you're getting now?"

Wilkerson ran his tongue back and forth behind his lower lip. "I'd like the money, Mr. Parker, but I'll be honest. I haven't got the head Brett has."

"He's not old enough," said Parker.

"He ain't old in years, but he's sure seven feet tall when he goes after an outlaw. He's been out in the hills so much he's like an Injun himself. And he knows how to organize and outguess 'em. You make him your chief deputy and you won't regret it."

Parker studied Malone. The boy did have an air of competence about him, and Parker had seen for himself that he wasn't cowardly and he wasn't stupid.

"Nearly every outlaw in the Territory is under twenty-one," Wilkerson said.

"They're more dangerous when they're younger. Take a feller like me with a tableful of kids — he gets cautious. He keeps thinkin' about what those kids will eat if he gets killed. Brett's your man, Mr. Parker."

Parker considered. "By the way, what about Art Stoddard?"

Wilkerson became wide-eyed, too wide-eyed. "He's in St. Louie."

"Doing what?"

Wilkerson shrugged. "He went up there when he heard that Judge Story was about to lose his job."

"Stoddard was Story's brother-in-law," Malone said.

"Oh." Parker nodded slowly. "How long has he been gone now?"

"Quite a while," said Wilkerson.

Parker became impatient. "How long is 'quite a while'? A month?"

Wilkerson looked at Malone, who in turn looked out the window toward the gallows. "More like six weeks," Wilkerson said finally.

"On business?"

Wilkerson frowned. "I don't rightly know, your honor."

"If you men won't tell me, I'll have to figure it out for myself." Parker waited a moment for them to speak, but there was silence from both of them. "It is obvious," he said dryly, "that if you two men had any defense to offer for him, you would do so now. Therefore I am justified in concluding there is no defense. Six weeks away from the job of marshal is far too long unless the circumstances are most unusual. Therefore I am forced to conclude that Mr. Stoddard is no longer enthusiastic about his appointment and I shall consider the post of marshal vacant. In due time I shall select a man to take his place. In the meantime, the physical necessities of judicial affairs in the Indian Territory must depend on the deputies." He stared hard at Malone who slowly lifted his eyes and stared back. "Brett Malone," said Parker in a loud voice, "consider yourself chief deputy. I'll give you a tryout. If you make good, the job is yours permanently."

Brett seemed unmoved by this announcement. He continued to return Parker's stare until the silence became uncomfortable. Then Wilkerson jumped in. "He'll do the job, your honor. I'll vouch for that. I've knowed Brett since he was knee-high to a milkin' stool, and I can guarantee you'll never regret this. I seen Brett trail a shot-up bobcat into the brush, Mr. Parker. Ain't kill unless you have to."

"I ain't never killed a man," said Malone, "and I don't especially want to — but I ain't afraid to, neither."

"If you are doubtful," Parker said, "of your own feelings in this matter —"

"I ain't doubtful," said Malone. "I know my feelings. But I want to go by the law too. I just ain't sure how far I can git with my hands tied."

Parker got up hastily. "I don't want you to feel that way. Any man who rides under Parker will have the full and complete support of this court. I ask only that he remember he is a marshal and not a hired killer. If you do not —"

"He'll do it if he says so," Wilkerson said quickly. "He's just a feller that likes to know where he stands."

"How about it, Malone?"

The young man nodded. "I'll take the job. If I don't do right, you can fire me — or put me on trial."

Parker studied him. Malone was sincere, he saw, and went on to other matters. "The first thing is to get some more deputies."

"Deputies? We got three," said Wilkerson.

"Ridiculous! I want" — Parker paused and looked out at the gallows, then turned

much more you need to know."

"I'm not worried about his skill or his courage. I've seen those demonstrated." Parker studied the boy. "But a job like this requires restraint as well." He fixed his eyes on Malone. "You cannot go charging around with a knife and a rifle, shooting men haphazardly."

Malone said slowly, "You don't expect us to bring in killers with a lot of soft talk, do you, judge?"

"Of course not, but it involves using a certain amount of discretion."

"You mean to let the other guy shoot first?"

Parker looked at Malone. This young man was smarter than he had realized. "Not exactly — but you are not to shoot unless you feel it absolutely necessary."

"You'd rather have them alive," said Wilkerson.

"Isn't a murderer just as good dead from a bullet as from a rope?" asked Brett.

"A man's life is to be taken only according to the law," said Parker, "by which he will receive a fair trial. You as a deputy have no power to decide a man's guilt."

"Who decides," asked Brett, "if my life is in enough danger that I can shoot?"

"The court."

"You mean I can be tried for murder if I shoot a criminal?"

"Absolutely. The law plays no favorites."

Malone said dubiously, "It doesn't sound like a very good job to me. It sounds like a good way to get killed."

"I'll try to explain. Any man has a right to defend himself or his family or his property. In addition an officer of the law has a right to shoot a man who resists arrest or tries to escape. Otherwise the most out-and-out criminal in the world may be killed legally only according to the form prescribed by law. He gets a jury trial. If convicted, the court fixes the time and place and manner of his death and until that moment the law protects his life as carefully as it protects your own."

Malone said stubbornly, "I don't see no sense in protecting a murderer or a rapist."

"If the law didn't do that," said Parker, "then anybody could shoot anybody and claim it was needed."

"Then if I shoot a man trying to arrest him, I might be held for murder myself."

"That is possible."

Malone turned to Wilkerson, shaking his head. "It looks to me like a loaded gun, Jim."

Wilkerson said, "I don't think the judge

means it the way it sounds." He turned to Parker and said earnestly, "Brett's young Mr. Parker, and he takes things just the way you say 'em. You ain't aimin' to put a deputy on trial every time he kills a criminal are you? Because if you are, you won't have no deputies. Nobody can go over in the Territory and arrest men like the Kid and John Duck and Blue Snake without a rifle or a six-shooter pointing at them — and he may have to use it."

"The Kid has been brought in before," Parker pointed out.

"Sure — because he knew nothing would happen to him. It gave him somethin' to do. But if the word gets around that these men are going on trial for their lives, Mr. Parker, us deputies are goin' to have a real job on our hands."

Parker glanced at Malone, who nodded.

"Let me put it a different way," said Parker. "The law will presume that its deputies will abide by their oath and will strive to bring criminals in alive — but I don't want you to be careless. If complaints are made and if a grand jury thinks there's a chance you killed unnecessarily, an indictment will be returned and you will have to stand trial. But," he added with a slight smile, "I do not think either of you men

around — "I want twelve more. How soon can you get them, Malone?"

Wilkerson whistled. "Twelve!"

Malone showed no reaction. "Pretty soon," he said.

"Do you think you know twelve men who are not afraid to risk their lives for twenty-five dollars a month?"

"Some of them risked their lives during the war for nothing," Malone said. "Some of them been in trouble with the law too — some of the best ones."

"And yet they would work with the law?"

"Sure. They haven't done anything serious — a little whisky smuggling, knife fighting — no murders."

"Are these men who will remember their oath?"

"Most of 'em."

"All right. The court will not investigate their past records too minutely."

"In that case," said Malone, "I'll pick out twelve men that will do the job as long as they're under oath."

"That's all I ask. How long will it take?"

"Give me a week."

"All right." Parker suddenly felt elated. "Now," he said to Wilkerson, "who's in charge of the jail?"

"Maledon — but Hans Eoff is the turnkey."

"I would like to visit the jail."

Wilkerson got up. "I'll take you downstairs. It ain't very pretty," he warned.

"My esthetics can be controlled for the purpose of this visit," Parker said firmly.

Malone had arisen and was staring out at the whitewashed gallows gleaming in the sun. "It stinks down there," he said bluntly.

"I am going to inspect it," Parker said again, firmly.

Wilkerson said in resignation, "Follow me, Mr. Parker."

Chapter 6

They went along the hall and down a narrow stairway. The stench hit Parker's nostrils and made him gasp for breath, but he said nothing.

The basement ceiling was low, and there was no light except what filtered in through dirty windows set high in the walls. A long hall ran lengthwise down the middle, and on each side were small cells partitioned by steel bars. A Negro picked up two pails that obviously served as slop jars and carried them past Parker and up the stairway. All around him, men sat in the cells or played cards through the bars. They eyed Parker suspiciously and silently as he went by, their eyes gleaming with unspoken thoughts. Most were unshaved, uncombed, dressed in ragged, dirty clothing; many were barefoot. Some were Negroes; others were obviously Indians; some were white. But over all rose the stench of unwashed bodies, human excreta and spoiled food.

A man was sitting on a stool at the far end of the basement, reading a paper in the dim light. He looked up, put down his paper, and came to meet them. Wilkerson introduced him: "Hans Eoff, Mr. Parker." He pronounced it "oaf."

Eoff was a big, square-framed man with reddish side whiskers and a sweeping red mustache. He talked with an accent. "Yah, I'm the turnkey. We don't lock the prisoners in their cells in the daytime except for the murderers, and they don't try to escape."

"They look well fed," Parker observed.

"We feed them fine. I raise five hogs from the scraps left over."

"But this," said Parker emphatically, "is the filthiest place I have ever seen in my life. It is not fit for hogs, to say nothing of human beings."

Eoff pursed his lips. "I'm sorry, your honor. We have no money, we have no room. It's not my responsibility anyhow."

"You could keep it clean."

"I'm not hired out for a janitor," said Eoff. "Anyhow, who is going to watch the prisoners while I am scrubbing the floor?"

"How about the Negro?"

"He works all he can, but it isn't enough. We need three-four men."

"You'll get them," Parker said curtly. "How do the prisoners sleep?"

"On the floor — one blanket apiece."

"They must freeze in the wintertime."

"We usually turn them loose in December. Anyhow, it doesn't get so cold down here."

"I know it is not your responsibility," Parker said coldly, "but I want you to keep this place as clean as possible. This is a disgrace to humanity."

"Yes, sir." Eoff swung his head. "I'm sorry, sir. I often showed it to Judge Story."

Parker turned to Wilkerson. "I've got to get out of here. I can't breathe this foul air any longer."

Wilkerson led him back up the stairway. Parker stood outside in the cleansing sunlight and breathed fresh air in great lungfuls.

"One thing bothers me, Mr. Parker," said Wilkerson.

"What's that?"

"You're fixin' to hire twelve new deputies, and inside of six months you'll have two hundred prisoners on your hands." He gestured toward the building behind them. "There's only eighteen in there now. Where will we put two hundred?"

Parker glared at him. "Double them up, triple them, quadruple them. Some day we'll get a new jail."

"It will take more men to feed them — and this place won't be any cleaner," Wilkerson noted.

Parker said, "I don't care if it takes ten or fifteen years to clean up this mess in the basement. It's the mess over in the Territory that worries me most. You bring the prisoners in. We'll worry later about where to keep them."

He left the grounds of the old fort — still partially enclosed by a stone wall — and went back up Garrison. He reached a gaunt, box-like structure on a corner and noted the farmers and cowboys standing around. The front of the building on the lower floor was all glass windows, and a painted sign above them, clear across the front, said "Thompson Pharmacy." Above were three windows with rounded tops, and above those another sign in three-foot letters that followed the curve of the windows: "DRUG STORE." He stepped inside, into the smell of medicines and horse tonic and mange remedy and liniment. It was a hot day and he wished he could shed his outer coat, but it would not do, for the dignity of the federal court required certain concessions to comfort. Regardless of his conspicuousness he pushed in between two blanket Indians, laid both forearms on the marble counter-top and ordered soda water. It was refreshingly cool, and he drained the glass. The Indians were watching him intently, openly. He set the glass down, paid for the drink, and went out. No doubt, he thought, the entire countryside would soon know about him. That was as it should be. Every person in the Indian Territory would very soon know about his court. Those who had reason to fear it would shudder; those whose hands were free of iniquity would be able to breathe a sigh of relief and set aside their rifles.

He stopped to visit the banker, had dinner, and finally went on to the hotel. There was no mail, and he went upstairs. Mary fell into his arms when he opened the door.

He lifted her head with his forefinger. "Mary, you're crying," he said in amazement.

"I was afraid for you, Isaac. I heard shots outside somewhere, and I know how uncompromising you are with criminals, and I thought —"

"Never mind," he said. "If anything happens to the judge, the President will send another."

She hit his chest with her fist. "I don't care about the court, Isaac. I care about you!"

He hugged her briefly and set his hat on the bureau. "Let's have a glass of wine, dear. It's been an exhausting morning."

She poured the wine, and he sat back as well as he could in a straight chair; his legs were too long even for that. "I like that young fellow, Brett Malone," he said, resting his glass on his knee. "Nice fellow, very appealing somehow — honest and aboveboard." He looked absently at her. "I'm not sure how he will respond to authority. There seems to be a little rebellion still inside of him. Left over from the war, I suppose." He tasted the wine and said thoughtfully, "I'd like a son like him."

"You have a son," Mary reminded him.

"I saw him when I came in. He was playing with a girl in the vacant lot."

She stood directly before him and demanded belligerently, "Do you know *what* girl, Isaac?"

"No." He looked up at her. "I can't say that I do."

"Annie Maledon, daughter of the hangman."

"I have talked to George Maledon. A very nice fellow."

She paid no attention. "That's the kind of children Charlie will have to associate with in Fort Smith." Without warning she burst into tears. "Isaac, I can't stand it!"

He was on his feet, comforting her.

"Now, now, Mary, you mustn't give way to your feelings like this. Conditions will improve. It isn't that Fort Smith itself is so bad, but the Territory — conditions are terrible over there and they extend to Fort Smith. All that will be remedied." He took his arms from around her and began to pace the floor. "Crime will be stopped," he said. "Not only Fort Smith will be a safe and pleasant place to live, but all of Indian Territory, that great cesspool of crime, will be purged whiter than the driven snow." He paced on. "For every time and every place there is a man who is equipped by nature, by temperament and by talent to perform the exacting requirements of the problem before him." He waved his arm in a semicircle. "This is a great frontier area, lawless and violent, and undoubtedly the appointment of Isaac C. Parker to this task was guided by the divine hand of providence. I shall live up to that great responsibility. The men before me have failed. Let them go back to their civilized courts. Isaac C. Parker will stay here in Fort Smith and bring order out of chaos. That is my task — order out of chaos. To that ideal I shall be ever true!"

"Isaac," Mary said quietly, "you're making a speech." He had been a prominent and much-sought speaker in St. Joe, and he had been on his feet many times in Congress and had read his remarks subsequently in the *New York Tribune.*

He laughed, not really embarrassed. "So I was — but I firmly believe that I am the right man in the right place."

"Isaac," she said, and he stopped, looking at her in puzzlement as he heard the strange note in her voice. "I'm afraid the people of Fort Smith are not going to help you very much." She handed him a large piece of printed paper. The heading across the top read, *The Western Independent.* "On the front page," she said. "You had better read that paragraph, Isaac."

He took the paper and began to read it to himself:

"PRESIDENT GRANT'S latest carpetbag officeholder, a Yankee from St. Joseph, Missouri, has arrived to take over the judgeship of the federal court for the Western District of Arkansas. It is presumed that his first move will be to find out what Bentley Garth is carrying into the Territory *via* Garth Freight Lines. Some say he takes rifles; others say whisky; Garth says he takes goods for the Indian agencies. This office knows not, but assumes for purposes of publication that Garth is telling the truth.

Perhaps Judge Isaac C. Parker will ferret out the answer. But let us not expect too much of him, for a look at his record will clear away the fog. GRANT has sent us another castoff. His new judge has never been a real judge before. He was county judge in Missouri, but that office in our sister state has nothing to do with lawyers and juries. He served in the U.S. Congress but was recently defeated for the Senate, so since his own people won't have him, and since he is a good Republican, GRANT found it necessary to arrange a political job for him. Meanwhile, crime in the Territory is the rule, not the exception. A man's life is not worth a hatful of green persimmons across the river; men are killed every day for a few paltry pennies; the Territory is a blot on the face of the continent. And the President continues to send us his castoff carpetbaggers. Those of us who have watched the course of Yankee-dominated rule since the War will not expect very much. We freely predict the Kiamichi Kid will take His Honor's measure."

Parker stared at the paper with his mouth open. It was grossly unfair. He'd hardly put foot in this town. He dropped the paper on the table and went to the window, hardly seeing Mary as she came alongside and put her arm comfortingly around him. He stood at the window and looked down and saw the grim building that marked his courthouse and jail, and he thought about the gallows that would hang twelve men. "I'll show them!" he said harshly. "Twelve men at once! I'll show them. Before I am through, they will admit on bended knee that they were wrong — terribly wrong." He picked up his Bible. "The Indian Territory shall live by the Word." He released the big gold clasp and opened the Book, turned a few pages and ran down a column with his forefinger.

" 'Be not deceived; God is not mocked: for whatsoever a man soweth, that shall he also reap,' " he read. " 'For he that soweth to his flesh, shall of the flesh reap corruption; but he that soweth to the Spirit, shall of the Spirit reap life everlasting.' " He closed the book with a slap. "Mary," he said, pacing the floor, "this will be my great work, and I shall not be found wanting."

God is not mocked: for whatsoever a man soweth, that shall he also reap.

Chapter 7

Judge Parker, wearing a sober black suit and a maroon vest of brocaded silk, sat erect in the courtroom that was to be his and looked out at a dozen or so attorneys gathered informally to hear what the new judge might have to say. He noted their apparent lethargy, their seeming indifference, but he was patient. They would learn soon enough. He looked again at his big gold watch. Two of the lawyers stood by the door, discussing Daniel Evans' case in audible tones. Parker heard the word "acquittal" and listened no further. A fat man sat in the spectator seats reading *The Western Independent*. A short, square man who looked very businesslike had an open briefcase on his lap and was going over some papers, occasionally making a mark with a pencil. Parker glanced briefly at his watch again and cleared his throat. No one looked up. At that moment young Clayton sauntered leisurely into the room, and Parker frowned momentarily. He looked back at the scattered attorneys and began:

"Gentlemen, I have called you to introduce myself and to advise you as to my future method of procedure." He saw the fat man still reading his paper and the squarish man still making notes, and the two men at the door continuing to talk. Clayton moved rather noisily across the room and took a seat in the front row; he was the only one who seemed to be listening. Parker paused and then went on without raising his voice. "I am Isaac Charles Parker of Missouri, where I practiced law and from where I was elected to Congress. As you may have noted, I was defeated for the Senate," he said dryly, "but as you may not realize, this appointment is not considered a sinecure by either the President or myself. The President is very perturbed over the unhealthy condition of law and order in the Territory and he is determined that it must be improved."

The fat man looked up rather blankly and went back to reading his paper.

Parker was becoming nettled. "The conduct and procedure of this court may be slightly different from what you are accustomed to. I shall not ask deputies to risk their lives bringing in prisoners who are predestined to acquittal."

The squarish man looked up sharply, his pencil poised. He observed Parker briefly, then went back to his notes. Clayton looked at his watch.

Parker drew a full breath. "I will ask each gentleman here to identify himself. I am acquainted with Mr. Clayton, naturally, and I have met Mr. Wilson, who is not here. I understand he had important business at the end of a pole baited for catfish."

Clayton snickered, but the squarish man looked up at Parker's face, considered it, and put his pencil in his vest pocket.

Parker waited a moment. "I have asked you to identify yourselves." He looked at the black-bearded man sitting near the wall on his left. "Colonel DuVal, you are an attorney as well as a doctor?"

"Yes, your honor. I have had training in both professions, and when I came to Fort Smith there was not enough practice in either to keep me busy. At present I practice medicine only as medical officer of the court."

"Thank you." Parker's eyes moved to the fat man, who sensed the silence, looked up quickly, and then said, "I am Thomas H. Barnes, your honor."

Parker nodded and said pleasantly, "I realize this is not a court session, but I will expect counselors to stand when they address the court."

Barnes began to struggle to his feet, but Parker stopped him. "You have already introduced yourself. Next, please."

The squarish man got up. His movements were quick and sure and indicative of strength and vigor. He wore a wide cravat tied in a bow so that both ends formed long diamond-shaped patterns against the small area of his exposed shirt. He had a flowing mustache and equally flowing, glossy black hair that fell over his shoulders. "I am Colonel Boudinot, your honor."

Parker bowed slightly. "Thank you, colonel. I have heard of your long and distinguished service as a leader of your people, the Cherokees. I am pleased to have you in this court."

The others, now following Boudinot's lead, got to their feet as their turns came: Alfred W. Arlington, Wilbur D. Reagan, and half a dozen more. Finally all had given their names but the two near the doorway. Parker fixed his gaze on them and waited. There was silence in the room. Parker looked back at his desk and then at the lawyers in the courtroom, and said pleasantly: "I have asked all gentlemen to identify themselves. Therefore if any declines to identify himself I shall be compelled to assume that he is not a gentleman and I shall, if he appears to practice in my court, be compelled to examine his credentials with great care."

Again there was silence — but more than that: an unconscious holding of breath throughout the courtroom. Finally it became apparent even to the men at the doorway. One of them looked up puzzled; the other turned his head sharply. "Have I missed something?" asked the first one, a grizzle-haired man, clean-shaven but with the black stubs of whiskers showing in such a way as to give his skin a raw look.

Parker, still pleasant, said, "I'm sure what you have missed is not as important to you as what your partner has been saying."

The second man, a nervous-looking man with a full beard, spoke up quickly: "We were discussing a case that comes up in the next session."

"What case?"

"Daniel Evans."

Parker said, "I can appreciate your laudable concern for your client. Am I correct in assuming he *is* your client?"

"Yes, sir. We're McClosky and Hickok."

Parker inclined his head. "It is indeed a great favor you have conferred upon this court by divulging your identities. I will not reveal mine, for I am sure it is not important to you, although you may be puzzled at my station in this courtroom. However, I will not burden you with any memory-taxing data on that subject except to say that if you perchance are in this area when the next session of court opens, your ignorance may be refreshed. In the meantime, my advice to your client is to consider carefully his situation with respect to the coming trial. He may find that in his selection of counsel he has demonstrated that his defenders have a fool for a client."

The courtroom was quite still. Hickok, the man with the raw skin, stood with his mouth still open, bewildered. McClosky's Adam's apple bobbed up and down as he felt the impact of Parker's sarcasm. Finally he said, "We were discussing the case."

Parker said, unperturbed, "The courtroom is not for conferences of counsel. I believe you have quarters for that purpose."

Hickok now brought a burning cigar from behind his back, put it in his mouth and drew on it slowly, obviously trying to get his bearings in a situation that suddenly had become fraught with danger.

Parker said, without looking at either McClosky or Hickok, "Certain forms of court procedure will be followed in this room. I prefer counsel, when addressing the court, to use the time-honored phrase 'your honor' — not, I hasten to add, in deference to the man on the bench but as a mark of respect to the court itself. Likewise, I will request counsel to refrain from smoking during sessions of the court. I am aware that on a somewhat primitive frontier certain forms of conduct may be disregarded by the general public, but I shall expect the attorneys who by law are officers of this court to set an example by their conduct."

Hickok slowly took the cigar from his mouth and put it behind his back.

"Whatever is the nature of your presence here," Parker said, looking up at the two, "I would suggest you remove yourselves from the doorway. In case of a fire or other emergency you might find yourselves in danger of being trampled, and I doubt that the court could be held responsible."

McClosky recovered his wits and moved quickly to sit down. Hickok followed him, still holding the cigar behind him.

"I would suggest you dispose of your cigar," said Parker. "Otherwise you may absent-mindedly sit on it, and the result might be very painful."

Hickok finally came to. He went to a window and carefully laid the cigar on the ledge, then went back and sat down, studying Parker as if his mind would not accept what his eyes and ears were telling him.

Parker looked at a sheet of paper on the big desk before him. "Court will commence promptly at eight a.m., next Monday," he announced. "The first case on the calendar is the case of the United States versus Daniel Evans, in which the government alleges murder. Mr. Clayton, are you ready to prosecute this case?"

Clayton said quickly, "Yes, your honor."

"Who is chief counsel for Daniel Evans?"

"I am, your honor," said Barnes, the fat man, and got slowly to his feet, not without considerable wheezing. "This is very short notice, your honor. I cannot be ready to try the case so soon."

Parker referred to a paper at his side. "The indictment was returned in November, seven months ago," he said. Barnes had sat down. "Evans has had one trial, and the jury has disagreed. The additional burden of a second trial is on the prosecution, and I see no reason for delay on the part of the defense. Today is Thursday, May sixth. Daniel Evans will go on trial Monday, May tenth."

Barnes started to struggle to his feet again, but McClosky was ahead of him. "Your honor, as associate counsel for Evans, I move for a continuance."

"Denied," Parker said promptly.

McClosky froze in the act of sitting down and stared at Parker.

Barnes got to his feet. "Your honor, there is a great deal of work to do on this case. We must produce witnesses, and we may have to subpoena some of them from the Territory. We cannot possibly cover so much ground in three days."

"The calendar has been available to you at all times," Parker said quietly. "If you wish to plead negligence, I will allow a short postponement."

"Your honor —" Barnes wheezed. "I'm sure your honor would not ask me to disqualify myself from practice in this court."

"Not at all."

"Then —" Barnes seemed genuinely nonplused. "My client is without funds, your honor. I request the court to appoint further counsel for the great amount of work that must be done on his case in the next three days."

A very neat scramble, thought Parker, but he said, "Very well. Who is the newest attorney in this court?"

They looked at one another. Then a young man with neatly trimmed chin whiskers arose. "Your honor, I believe I am the newest man here."

Parker studied his clean, crisp face. "You

are Rudolph Clyman. How long have you been here?"

"About a month, your honor. I read law with a firm in Atlanta."

Parker liked his appearance, his alertness, and the musical Southern drawl of his speech. "The court will appoint you associate counsel, even though the court is under the impression that Daniel Evans is well represented in numbers if not in competence."

"Your honor —" Hickok finally came to life. "I object to the court's remarks. The court is not only exhibiting bias toward Evans' counsel but it is prematurely, in effect, judging Evans himself."

Parker turned his unperturbed gaze on Hickok. "The court is fully aware of the implications. It is also painfully apparent to the court why the previous court enjoyed an unsavory reputation. You may sit down, counselor."

There was not an eye in the courtroom now that was not fixed on the bench, not an ear that was not straining to hear every word. Parker said, still pleasantly, "I am new myself, and unacquainted, but I shall go ahead with the legal business of the Western District of Arkansas. I shall pray that the court's mistakes will be small ones

— but justice must be done."

"Your honor —" Colonel Boudinot got to his feet. "Did I understand correctly — did your honor say eight o'clock?"

"You heard correctly, Colonel Boudinot. There is a top-heavy docket in this court, and it is essential to dispose of every case possible. It may interest you gentlemen to know that the court has ordered the appointment of twelve more deputy marshals, as reported in the press, and it may be anticipated that not only will the work of the court be vastly increased but also the work of the counselors will be multiplied. This will be a working court, gentlemen. Delays and continuances will not be countenanced without very good reason. We will open court at eight o'clock, have one hour for dinner and continue until dark or until the calendar is clear. Saturdays will be the same — Sundays too, if necessary."

Boudinot was still standing. "Your honor, with such a heavy schedule, the attorneys will have no time to prepare their cases."

Parker smiled briefly. "I doubt, Colonel Boudinot, that any attorney in Fort Smith is indispensable to the trial of every case. Between cases in which you appear, I think you will have time to prepare your defenses."

"But a case may take six or eight weeks, your honor."

"I doubt," said Parker, "that cases in this court will take so long. It is hardly necessary to study a man for six weeks to form a conclusion as to his guilt or lack of guilt."

"Your honor —" Colonel Boudinot, Thomas Barnes, and Colonel DuVal had spoken simultaneously.

"One at a time, please, gentlemen."

Colonel DuVal took the floor. "The court's last remark is disturbing. Does not the court expect to decide a trial by the evidence?"

Parker smiled. "By *all* evidence, counselor. I believe that is standard practice in American jurisprudence, and I think it is well known that a witness's appearance may have more influence on a jury than his words."

Colonel Boudinot jumped up. "What is the court's theory of guilt in criminal cases?"

Parker hesitated for a moment. "If you want to know whether this court will be as careless or as easily influenced as the preceding court," he said, "the answer is no. I have seen the deathly pall of terror hanging over the Territory with my own eyes, and I am resolved with all my strength to sweep it away so that the sun of justice and righteousness may shine again, and the downtrodden and afflicted may once more walk the streets without fear.

"Gentlemen, you have asked my theory of the law. The answer is brief. I am determined to uphold and enforce the law of the United States and the Word of God. My one unswerving principle will be: let no innocent man be punished; let no guilty man escape." His gaze ranged the entire room, and he looked at each man in it. "You are dismissed until Monday morning."

Chapter 8

They filed out silently. It was considerable satisfaction to Parker to know that he had given them something to think about. It rather seemed that the first session of court would get off to a good start. He gathered his papers and got up. He heard a step at the courtroom door and saw Brett Malone. "Come in," he said cordially, for somehow the sight of the young-old deputy warmed him.

Brett entered, removing his hat. "Mr. Parker, I got your deputies."

"How many?" asked Parker.

"Twelve — like you asked for."

"Where are they?"

"In the marshal's office."

"Bring them in here."

Malone disappeared, and Parker sat down, well pleased. The deputies filed in behind Malone a few minutes later, and Parker looked them over. They were unprepossessing at first appearance, for most of them were rudely, even raggedly dressed, in wool shirts, scuffed and wrinkled boots, shapeless pants, beaten felt hats or no hats at all. But, Parker observed, they were all clear-eyed and intelligent-looking and young. Five were white, four Indian, and three Negro. Parker finished scrutinizing them. "Malone," he asked, "do you vouch for all of these men?"

"Yes, sir," said Malone.

"Do all of you know what your duties will be?"

Malone said, "You better tell 'em what you told me, judge."

"Very well. I want men brought in for trial. I want them alive if possible, and I do not expect any deputy to kill a prisoner or a suspected or known criminal without absolute necessity. If any man kills carelessly, he will be tried for murder in this court. I expect you to use the greatest discretion in such matters — but I am not asking you to commit suicide. Above all, bring the prisoners to Fort Smith. If it is absolutely necessary to bring them in dead, do so — but bring them in. Does everybody understand?"

A big Negro stepped forward. "Your honor, you means you wants criminals brought to Fort Smith, an' you hope we don't have to kill 'em, but you ain't askin' us to let the other guy take first shot."

Parker nodded. "Exactly. What's your name?"

"Will Sunshine, your honor. That's my Choctaw name. I was a slave in Virginia before the wah, just name' Will. I come west an' married a Choctaw woman, and now I got a last name."

Parker felt pleased at this visible operation of the principle of freedom. "Thank you." He spoke to them all. "I take it you are acquainted with your duties and your pay, and you are willing to subscribe to the oath."

They nodded.

"Raise your right hands and repeat after me: 'I' — each man will repeat his name — 'do swear and affirm' —"

Then each man stepped up, and Parker pinned a badge on him. "All right," he said. "You will get further orders from Chief Deputy Malone. You may go now."

Malone was the last one out, and Parker stopped him. "I take it that your feeling about the necessity of putting the Kiamichi Kid on trial has not changed."

"Yes, sir, judge, that's about it."

"Then one of our first jobs is to get the Kid."

"It won't be no cinch. The Kid holes up over there in Indian country, and everybody gives him a high sign when a deputy gets anywhere in the country. He can run or he can stay and fight it out — and it would take artillery to blast him out if he decides to stay and fight. I've seen his cabin up in the Kiamichi Mountains and it's a regular fort; he just laughs at us."

Parker considered. "Let's put it this way, then: we want him and we are going to get him, but we can afford to be patient. In other words, I don't want any deputies killed trying to take him by fighting it out. Just let your men know that they are to keep their eyes open and watch for a chance to capture him."

"Yes, sir."

"That reference to Garth's Freight Lines — what do you know about that?"

Malone looked uncomfortable. "There's talk — lots of talk. There always is about any man who runs a freight line into the Territory and doesn't go broke. I don't rightly know. We never got anything on him since I been in the office. Of course, he was a friend of Judge Story, but how much that means I don't know neither. He raised Ann, you know. She was a baby when their folks died."

"We'll consider Garth a future order of business, then. We won't do anything but keep our eyes open. If he's smuggling whisky into the Nation, or rifles and ammunition, we'll find it out and we'll make an example of him. What's the matter, Malone? You look hesitant."

"Nothing's the matter, judge. I'd hate to arrest Garth on account of Ann, but I reckon I would if I had reason to."

Parker nodded approval. "That's all I ask."

At exactly eight o'clock on Monday morning, May 10, Parker raised his eyes from his big gold watch and nodded to the court caller, J. G. Hammersley. Hammersley, a small, slightly built, neat-looking man, got to his feet and sang out:

"Oyes! Oyes! The honorable district and circuit courts of the United States for the Western District of Arkansas, having criminal jurisdiction over the Indian Territory, are now in session. God bless the United States and the honorable courts."

The buzz of voices ceased, and Parker looked around to impress the scene indelibly on his mind — his first court. He was sitting in a high-backed, leather-bottomed chair, behind a huge, cherry-paneled desk. At his left hand was his big Bible, its heavy backs held together by an ornate gold clasp.

Further to his left, behind a railing, were twelve chairs for the jurymen. In front of him were oak tables for the clerk, the reporter, and the lawyers. Beyond them, and filling the small courtroom, were benches and chairs — now very scantily occupied. He thought as he glanced around the room that there were not over a dozen spectators in court. Evidently the opening of court had very little significance in Fort Smith.

"The clerk will read the first case."

The clerk, a roly-poly little man with a deep voice, jumped to his feet. "The United States of America versus Daniel Evans."

Parker looked down at the lawyers. "Mr. Barnes, are you ready?"

The fat man nodded. "Yes, your honor."

"Mr. McClosky, are you ready?"

McClosky nodded nervously.

"Yes, your honor."

"Mr. Clyman?"

"Yes, your honor."

Barnes got to his feet with some effort. "Your honor, my colleague, Mr. Clyman, will be our trial lawyer."

"Very good." Parker sniffed. There was the odor of a rank pipe. He glanced at the lawyers, then at the spectators. An old man, gray-haired and leather-faced, was puffing away methodically.

"There will be no smoking in the courtroom while the court is in session," Parker said loudly. "The bailiff will be instructed to enforce this ruling."

The old man did not seem to hear, but Parker was patient. Perhaps the old fellow wanted a moment to get used to the idea. "We will proceed to empanel a jury."

The clerk called out, "Sam Green."

The old man with the pipe leaned forward. "Present," he said.

"Will you come up here, Mr. Green?"

He left his bench with some difficulty and made his way forward, dragging his left foot.

The clerk said, "Sit there, Mr. Green."

He sat down, still puffing at his pipe. He took it from his mouth and looked at it, then carefully tamped it with the end of his little finger and continued smoking.

Parker looked at the bailiff and nodded. The bailiff tiptoed over and whispered to the old man.

Sam Green drew back indignantly. "You mean I can't smoke my pipe in this here courtroom?"

"That's the ruling, Mr. Green."

Sam Green glared at them all. "Well, I'm damned. This is the kind of things we fit the war over, but I didn't know they'd send a carpetbag judge down here to pestercate us over smoking."

Parker looked coldly down at the lawyers,

challenging them to smile. They kept their faces straight. Sam Green slowly knocked out his pipe on his heel.

Clayton asked Green a few questions. "Do you believe in capital punishment, Mr. Green?"

"If a man is guilty of murder, he needs hangin'," said Green.

Clayton indicated the defendant, a pale, sullen young man. "Do you know this man?"

"Never seen him before in my life," Green said without looking up from his pipe.

"Your panelman, Mr. Clyman."

The young lawyer looked thoughtfully at Sam Green. "Have you lived in Fort Smith long, Mr. Green?"

"Thirty-three year, come November."

"You were in the war on the Confederate side, I take it."

"They waren't no other side worth havin'!" the old man said fiercely.

"Is that a bullet in your leg?"

"No, sir. That's from a busted ankle. Cavalry horse fell on me at Pea Ridge."

Clyman nodded as if well satisfied. "No challenge," he said.

The bailiff led Green to a seat in the jury box, but the old man turned at the last

moment and addressed Parker: "Your
honor, can I send out fer a plug of tobaccer?
If I ain't allowed to smoke in this here
Yankee court I got to have something to
keep my jaws busy."

Parker wondered for a moment if one of
the lawyers had put Sam Green up to that,
but he decided against it. "The bailiff will
send out for you," he said.

Green sat down. "If I'd a-knowed a man's
rights was goin' to be trampled on, I'd never
a-come in today."

Parker sat tall and straight. "Mr. Green, I
would like to remind you that you are addressing the court of the United States.
These black robes do not ornament a man:
they clothe this court with the dignity and
majesty of the law, and I feel it my duty to
warn you that lack of respect in this court
will be treated according to law. Likewise,
Mr. Green, I would remind you that jury
duty is a duty as well as a privilege. When
any person is called for jury service in this
court, they will be expected to serve unless
there is a good reason for not doing so."

The jury box was filled in twenty minutes.
Parker had been dubious about selecting a
jury from the small number of persons
present, but more drifted in, and there was
only one challenge.

Parker, now presiding for the very first time in all his life, felt a great sense of responsibility and no little humility as he surveyed the courtroom. "The clerk will call the first witness."

Clayton established the facts of the case. A boy about nineteen years old had been found in a strip of timber by a small stream in the Creek Nation. He was dead and without shoes. A pair of heavy, coarse shoes were found nearby, and the carcass of a small gray pony with a bullet through its brain. Witnesses had seen this boy, wearing a pair of new boots with high heels and fancy tops, riding a large bay gelding with a new saddle, accompanied by an older man wearing heavy shoes and riding a small gray pony with an old saddle.

Jim Wilkerson testified that he had arrested Evans at Eufaula, wearing the boots and riding the horse. On cross examination he said Evans had told a story of having traded for the boots and horse and then having parted company with the dead boy.

Parker listened very closely to the testimony, and watched Evans studiously. He did not think Evans' attorneys would put him on the stand, and he was determined to be sure in his own mind whether the man was guilty. Evans appeared light-hearted over the entire proceeding, and carelessly oblivious. Parker began to form a serious dislike of him. He realized of course that such a dislike must not be allowed to influence his opinion of Evans' guilt or innocence, and so he put it out of his mind and concentrated on culpability. He could not escape the conclusion that the man was guilty.

The trial went along very fast under Parker's urging. Word went out that a new and different judge was at work in the courtroom, and after dinner more spectators drifted in. The bailiff had to stop many of them from smoking, and at his suggestion Parker sent out for half a dozen spittoons. It seemed that men accustomed to using tobacco constantly were bound to chew if they could not smoke.

To Parker's astonishment, Clyman put Evans on the witness stand late in the afternoon, and the man told the same story he had told before; he had bought the boots and the horse from young Seabolt, and probably young Seabolt had later been killed for his money. On both direct and cross examination he denied absolutely that he had harmed Seabolt in any way, to say nothing of killing him.

Parker adjourned court at six o'clock,

well pleased with his progress. He was quite aware that he had promulgated a revolution in court procedure in Fort Smith. He gathered up his few papers — for he had kept no notes — and his big Bible and prepared to leave, when Clayton stepped back in. The courtroom was empty but for the two of them, and Clayton said, "Your honor, I'm worried about this case."

"There's nothing to worry about," said Parker. "The man is guilty."

"I think so too — but I have no evidence to prove it. His story is a common one, and everybody here knows it could be true."

"I know it isn't," said Parker.

"But your function is to interpret the law — not to judge the evidence."

Parker chuckled. "Was there ever a judge who didn't have an opinion?"

"Possibly not," Clayton admitted. "But you are not supposed to let the jury know what you think about it."

"Why not?" Parker scoffed. "Any jury looks to the court for guidance. They expect to be prompted, and they will bring in the verdict the judge wants."

"Your honor, allowing what the judge wants to be a factor in a jury's verdict is a dangerous precedent."

"This is a dangerous country," Parker

said. "Your namby-pamby rules of court procedure will accomplish nothing but the bogging-down of justice. Know one thing, Mr. Clayton: the President has ordered the establishment of order in the Indian Territory. Whatever is necessary to accomplish that end you may expect to see done in my court."

"Very well, sir, but —"

"A man is waiting in your office, Mr. Clayton," said Brett Malone from the doorway.

"All right, I'll be right there." Clayton hurried out.

Malone came on in. "What's worrying him?"

For some reason Parker liked the informality shown by Malone. "He's carrying the weight of the world on his shoulders," Parker said. "He has a murderer at the bar and he is afraid he can't convict him."

"You're sure Evans is guilty?"

"Quite sure," said Parker. "I've been watching him all day. He is thoroughly no good, impudent and insolent. He's as guilty as he can be."

"Then what's Mr. Clayton worryin' about?"

"Because he hasn't been able to prove it."

"You mean Evans will go free?"

"Not in the least." Parker stood up. "Not while I am judge of this court."

"Can you tell the jury to convict him?"

"I certainly can — and I shall if it is necessary. I am a judge. The very title is indicative of my position — to judge guilt or innocence. And if I see the defense attorneys getting the jury confused, I believe it to be a part of my work to straighten them out."

Malone nodded soberly. "I always wondered why a judge didn't do that. I seen several juries mixed up."

"Probably because it's easier to say nothing. Goodnight, Malone."

"Goodnight, Mr. Parker."

He started out. "By the way, have you seen Ann over the week-end?"

A blush spread over Malone's wind-tanned face. "We was riding yesterday over to Van Buren. Went to church last night."

"A very good place to go," Parker said approvingly. "And a nice ride home in the moonlight."

Malone blushed again. "Yes, sir — but there isn't no moon till morning."

"Oh. Well, goodnight."

Chapter 9

Mary was interested and solicitous — as she always was — when Parker reached the hotel. She brought him a glass of wine, and sat across the table from him, asking all about his first day in court. She would have been there, she said, if she had found someone to take care of Charlie. Was it hard work? Did he like it? Who was on trial? How were the lawyers accepting the new judge?

To all of which he answered patiently and pleasantly, dwelling on the many occurrences of the day with some pleasure and quite a bit of gratification. "They had to learn that the judge — not the attorneys — controls the court," he remarked, sipping the wine.

Presently, when he was through talking, she said, "Isaac, I have found a nice house for us, but it is not for rent. We'll have to buy it."

He nodded thoughtfully. "We can manage, I think, though it may take some careful economy. My salary here is considerably less than it has been, you know."

"I know," she said, pouring more wine. "I will do my part, Isaac. Whatever you say."

"I'm sure you will. By the way, where is Charlie this evening?"

She answered distastefully, "Playing with Annie Maledon. Isaac," — she faced him — "I wish he had someone besides that hangman's daughter to play with."

"George Maledon is very highly thought of in Fort Smith."

She shuddered. "Yes, but he — he hangs people."

"Not he — the government."

She shook her head. "He hangs people, Isaac, and you cannot argue your way out of that. He hangs them and I have heard he gets a hundred dollars for every man he kills."

Parker frowned. He watched Mary as she went across the room to look out of the window for Charlie. She was a large woman as women went, but she lacked three inches of being as tall as he was, and she was strong and moved gracefully, and he still felt a glow of pride over her. In money matters too she was very cooperative; she adjusted herself to his income, whatever it was, and always managed to look very stylish and attractive and to keep Charlie nicely dressed. He was very fortunate, he realized, in having Mary as a wife. He felt sure it would be only a matter of a few weeks until she would adjust herself to life in Fort Smith.

She turned back, avoiding his eyes. She went to the bureau and poured more wine. He watched her lift the glass, and said thoughtfully, "Mary, you seem unsteady. Are you sure you haven't had enough?"

She tossed the wine down. "I'm trying to forget about that man killing people for a hundred dollars apiece," she said a little thickly.

He didn't answer. This was a passing mood — probably a reaction from the long and arduous trip from Washington. That, he reflected, was enough to color anyone's outlook. . . .

In court the next day Clayton showed that Evans had been wearing Seabolt's boots; they were pretty thoroughly identified by a heel that had come loose and been nailed back on with horseshoe nails. He showed that Seabolt and Evans had traveled together, and that soon after the time Seabolt was killed, Evans was seen with the boots and the horse. But dinnertime came and Clayton stopped in the courtroom for a moment. "I'll never get a conviction in this case," he said.

"Do you think he's guilty?" Parker asked.

"I can't think anything else."

"Then what are you worrying about?"

"Well, look, your honor. I've shown all these connections with the murdered man — but Evans has never denied them. He has an explanation, and although I don't believe it for a minute, I am bound to say that from a legal standpoint it is my opinion that we must produce some evidence to tear down his explanation or we shall lose the case."

Parker got up and slipped the black robe from his shoulders. "Go ahead with your case," he advised. "Have faith in eventual justice." He smiled at Clayton. "How's your youngster? Over the measles yet?"

"Apparently," said Clayton. "That's a load off of my mind, too."

"I should imagine it would be. If you'll wait a minute I'll get on my coat and walk as far as the drug store with you. Since we have no cooking facilities, I'm eating at the Oyster Saloon."

"I'd be honored to have you at our house for dinner, but —"

"No, no, I wouldn't think of it. Your wife has enough on her hands with a sick baby. I'll just walk up the street with you. It probably will be frowned on by defense attorneys, but for the moment we won't worry about it."

After dinner Evans was called for redirect examination. Parker watched young

Clayton batter the man with questions but apparently fail to make a dent in the man's self-assured insolence. Finally Clayton said wearily, "Prosecution rests, your honor."

"No more questions," said Clyman.

"There will be a five-minute recess before the jury is addressed," said Parker.

There was a rather full courtroom by now, and Parker was well pleased, for what he had in mind would be most beneficial before a large audience. He resumed his seat behind the big desk and said pleasantly, "It has been called to my attention that the floor of the courtroom has been used as a cuspidor. I will ask spectators to please observe that spittoons are provided for their use. This is a federal court and not a cave in the mountains. If you cannot spit in the proper receptacles, kindly refrain from using tobacco."

He heard muttering as he looked at his watch, but he did not mind. It was his court and he would run it as he deemed proper — not like a cockfight.

Clayton addressed the jury. His talk was faltering, however, and Parker saw that he had no confidence in the case. He was young and conscientious, but he would have to learn better oratory if he expected to make a good prosecutor.

Clyman spoke, and in a short but forceful summary put his finger on every flaw in Clayton's case, exactly as Clayton had done at noon.

Finally they were through, and Parker took a drink of water and arose to his feet. This would be his first charge to a jury. He cleared his throat, adjusted the black robe so that it hung in graceful folds from his shoulders, and prepared to deliver his charge.

"Gentlemen of the jury," he began, "in addressing you on this occasion I am impressed with the greatness of the government of the United States of America. Its greatness consists in the fact that all of its power is in the hands of those who are to be benefited or injured — in the hands of the people. A government like this will always be strong and will not perish.

"This is my unfaltering belief. Likewise it is my firm belief that every accused person shall have the right to speedy and just trial; this is guaranteed in the Constitution of the United States, and I, as judge of a federal court, am bound to uphold this right." He glanced at Daniel Evans and his jaws tightened. "We are here today to call to judgment a man who murdered his companion for a horse and a pair of boots," he said, "and I wish to call your attention to the salient facts." He launched into a summary of the case. He had no notes and needed none; his memory was clear and accurate, and it functioned at its best when he was addressing an audience. After an hour of reviewing the evidence, he advised the jury of its possible decisions.

"You could, of course, find this defendant innocent, but I am sure you will not do so." He heard a sharp intake of breath from Clyman. "You have observed the defendant for two days," he said inexorably, "and you know as well as I do that he is completely and unalterably guilty of murder." He glanced at Evans and was gratified to see that the man had been jarred at last. He went on with considerable satisfaction. "If you find this man guilty of murder, as I am sure you will, then it will be the duty of the court to determine his punishment."

The bailiff, Frank Sinclair, escorted the twelve men to the jury room, and Parker resumed his seat.

Clyman was up. "Your honor," he said, "I move for a retrial on the ground of the following errors made in the rulings of the court."

He enumerated eighteen so-called errors,

and Parker listened attentively.

"And finally," said Clyman, "I respectfully object to the court's charge to the jury, in which the defendant was referred to as a 'murderer,' and in which the court stated that it had no doubt the jury would return a verdict of guilty, and in which the court also discussed the case as if there could be no other verdict, to wit: by advising the jury that it was the court's prerogative to fix the punishment, in such a manner as to exclude from the jury's mind any consideration of the case except as to the punishment. Your honor, I ask the court to consider these points, and I respectfully move for a retrial on the grounds stated."

"Denied," Parker said promptly.

Clyman was in the act of sitting down. He glanced up at Parker with his mouth open, then finally said abruptly, "Exception!" and sat down.

Parker was not perturbed. He leaned back in the big chair and put his fingertips together. "The court takes into consideration counselor's youth and inexperience and also the fact that counselor has had no previous legal work in this section of the country."

Clyman jumped to his feet, but Parker ignored him and continued. "It is a waste of breath to take an exception in this court," he said.

Clyman was standing. "I'm afraid I don't understand, your honor."

"There is no appeal from the decisions of this court," Parker said.

Clyman slowly turned white. "Your honor, I —" He stopped, seemingly aghast at the awful implication of Parker's words. "Perhaps," he said shakily, "the court will enlighten me further."

"Gladly," Parker said, pleased at the sensation his words had created. "This court, in trying criminal cases, sits as a circuit court, and the federal statutes fail to provide for appeal of a circuit court's decisions to the supreme court of the United States in criminal cases."

"Your honor, I was not aware —"

Parker smiled faintly. The courtroom was buzzing now. Only the attorneys who had known this all the time were silent. Perhaps, he thought, they had hoped he would not be aware of this power.

"But this — surely, your honor, this is an unintentional omission from the statutes, and —"

"This court," Parker said firmly, "does not question the statutes or inquire into omissions or errors. This court *interprets* the statutes. Again I remind counselor that there is no appeal from the decisions of this court." He sat straight and tall and sternfaced as he said that, for he knew fully what power he held in his judicial hands, and it gave him a God-like feeling that he never had experienced before.

"But *surely,* your honor, there is some recourse. If what you say is unqualifiedly accurate, then this must be the only trial court in modern history from whose decisions there is no appeal."

"It may be the only one," Parker conceded. "My familiarity with judicial history does not, I regret, extend far enough to give me personal knowledge of that aspect. However, this court's decisions are absolutely final. It may be that the Congress meant them to be so, for this is a violent country, and violent means are necessary to bring order."

Barnes got to his feet with some difficulty. "Your honor, may I ask for information?"

"You may."

"Is it the court's opinion also that the President cannot commute or pardon men convicted in this court?"

Parker was complete master of the situation. "Of course he has that right," he answered, "but I can assure you it is not an avenue of relief to be relied upon, for the President is heartily sick of conditions in the Territory, and he has told me personally there will be very little executive interference with the functions of this court. In other words, gentlemen, he has told me to clean up this mess you have allowed to brew here in Fort Smith — and I am going to do it!"

There was silence for a moment. Then Clyman, still on his feet, said pleadingly, "Your honor, there are certain safeguards of standard court procedure that have evolved under the Constitution of the United States. One is that the fact of guilt is to be judged by a jury, and the court's role —"

"Do you mean to say," asked Parker sternly, "that the court is not as well qualified to judge the facts as a man following a mule in a furrow?"

Clyman floundered. "No, your honor. I —"

Parker leaned forward, narrow-eyed. "Does counsel wish to subject himself to a charge of contempt?"

"No, your honor. It is only — my client's life may depend on this ruling."

"His victim's life depended on his mercy," Parker said implacably, "of which there was none." He felt a little sorry for Clyman, and tried to lighten the blow.

"For counsel's information, I will say that the rules of court procedure he mentions were designed and evolved for courts in a civilized country; this court is not in a civilized country. I am aware that there will be charges of 'leading the jury,' but I am compelled in all candor to say that the court will not be responsive to such charges. This court is interested only in the guilt or innocence of a man on trial. Further, this court will not be prejudiced by his race or by his color or by his associations. His guilt or innocence is all that matters."

"But your honor —" Clyman was desperate. "The impartial determination of a man's guilt or innocence is at the very foundation of our legal structure, and those safeguards —"

Parker, finally annoyed by this haggling, glared at Clyman. Clyman saw the displeasure in Parker's eyes and abruptly stopped talking. He sat down, obviously reluctant but finally submitting to the will of the court.

Parker looked at his watch, idly wondering if by chance this was Clyman's first case. He was about to announce a recess when the bailiff came in. "Your honor, the jury wishes to return."

Parker looked at him, hardly able to conceal his elation. Such a quick decision could mean only one thing. "Bring them in," he said.

The jury filed in, led by Sam Green.

"Have you reached a verdict?" asked Parker.

"We have, your honor," said Sam Green.

"Will you hand your verdict to the clerk?"

Green shifted the cud of tobacco from one cheek to the other and handed the folded paper to Glen Holbrook. The rolypoly little man unfolded it and began to read in his startlingly deep voice: "We, the jury, find the defendant Daniel Evans guilty of murder."

A woman gave a little scream in the back of the court. There was a buzz of voices. The jury looked well satisfied. The attorneys were quiet. Clyman's head was down as he stared at the floor. Parker looked at Evans. For the first time the man seemed to be serious and apparently somewhat flabbergasted.

"This prisoner will be returned to his cell, and extra precautions will be taken to prevent escape," Parker said. "Sentence will be passed later, after the court has taken the facts and the law under advisement."

Chapter 10

Malone, standing at the door, came up and got the prisoner, moving silently in his moccasins. The lawyers arose and drifted out. The audience broke up into little knots, each one clustered around some individual who had the floor.

It was pretty late for the next case, and anyway Parker did not want an anti-climax. He arose and went to his chambers, carrying the big Bible. His "chambers" were an office room opening off of the courtroom; it was similar to Clayton's but a little larger. He hung up his robe and put on his coat and his silk hat. He had thought of discarding the silk hat as pretentious in a town like Fort Smith, but he had decided it would be more dramatic to keep it. Since he had been conspicuously identified with it from the first, let them be constantly aware of it as a badge of his office, as a reminder of the justice that he would dispense from his courtroom in the old military barracks. He set the hat straight on his head and pulled it tight.

Outside, he ran into Clayton, who said doubtfully, "I did not think we would get a conviction in that case."

"Is there any doubt in your mind about the man's guilt?"

"No, not really."

"What are the lawyers saying?"

Clayton shook his head. "They're grumbling. The older heads knew it all along, of course, but nobody ever cared, because if a convicted man could afford an appeal he could also afford a direct application to the judge — which in Fort Smith was far more reliable than an appeal."

"Let them grumble," Parker said. "They have much more to learn." He smiled at Clayton's wide eyes, and stepped back to get his Bible.

He walked to the hotel, smiling pleasantly when he passed anyone. He reached the office of *The Western Independent*, and Weaver came running out with a dirty printer's apron tied around him. "Hear you finished Evans' case, judge?" he said.

"Yes."

"Come in and sit down." Weaver seemed pleased over something, and Parker followed him into the little shop. It was only one room, and a tiny one at that, with typecases along one wall, a rolltop desk at the front, a small pile of newsprint near the water bucket on a bench at the back, a hand-press taller than Parker, and over all the fragrance of fresh paper and the spicy aroma of printer's ink. Parker sat in one of the two chairs.

"I understand you charged the jury to find him guilty," said Weaver, taking off his apron.

"Not exactly. I merely indicated what I thought the evidence showed."

Weaver laid his apron across a type-case. "You feel there's no doubt of Evans' guilt?"

"I know there isn't."

Weaver put one foot on the rung of the high-stool, pulled up his sock and tightened the garter. "You're not afraid of setting a precedent?"

"I am my own precedent," said Parker quietly. "The situation warrants it."

"You mind if I quote you on that?"

"Not at all."

"You realize," said Weaver, standing up, "that I am forced to print both sides of this, no matter where my sympathy lies."

"I hadn't given it any thought."

"I'm running a newspaper, you know, and I try to print all sides. I have my own personal convictions about crime in the Territory and consequently in Fort Smith, but I print opinions from all who have anything to say."

"So I noticed," said Parker. "Including your own."

Weaver colored. "Naturally."

"You were not very charitable," Parker observed.

"No. I think our past experience in Fort Smith explains that."

"Possibly."

"You must realize one thing, judge. I could be all for you but I wouldn't dare to say so in my paper. My readers expect me to raise hell, and that's what I do. Mostly it's been justified, because conditions here under carpetbag rule have been terrible. I'll give your side when you want me to, but don't be surprised if I express doubt. Anything else would be looked on here as Yankee talk." Weaver was putting on his coat. "I'll buy you a drink, judge."

"No, thanks," said Parker. "I am not a user of hard liquor."

Gil Weaver chuckled. "Well, every man to his own poison, I always say."

Parker followed him out.

Weaver didn't lock the door. "If anybody wants in they'll break a window anyway — so why tempt them?"

The street was dry, and the ridges of mud thrown up several days before by wagon wheels were iron hard and difficult to walk on. Parker stumbled once, and Weaver caught his arm.

144

"Well, I leave you here," said Weaver finally. "Stop in whenever you come by this way. And if you ever change your mind about that drink, let me know."

"I will," said Parker.

He went on, feeling warmer toward the editor. Weaver's friendliness, he felt sure, was a symbol of what all would feel before he finished his task — all except the criminals and the defense lawyers.

When he reached the hotel, Mary took his hat and coat. "Did you finish the case today?"

"It's finished," he said, sitting down.

"What — what was the verdict?"

"Guilty."

"What are you going to do now?"

He glanced at her face. "Mary, you look almost fearful. Did you know Evans, by any chance?"

"Not at all," she said. "I've never seen him."

He relaxed. "You acted as though he might be a long-lost brother of yours."

"No." But still she stood there. "What *are* you going to do, Isaac?"

He spoke absently. "Sentence him, of course — as the law provides." He reached for the Bible, unfastened the clasp, and opened it to Revelations. He started down one column with his forefinger. . . .

The next morning at eight o'clock the case of Edmund Campbell came to the bar of justice. This morning, Parker noticed, the courtroom was filled, and he was pleased to see a difference in the attitude of the lawyers. There was an alertness now that had not been there before, and Thomas Barnes no longer sprawled his huge bulk in his chair but sat up straight. Colonel Boudinot seemed brighter-eyed and those others in the front rows of seats, who obviously had appeared the first two days only to see how the new judge would conduct his court, were back again — this time to learn everything they could. The fact of not being able to make an appeal, Parker thought wryly, had had quite an effect on their attentiveness.

Campbell's trial lasted a day and a half, and he was found guilty, with Parker, as before, giving the jury the benefit of his own conclusions about the man.

James Moore, an outlaw with a record of crimes in the Territory, had robbed an old man; a posse had pursued him and he had killed one of the men. He expressed no regret, saying that the dead man was the eighth he had killed — not counting "niggers and Indians." Parker felt that justice had been done when the jury found him guilty.

Smoker Man-Killer was a Cherokee who spoke no English, and Parker hired an interpreter for him, a halfbreed named High Wind Blows. High Wind looked like a renegade himself, Parker thought, but Malone, who listened to his interpretations, said he was honest.

Parker was frequently astonished at the great fund of information which Malone had at his command. He knew several Indian languages — not well enough to interpret, he said, but well enough to understand. And he was getting along well with his deputies — all older men. At this moment the twelve were over in the Territory looking for lawbreakers; George Ishaharjo was limping around with the help of a cane; and Jim Wilkerson was up in northwest Arkansas serving some papers.

Smoker Man-Killer's wife and child and two sisters were very prominent in the courtroom, and wept silently most of the day, but the jury was not moved. Smoker had killed a neighbor without apparent motivation, and he was found guilty.

John Whittington had a wife and two children; he had killed an old man, cutting his throat to obtain a hundred dollars; his knife, with the victim's blood on it, was found by the body, and the jury, under Parker's guidance, found Whittington guilty.

Samuel Fooy was the last man tried for murder at that session. He was half Cherokee and half white, and he had killed a barefoot itinerant school teacher for $250. He had a wife and three children, but one of the chief witnesses against him was a woman to whom he had boasted of the killing, and Parker wasted no words in telling the jury what he thought. The jury found Fooy guilty.

The Western Independent that week commented on the six convictions. Parker read the item while he was standing alone in the drug store having a vanilla soda.

"It is notable that Fort Smith's new federal judge exhibits no misplaced sympathy and no tendency toward softness in the cases of men tried for murder. Attorneys of Fort Smith are freely complaining that Judge Parker's methods are high-handed, but privately most of them are not slow to admit that some such tactics are absolutely necessary to cope with the carnival of crime that has reigned in the Indian Territory since Arkansas was first admitted to statehood."

The next day Parker announced that the

six convicted men would be sentenced the following morning at eight o'clock, and listened to a plea by Clyman for a light sentence for Daniel Evans by reason of circumstantial evidence.

Parker noted coldly that Evans had shown no clemency toward young Seabolt, and he pointed out that the time for consideration of such things was before a crime was committed.

That night he sat up late, reading the Bible. Long after Mary was asleep he continued, by the light of the coal-oil lamp, to turn the pages and peruse the columns, noting chapters and verses. A rooster was crowing off to the east when he finally arose, closed the Bible quietly, and got into bed beside Mary.

It seemed only minutes later that Mary was shaking him. "Isaac, you must get up at once or you'll be late!"

He got up, yawning. The sleep of the just, he thought.

He shaved and put on his coat and hat. He said, "Kiss me, Mary."

She kissed him warmly.

"You're a great comfort."

"You're worried, aren't you, Isaac?"

"No," he said honestly. "I do not worry. I make my decisions according to the law and the Word, and then I worry no more about them."

"I'm sure you will do what is right, Isaac."

"Thank you, Mary. I appreciate your confidence."

He walked his usual route to the courthouse, went into his chambers at ten minutes to eight, put on his robe, read a page in the Bible, and then walked into the courtroom.

It was crowded. All the lawyers were present, and men and women and some children were standing in the aisles and sitting in the open windows, for it was a warm day.

He walked to his big chair, laid the Bible on his left, his watch on the right, and sat down. For a moment he closed his eyes, asking for divine guidance. Then he looked at his watch and turned to Hammersley. "Ask Deputy Malone to bring in the prisoners."

Five minutes later the six men appeared. All were shackled with their hands behind them. They were guarded by Brett Malone, tall, lean, and as tough as a young oak tree in a storm; Jim Wilkerson, big, shambling, easy-going; and George Maledon, unsmiling, sharp-eyed, with two pistols in the belt around the outside of his coat, a strange-looking little man with his huge beard the size and shape of a patriarch beaver's tail.

Unexpectedly Parker felt a great affection as he looked at Malone; he wondered if Charlie would grow up to be like him. Briefly he thought that Malone was nearer the age his son should be; there were thirty-four years between himself and Charlie, but only twenty-two between himself and Malone. He had begun to see, since Charlie had been born, that such a wide gap of years as thirty-four created was hard to bridge.

The six men walked up to the big cherry-paneled desk and faced the judge.

He stood up.

"John Whittington, step forward."

The man took two shuffling steps toward him. He was apprehensive but plainly defiant.

Parker, his left hand on the Bible, held Whittington's eyes with his own, determined to burn into the man's very soul the words he was about to speak.

"John Whittington," he said in a ringing tone that filled the courtroom, "there is but One who can pardon your offense; this is the Savior whose blood is sufficient to wash from your soul the guilty stain. Let me therefore beg of you to fly to Him for that mercy and that pardon which you cannot expect of mortals. When you return to the solitude of your prison, let me entreat you by all that is still dear to you that you seriously reflect on the conduct of your past life. Bring to your mind all the aggravated horrors of that dreadful hour when the soul of the murdered Turner was sent unprepared into the presence of its God. Think of the dreadful agony of the unnatural widowhood to which you reduced the unfortunate partner of his bed and board. Think upon the poor orphan child who is now left fatherless to the mercy of the world. And when, by such reflection as these, your heart shall become softened, let me again beseech you, before your bloodstained hands are raised in supplication before the judgment seat of Christ, that you fly to the arms of the Savior and endeavor to seize upon the salvation of His cross."

Parker now was filled almost to bursting with the tremendous emotion of that moment. It had been building up inside of him for days and now in one blinding flash of righteousness he felt lifted to the highest peaks, and for a moment he was unable to speak.

The courtroom was as still as death, but Parker saw nothing but the man before him and the great crime he had committed against God and Nature.

"John Whittington, you have been found guilty of the crime of murder. Have you anything to say before sentence is pronounced upon you?"

He would never know whether John Whittington answered or not, for the pressure building up within him was almost unbearable. He swallowed and gasped for breath, and then he brought his iron control to bear.

"John Whittington, I sentence you to be hanged by the neck until you are dead, *dead,* DEAD!"

He stood straight and tall, his eyes blazing with righteous fury. Through dimmed vision he saw Malone step up and take Whittington back to his place in line, and then suddenly Parker felt limp. He had said the dreadful words, and now came the reaction that even he had not been prepared for. He sat down in the big chair, buried his face in his arms, and wept. He sobbed aloud, and great tears poured from his eyes and wet the desk.

After a moment he looked up. There was a strange silence in the courtroom. No one moved. Parker stood up again. "Daniel Evans, step forward."

Five times more he lectured the convicted men on the terrible error of their ways. Five times he pronounced the dreadful words of death. And five times more he felt the great, tumultuous building up of pressure within himself, and the sudden letdown after he had spoken the ominous words: ". . . until you are dead, dead, dead!"

Then, as in a haze, he knew the six men were taken away. He adjourned court. He was completely exhausted. He had intended to go on with minor cases that day, but he needed time to regather his strength. He left the courtroom, went into his chambers and sat down, resting his face in his hands, trying to overcome the lethargy that had descended upon him.

Presently there was a soft knock on the door. He raised his head and said, "Come in."

Brett Malone entered, his big, ragged hat pushed to the back of his head. His eyes were shining.

"Judge," he said. "I gotta hand it to you." He put a friendly hand on Parker's shoulder. "Most people didn't think you had the nerve. They were making bets around town."

"What kind of bets, Malone?"

"They were offering two to one you'd let

at least one of them off, and they offered even money you wouldn't sentence more than one to hang."

"And what were the odds, Brett, against my sentencing all of them to hang?"

Malone shook his head. "Ten to one, sir."

"Did you take any of them, Brett?"

"All I could. I borrowed a hundred and seventy dollars from Jim Wilkerson, and I bet thirty of it that you would hang all six. I cleared about seven hundred dollars today."

Parker frowned. "It's a terrible thing to bet on men's lives."

"We were betting on you. I knew a man with your kind of face would have a backbone like a poker. My old man had that kind of face — a little bony, and not a weak spot in it anywhere. I'm real proud of you, judge."

Parker basked for a moment in this unexpected approval.

"Of course," he said, "you're happy because you won a lot of money. But it must have seemed an awful risk to you."

"Not too much risk." Malone's eyes were thoughtful. "Not too much. I was bettin' on the man — not on nothin' else."

Chapter 11

Eventually Parker left his chambers and went up Garrison. He walked a little unsteadily at first, but after a block or so he got his legs under him. He passed the House of Lords Saloon, and noted an unusual number of saddled horses in front of it. Everywhere along the street, however, there was dead silence as he went by. He stopped at the Thompson Drug Store for a soda, and there met Gil Weaver.

"Judge," said Weaver, "I have to hand it to you. I never thought you'd do it."

"Have a soda?" asked Parker.

"I'd appreciate it — if I can pay for it."

"Suit yourself," said Parker. "Are you one of those who lost to young Malone?"

"I'm ashamed to say I am — but I'll be proud to pay up, for this is a great day. Law and order are coming to Fort Smith at last!"

"I'm glad you approve."

"Approve! Hell, I'd help string 'em up!"

The sodas were pushed across the marble counter, and Weaver dropped a twenty-cent piece down beside them.

"That young deputy of yours — he's sure sold on you. I never seen anybody argue for somebody as hard as he did for you. Understand he had a fight down at the Two Brothers."

"I'm sorry to hear that."

"Don't worry about Brett. He can take better care of himself than any man in Arkansas — and that's taking in considerable territory."

Parker felt better after the soda, and decided to return to his chambers and get his work lined up for the next day. But after he got there he was restless, and went back into the courtroom and stood behind the high-backed chair. Then he went to an open window, and was standing there when Clayton came in. Clayton said, "You acted admirably, your honor. It was indeed high time."

"Thank you."

"I suppose you are aware that you didn't set a date, your honor."

Parker looked out at the massive gallows. "Yes, I am aware of that. How many more murder indictments are coming up at this term of court?"

"There are none, your honor."

Parker said thoughtfully, "I have no doubt the sentencing of six men to death will have a profound influence throughout the Territory."

"Yes, your honor — and now the Territory will wait to see what happens."

Parker swung around, his hands clasped behind him. "What do you mean — what will happen?"

"They will wait to see if you will actually hang them."

"Why should I have sentenced them?"

"Men have been sentenced before," said Clayton, "but very few of them have dangled at the ends of George Maledon's ropes."

Parker started to answer, but thought better of it. Let them wonder. The impact of the execution would be all the greater when it came. He looked out once more at the gallows. "The new deputies will be returning presently," he said. "They may have some more candidates for the grand jury."

He made his way back up the street an hour before his usual time, spoke to all he met whom he knew. The banker came out on the wooden sidewalk to shake his hand. "It was a good day for Fort Smith when you came here, judge."

"Thank you."

"By the way, we're going to finance that house for you. Thought you'd like to know."

Parker nodded, smiling. "It will make

Mary happy," he said.

"You can come in any time to sign the papers."

Parker nodded absently. "I'll be in."

At the hotel Parker went upstairs. Mary did not answer the door, and he turned the knob and went on in.

"Mary!" he cried incredulously.

She was sitting near the window, her face in her hands, sobbing loudly.

He crossed the room quickly and put his hands on her shoulders. "Mary, what's the trouble?"

She didn't look up. "I heard what you did," she said finally.

"What I did?" he repeated.

"Yes." She sobbed. "You sentenced six men to death!"

It made him think for a moment, and then he understood. Mary was showing the natural sentimental weakness of her sex. He humored her. "There, there. It's not as bad as it sounds. All these men were convicted by a jury. All were found guilty of murder. The law prescribes the penalty. All I did was pronounce it."

"They say you told the juries what to do."

He opened his mouth, then closed it. Her face was still buried in her hands. "Isaac, I never thought I'd see the day."

159

"You knew what a judgeship involved, didn't you?"

"I guess not."

"Have you seen any of these men?" he demanded.

"No."

"Then why —"

"It's a life, Isaac. A human life! And you are taking it!"

"Not I," he said. "The law is taking it. And you are forgetting something: the wives made into widows by the vicious greed of killers; the children made fatherless."

"Two wrongs don't make a right, Isaac."

He became a little impatient. "I have sworn to administer the law," he said. "If I am to keep that oath, I have no choice. I have promised the President that I will establish order in the Territory. I cannot do that with a slap on the hand. Criminals must be punished — in a dramatic fashion so that all the world may know that murder and rape are no longer countenanced in the Territory."

She had stopped crying. "I suppose there is no use talking to you," she said tearfully.

"None whatever. Where is Charlie?"

"Locked in the wardrobe."

"Why?"

She looked up, facing him. "Isaac, do you

know where your son was today?"

"I'm sure I don't."

"I missed him," she said, "at noon, and I went to look for him. Annie Maledon told me where he was — down at the house of that awful Indian Rose!"

"Well, after all," he said uncertainly, "Charlie's only four."

"Isaac," she said severely, "do you want your son to grow up among women like that?"

"Well — of course not."

"Then now is the time to stop it. I demand that you give him a strapping."

Parker frowned. "He's too young to know what it means."

"He's not too young to mind, Isaac. It's not the first time this has happened."

"You haven't told me."

"You were filled with your own problems and I didn't want to worry you. But Charlie was down there a week ago, and I told him not to go back. Just yesterday I caught him within a block of that awful house."

"Well, let's get him out of the wardrobe."

He opened the flimsy door. Charlie was sitting with his back against the wall. He looked up, his blue eyes — like Mary's — bright with anticipation, his tawny hair — like his father's — badly mussed.

"Isaac," said Mary loudly, "I demand that you give him a strapping!" Her voice was becoming shrill.

Parker temporized. "He's only four years old."

"He disobeyed me."

"He's in a strange place, in a strange town, among strange people. You can hardly expect —"

"He will come to a bad end in company like that," Mary insisted.

Parker took Charlie into his arms. "You won't go down there again, will you, son?"

Charlie's eyes were brighter as he shook his head. Parker hugged him briefly and set him down. "Mr. Hoffman just spoke to me, Mary." He watched Charlie go out of the room. "The bank is going to help us buy our house." He put his arms around her. "We'll have a place of our own — in a better part of town. This is no fair test for any child."

She looked at him. Some strange emotion was in her eyes, but he could not tell what it was. Then she turned and went to the wine bottle. "Isaac," she said as she pulled the cork with a little pop, "about Evans. How can you know he is guilty?"

"I know," he said. "That's my business as a judge." He took off his coat. "I watched Evans for two days, and I know. There is no shadow of a doubt, no reason to reconsider."

"And the other five?"

He tasted the wine. "Likewise," he assured her.

She sat in a straight chair, facing him, studying him, with a look he never had seen in her face before. It was as if she was reserving part of her thoughts, keeping some of herself a secret from him.

A little uncomfortable under her scrutiny, he began to review the six cases, stressing the viciousness of the various crimes, and feeling, in the telling, more sure of his rightness in handling them the way he had. . . .

The next day Malone stopped in to see him. "I'm going up to Tahlequah to bring back some prisoners," he said. "Be gone three or four days."

"What kind of prisoners?" Parker asked.

"I don't know about that. Will Sunshine rode in last night with a bullet in his leg and said they had rounded up quite a bunch, and I thought I'd better ride up there and be sure they get here."

"Who shot Sunshine?"

"The Kiamichi Kid or somebody with him. They weren't after the Kid just then, neither. But that's the way the Kid works. He shoots first." Malone shook his head. "If

I ever get him in my rifle sights, it'll be a temptation."

Parker glanced up at Malone; then he rose and put an arm on Malone's sinewy shoulders. "I've become very fond of you in the last few weeks, Malone. I look on you practically as a son."

"Yes, sir. You've seemed more like a father to me than like a judge, I'm bound to admit."

"I think we'll be much closer in the years to come, and I think you'll make a fine chief deputy, and, when you're older, a good marshal. But right now, Brett, promise me something. Promise me you won't do any careless shooting."

Malone looked down at his moccasins. "I never intended to, Mr. Parker — but I don't aim to come home with a bullet in me like Will Sunshine."

Parker withdrew his arm. "How is Will?"

"He's all right — but he won't be walking for a month, the doc says."

"We'll keep him on the payroll," Parker decided.

Malone brightened. "That's nice of you, judge."

"It's only fair," said Parker. "He was wounded in the discharge of his duties."

During the next few days Parker continued to hold court from morning to night. He disposed of a prodigious number of cases. Colonel Boudinot appeared before him three times in one day. Boudinot was a very intelligent lawyer, rather quiet but always alert and forceful in addressing a jury.

On the afternoon of the fourth day, during a very slow and fumbling cross examination of a witness by the slow-thinking Hickok, Parker heard something of a tumult in the direction of town. It was a welcome opportunity for a recess, and he called it in the middle of one of Hickok's long, involved questions.

Parker left the courtroom through a side door and looked up Garrison. The shouting had died down now, and he saw Brett Malone riding a sorrel horse down the middle of the street. Behind him, at a distance of a hundred yards, was an open wagon driven by a single man. In the wagon-box appeared to be six or eight men sitting down. That was strange, thought Parker, for sitting in the bottom of a wagon was anything but comfortable.

Malone rode straight and tall on the sorrel, sitting easily in the saddle, his big hat pushed to the back of his head.

Now Parker began to sense a reason for

the sudden quiet that had followed the shouting. On each side of the open wagon was a deputy, riding as near the wooden walks and dirt footpaths as he could. Fifty yards behind the first wagon was a second, and then a third, both flanked by outriders, with two armed men bringing up the rear.

Parker felt a sudden elation. He knew instinctively that Malone's deputies had brought in prisoners, and he visualized the long sessions of court ahead. He watched the wagons rumble down the street toward the courthouse, with young Malone commanding like a veteran colonel of cavalry. The wagons kept their distance from one another, and the outriding deputies kept pace with the wagons. Malone turned into the grounds of the old fort, and the little train followed him. The courtroom was empty now, and Parker went across the hollow-sounding floor to watch from a window. The three wagons pulled up together in the shadow of the gallows. Men clambered out — men wearing handcuffs. Then the deputies closed in on horseback, rifles ready. The prisoners marched through a cordon of silent, watchful guards into the basement of the courthouse. The deputies followed them in, and Malone swung down, tied his horse to a wagon wheel, and all but bounded up the steps into the courthouse.

Parker met him at the door. "You've had good luck, I see."

"Yes, sir." Malone was grinning. "We brought them in the tumbleweed wagons — twenty-two men — and never lost a one."

"Twenty-two prisoners!" Parker felt a glow.

"We worked out a system," said Malone. "Send out three deputies with a tumble-weed wagon —"

"Why do you call them that?"

"People over in the Territory started it, because the wagon goes in any direction, wherever the deputies think they can scare up a criminal. We run three men and a driver. The driver isn't armed, so the criminals can't overpower him and get a rifle or a pistol. The outriders stay at a distance so as to have a clear shot if there is a break."

Parker nodded. "It sounds like a most intelligent system. And you keep them handcuffed all the time?"

Brett grinned and whipped his dusty hat against his ragged denim pants. "No, sir. It would make mighty hard ridin' for a man all day in a wagon-box with his hands tied together, so we let them ride with their hands free, and we put the cuffs on when we go through a town so the people won't think we're careless."

Parker smiled broadly, and put his hand on Malone's shoulder. He liked the feel of Malone's supple but tough musculature. "A diplomat too," he observed.

Malone shrugged. "Just try to use some sense."

"Why did you come in from the northeast?"

"I had a hunch some of these outlaws' friends might try to ambush us at the ferry, so we left the road and cut across to Van Buren."

"What gave you a hunch like that?"

Malone put his hat on and pulled it down carefully. "It don't sound very loyal," he said, "but Bentley Garth was in the Choctaw Country three days ago, and if there's anything to the talk about him running rifles, then I figgered this was an unhealthy time for me to find it out."

"You think there's something in that talk, then?"

"I don't know," said Malone. "I just don't like to take a chance. I had eight deputies and three drivers to look out for."

Parker nodded in approval and then said thoughtfully, "We're going to have to investigate Bentley Garth pretty soon."

"Yes, sir, I know it."

"The fact that he's Ann's older brother doesn't make it easy, does it?"

"No, sir, it doesn't — but I'll clamp down on him when the time comes no matter whose brother he is."

"I'm satisfied you will. You're doing a good job, Brett."

Malone brightened. "Thank you, judge."

"What kind of crimes are these men accused of?"

"Mostly whisky. One assault and battery. One mayhem."

"No murderers or rapists?"

"No. I think they're laying low, waiting to see what's going to happen in Fort Smith."

Parker said, "You're wondering too, aren't you, Brett?"

"I thought about it," Malone admitted. "But it ain't my problem really."

"What would happen if we hanged all six at once?"

"Well, I think for a little while things would quieten down. Then business would pick up again, and you'd have to string up another batch. Eventually I reckon you'd make believers out of them, and killin' would stop."

"We'll see pretty soon," said Parker, "if you are right. My own feeling is you have made a good guess." He frowned a little. "I wish you had some capital cases."

"We'll get them if there are any. In fact," said Brett, "I've got Jim Wilkerson working on a couple of old cases, now that we can expect support from the court. We'll have more for you," he promised.

Parker watched him go, his moccasins gritting faintly on the floor. To his notion, Malone had already grown taller, and certainly he had an air of confidence and command that he had not shown in May. Malone had been a wise choice. It was a shame that the boy's father could not see him now.

That brought Charlie to Parker's mind, and he frowned. Well, he thought as he went slowly back, Charlie wasn't the same type. He thought Charlie would be more delicate, probably — more interested in law and politics. It was a natural choice, considering his father.

Chapter 12

And so the jail began to fill up. The tumble-weed wagons rolled into town with their loads of prisoners; the court ground on all day and sometimes at night. The new prisoners were docketed and put through the mill without let-up. And then one day Clayton said with a strange tone in his voice: "Your honor, you haven't set the date for execution of the six murderers yet."

"No," said Parker. "No, I haven't."

Clayton said cheerfully, "Well, it's not my responsibility. Just thought I'd remind you."

The harsh, debilitating heat of summer was on them now in mid-August, and Parker felt smothered under his heavy woolen robe in the courtroom, but every day he watched them come and go, and gloried in the procession. The more prisoners, the more trials, and the harder Parker worked. Night sessions, midnight sessions — anything to keep the mills of the gods grinding out their portion of justice.

It was after one of those night sessions that Parker sat alone for a few minutes in his chambers to renew his strength and give his mind a chance to collect itself. Idly he opened the Bible and leafed through it, waiting for the last sounds to die from the courtroom and the halls, for he did not want to run into Clayton or any of the lawyers with whom he might have to discuss some phases of the case or at least pass some banal words of greeting. That night he was weary.

He sat there for a while, gathering his strength, and then, feeling refreshed, he blew out the lamp and stepped quietly into the hall.

Before he closed the door however, he heard a whispered voice. He looked back.

For a moment he saw nothing, but the whispering continued. There were two voices — a girl's and a man's. Then his eyes began to make out forms, and by the reflection from the lamp in the marshal's office, where the door was open, he saw Brett Malone and Ann Garth embracing. It was hardly a casual embrace, for Ann was standing on tiptoe, her arms around Brett's neck, and his head was bent as he kissed her.

Parker stood still for a moment. They broke the embrace and then went back into it promptly, and Parker smiled. Sunday night services had always had a good effect on love and romance, he remembered. He waited, but their enthusiasm did not abate. Finally he stepped back into his office and made a business of fumbling for the coat tree. He managed to knock it against the wall, but caught it. Then he went out and turned toward the marshal's office.

He caught a glimpse of a shadow disappearing toward the marshal's outside door, and knew it was cast by a floor-length gingham dress. Malone was standing at the door when he reached it.

"Miss Garth, I assume," Parker said quietly.

Even in the half-light of the hallway he saw Malone's face turn red. "Yes, sir."

"Is it now your opinion," asked Parker, "that Miss Garth shows indications of maturity?"

Malone looked very uncomfortable. "I ast her to marry me," he said.

Parker nodded his approval. "A good answer. A very good answer. When is the event to take place?"

"I don't know, judge. She works for her brother in the freight office, and if we was to get married and have younguns it would force him to hire a bookkeeper, and she says he can't afford it now."

"Well, I know you'll work it out. I doubt very much that the routine of bookkeeping will long prevail against the demands of love."

But Malone sounded dubious. "She's awful stuck on her brother — and I can't say I blame her."

Parker said warmly, "When you get ready for the final step, I would be most happy to perform the ceremony for you."

"Thank you, Judge Parker."

"Don't mention it. Goodnight."

"Goodnight, sir."

But that week, while Parker waited patiently for more capital defendants, he became aware of a growing feeling, a holding back, a let's-wait-and-see attitude.

He and Mary had bought the house, and he hired a warehouse in St. Joseph to ship their furniture. In the meantime, they still lived at the hotel, and it was one evening in front of the Oyster Saloon that he ran into Si Hampton, the farmer whose baby Malone and Parker had rescued. He stopped to inquire about the health of Mrs. Hampton, and was pleased to hear that the baby had fully recovered from its ordeal.

On an unusual impulse Parker asked Hampton what the people were saying about his court. He was taken aback at Hampton's answer:

"You want the truth, judge?"

"Why — yes, of course," Parker said.

Hampton's eyes narrowed slightly. "The Territory is waiting to see if you're really going to hang those men."

"They doubt it?"

Hampton hedged. "They're just waitin'," he repeated.

Parker thought seriously about this as he took Mary and Charlie out to see their new home so that Mary could plan the furnishing. Charlie ran from one empty room to another, sometimes screaming at the top of his voice — senselessly, it seemed to Parker.

"He's a regular wild Indian," Mary said disapprovingly.

"Uh — yes." Parker was thinking about what Hampton had said. This, Parker knew, was the voice of the people, and it behooved him to listen, for it was the people he wanted to reach.

That night he read the Bible until very late. Charlie was put to bed, and presently Mary had a glass of wine and went to bed also, and soon was asleep. He thought absently, watching her lie there with her glossy hair spread over the pillow, that Mary was drinking more wine than usual, but he supposed it wouldn't hurt her. As a matter of fact, the doctor in St. Joe had said a small glass of wine was good for her.

And so he sat in the big chair through the long hours of the night, reading, turning pages, reading again. And finally, when he closed the Book and fastened the clamp, he was certain of his position. No matter what the reaction of people in the Territory and in Fort Smith, he had not forgotten that he must perform his duties according to the law and the Word. The law was plain enough; the Word too was plain. Before he went to bed, he got on his knees and prayed long and silently. . . .

The next morning the sun was bright over Arkansas, and Parker in his high silk hat and his heavy double-breasted coat walked to the restaurant, withdrawn and alone in the recesses of his mind. He spoke to others automatically, and even tipped his hat to Indian Rose before he remembered who and what she was. He sat by himself until Gil Weaver came in, looked around, and made a bee-line for him.

"You look sober this morning, judge," said Weaver, sitting down at the small table. He emptied a glass of water. "Hardest water in the state of Arkansas," he said, "but not as hard as over in the Territory."

"You've been over there?" Parker asked politely.

"Last week, as a matter of fact. Heard that

Bentley Garth was held up by the Kiamichi Kid and robbed of two wagonloads of merchandise." He added with disappointment in his voice, "Nothing to it."

Parker allowed a faint tone of sarcasm to creep into his voice. "Could you possibly tell me why everybody out here boasts about how hard the water is?"

Weaver laughed. "It isn't very complicated, your honor. There's so little in Arkansas to be proud of — but a man's got to be proud of something." He pushed the glass toward the waitress. "You'll be a real Arkansawyer, your honor, when you take to bragging about how hard the water is."

After a moment Parker asked casually, "Are you planning to be in court this morning?"

Weaver looked up. "Is something important going to happen?"

Parker deprecated the idea. "Routine," he said.

Weaver studied him. "I haven't had enough sleep in a month of Sundays, and I planned on taking a nap this morning — but the way you said that sounds like a hint. I guess I better be there when court opens. Still eight o'clock?"

"Still eight o'clock," Parker said, getting up.

"I'll be right along."

Parker left his chambers at a minute before eight and walked into the courtroom by the door at the back of the rostrum. The courtroom was fairly empty that morning, the crowds naturally having fallen off after the capital trials were over. This morning Bill Clayton was in his usual place; Colonel Boudinot was there, making notes on some papers; Rudolph Clyman was reading a book of decisions. Parker sat down, careful to sweep his robe under him. Malone was in the doorway, looking toward him for orders. At exactly eight o'clock Parker spoke to him, "Bring in the six prisoners convicted of murder."

Malone nodded understandingly and disappeared silently.

Parker was satisfied with the stir that went through the courtroom. The spectators now sat up straight in their uncomfortable chairs. Clayton looked expectant; Rudolph Clyman closed his book and seemed to gather himself as if to receive a blow; Colonel Boudinot promptly put away his pencil and sat attentively.

At that moment Gil Weaver came in, stood in the door for a moment, sensed the tension, darted quick glances around, then tiptoed to the bailiff and whispered. The bailiff whispered back, and Weaver's eyebrows raised. He nodded rapidly and went at once to a seat.

Malone and Wilkerson appeared with the six convicted men. Parker thought they looked considerably run down. Malone lined them up in front of the big desk, and Parker sniffed as the foul odor from their skin and clothing reached him. Then he stood up. "The court had hoped," he said, "to allow the convicted men a little more time to make their peace with their Maker, but the requirements of justice demand that we go ahead with the executions." He looked at the Bible. " 'He that smiteth a man,' " he said, " 'so that he die, shall be surely put to death. . . . Eye for eye, tooth for tooth, hand for hand, foot for foot. Burning for burning, wound for wound, stripe for stripe. . . .' " He paused, glanced at a paper on the desk, then went on in a businesslike voice:

"These six men will be hanged," he said, "on Friday, September third, of this year."

Colonel Boudinot said quickly, "Your honor, that is only three weeks from now."

"I am aware of that," Parker said coldly.

"But —"

"Your one appeal for a commutation

was rejected by the President, was it not, Colonel Boudinot?"

"Yes, your honor."

"To my knowledge, there is none now pending. For the information of the press and of any interested, it will be a public hanging, so that the world may know and may remember that order once more is established in the Territory."

"Your honor," said Rudolph Clyman, "what will be the order of execution?"

Parker looked at him and let a few seconds elapse before he answered. "They will all be hanged together," he said.

There was silence for a moment. Daniel Evans shrugged exaggeratedly. Samuel Fooy glowered. Boudinot seemed to be thinking about it. Clyman's mouth was open. Weaver's eyebrows had shot up. Of them all, only Brett Malone seemed unmoved; he watched the prisoners carefully, perhaps anticipating an attempt to escape. Finally Clayton could resist no longer. "Six men at once!" he breathed.

Parker looked icily at him. "Take the prisoners back to their cells," he told Malone, and sat down. "The clerk will call the next case. . . ."

At noon he had a quick bowl of soup and went to see George Maledon. "You have heard the news?" he asked.

Maledon's face was business-like. "You're going to hang all six at once."

"Yes. I hope there will be no hitch in the proceedings."

The little man with the big beard looked up from a rope. "There won't be. Six men at once is easy."

That evening the town was buzzing; Parker knew that from the silence that preceded and followed him on his way home. He knew it from the fact that he seemed to meet no one who knew him well enough to speak to him. He knew it when he reached the hotel, from the elaborate casualness of the high-collared clerk. And he knew it when he went upstairs.

They now had two connecting rooms, which gave them a sitting room and a bedroom, pending arrival of their furniture. He knocked, so as not to frighten Mary, and let himself in. She was sitting by the window, red-eyed.

He tried to ignore it. "Where's Charlie?" he asked.

She shook her head, looking as if she bore the sadness of half the world. "He's playing with Annie Maledon again."

"The Maledons are highly respectable people," Parker said.

"But he's a hangman!" she whispered brokenly.

"The Maledons live only a block from our new house."

"I know," she said wearily. "We'll be living next door to a hangman."

Parker was getting somewhat nettled. "If you feel so strongly about the man who pulls the bolt, what about the man who sentences them to death?"

She stared at him for an instant, and in her eyes was a strangeness, as if she never had seen him before. Then she turned back to the window, buried her face in her hands, and burst into loud weeping.

Chapter 13

The *Western Independent* was out two days later, and Parker found one in his mail box at noon. The item on the scheduled hanging was down in the middle of the page:

"FORT SMITH'S HANGING JUDGE — Isaac C. Parker is about to make a real name for himself — one that will be remembered for a long time, if not with pleasure by all parties concerned. However, the parties most concerned will not remember anything at all unless their memories are better in Hell than they are on earth, for his honor has sentenced all six of them to be hanged at one and the same time. Six souls to be launched into eternity at the same instant. This may be the largest civil hanging ever held in America; 30-some Sioux Indians were hanged at Mankato, Minnesota, during the War but that was a military hanging, we understand. Surely such a *singular* event as this will have a salutary effect on crime in the Indian Territory, and undoubtedly George Maledon, who gets $100 apiece for the men executed, will come as near to a smile as he ever has — which is, in this editor's opinion, only about half as far

183

as from here to the nearest star."

Parker folded the newspaper and left the post office lobby. The round-faced man with the reddish chin whiskers had a considerable bite to him — more than a man might think from looking at him or talking to him.

Parker continued to hold court, and petty criminals continued to flow through the mill of justice. There was very little time wasted, for by now the lawyers, though they sometimes grumbled, seemed to have pretty well accepted the new regime and did not often try delaying tactics. The only one who really seemed to chafe under such conditions was young Clyman.

Parker was not very tolerant. This was a court of law, he reminded Clyman, with a trial-docket growing longer every day as a result of the activities of a new force of deputy marshals. He reminded them that he himself sat on the bench six days a week, from morning to night, without relief, and he suggested with mild sarcasm that surely the lawyers in Fort Smith, spelling each other as cases were disposed of and others came on for trial, could keep up with one single man on the bench.

And, truth to tell, the business of the court almost became an obsession with him. He gloried in the number of cases that came before him; he took an almost lascivious satisfaction in reading over the cases and their disposal at the end of the week. Already he had established a record approached by no other trial judge in America — and still he drove himself ever harder. At night he examined notes on the trials, and sometimes turned to the law, but largely he concentrated on watching defendants to decide whether or not they were guilty, to catch little telltale signs that would give them away. And as he became more adept at reading character, so he was able to cut down the time spent on trials, and this in turn allowed him to handle still more cases.

One evening, as he was leaving the courthouse, he had an impulse to go down into the jail and see the men in Murderers' Row, to find out if they were repenting of their sins or if they were still defiant of the laws of God and man.

In his silk hat and heavy coat he started down the hall to the jail door, but Malone stepped out before him. "Your honor, this is the way to the jail."

"I know it."

"You don't want to go down there," said Malone.

Parker looked at him. "I certainly do," he said.

"But — judge, it stinks terrible."

"I know that."

"But — judge, why don't you go some other time?"

"You are talking like an idiot!" Parker said coldly, and pushed past him.

He was aware that Malone stood behind him, watching, as he went on to the door to be met by the stench of almost unbreathable air. Nevertheless he set his lips firmly and marched down the stairway.

At first he noticed only that the cells were filled. He walked toward the end they called Murderers' Row and became aware of a sudden strange silence. He looked up and saw Mary.

Her back was toward him, but there was no mistaking that well-dressed, graceful figure. She had a plate of cake in one hand and a bouquet of flowers in the other — zinnias, tiger lilies, four o'clocks, and a few red roses. She was moving down the cells, apparently oblivious to the foul air, offering cake and flowers to each murderous occupant.

"Mary!" he cried, astounded.

She turned and looked at him with a strangely defiant look in her eyes as she waited for him to castigate her. That was the unkindest blow of all, for he never had been severe with her in their married life. Now she acted, for all these depraved men to see, as if she anticipated a tongue-lashing, at the very least, from him.

He said no word. He was stunned. He moistened his lips. She waited. He knew he ought to do something, say something to smooth it over for the time being, to show the world that he had not been caught off guard, but he could find no words. For the first time in his life he was completely speechless. His eyes slowly dropped. It was degrading to be watched in all his over-wrought emotion by these condemned men, but it was too much; he could not rise above it, for Mary — his own wife — He shook his head in bewilderment.

It seemed at that moment more than he would ever be able to forgive — her debasement of him before such an audience.

Then he raised his head high and proudly. He said, "I will wait for you in my chambers, Mary." He turned on his heel and walked blindly up the stairway.

Malone was at the top of the stairs. "I'm sorry, sir. I — I tried to keep you from going."

Parker, warmed by the real sympathy in Malone's voice, stopped. "Why didn't someone tell me?"

"It's nobody's business to come between a man and his wife," said Malone.

"Why was she allowed to go down there in the first place?"

"It was nothing out of the way," said Malone uncomfortably. "Lots of women of the town come down here. Some of them are wives or sisters or mothers of the prisoners; others come just for curiosity, to look at a murderer or a rapist."

"The female mind!" Parker said. "Why must a woman be so morbid!"

"I don't know," Malone said honestly.

Parker stared at him in the gloom of the hallway. He wanted to ask if Mary had been there before, but he had too much pride to reveal further his ignorance of what went on in his own household.

He went on to his chambers and sat down. It was warm but he did not take off his coat. He sat there unmoving and tried to make some sense out of it, without success. Presently he heard her step, and forced himself to get up and open the door. She stood there, still defiant, but he hardly saw her. "If you are ready," he said, "we'll go home."

At the hotel he took off his coat and hat and Mary hung them up. He seated himself in his favorite chair and opened a two-week-old copy of the *New York Tribune*, but his mind wasn't on it.

Mary was busy in the kitchen which they now had connecting with their hotel room — much busier, he was sure, than usual — and silent. In complete failure to understand her actions of that day, he got up and went to the kitchen, where she was peeling potatoes over a galvanized bucket.

"Mary," he said, trying to be objective, "do you have any explanation for your presence in the jail today?"

She did not look up. A long potato peeling rolled into the bucket as her capable hands worked the paring knife. "I thought some kindness was not out of place — even for men condemned to die," she said finally.

He considered. In the courtroom he had absolute and final authority over lawyers, jurymen, even criminals, and it was hard for him to understand that in his own room this authority was broken down by the woman who was his wife. Mary was defying him, and it was frustrating to realize that, from a judicial standpoint, there was nothing he could do about it.

All these thoughts went through his mind, but he had no intention of abandoning the subject. She would have to see that he was right.

"I don't wish to deny them kindness," he

said finally, "but you must be aware that it looks strange to the people to see the judge's wife practically defying his authority, and going so far as to put herself in contact with the filth and stench of the jail, and to subject herself to insult and indecent remarks."

"The men were very respectful toward me when they found out I was not taking advantage of their unfortunate situation."

"They would be that in any event," he commented, "for you are the wife of the judge, and they would not take a chance on destroying their hopes for a reprieve from the rope."

"I did nothing," she said, keeping her head down.

"But Mary —" He was nettled at her stubbornness. "Surely you must see —"

Finally she raised her head and faced him, and for a moment her hands ceased to work. "Isaac Charles Parker," she said defiantly, "you may sit as a judge and you may think you are God himself with the power of life and death over human beings, but as long as you sentence men to death over that terrible gallows, just so long will I continue to obey the voice of my conscience. I can do nothing to stay the execution of the sentence, but I can lighten their last few hours on this earth."

"Mary!" he cried helplessly.

But she neither seemed to hear him nor to encourage him. Her head dropped; her hands flew again, and a long peeling rolled into the bucket.

He stood there for a few minutes, trying to think of something to say. In the end he was forced to turn away, baffled at this strange demonstration of Mary's opposition. It seemed to him then, as he went back to his chair, that something had sprung up between them, to keep them apart. Always before they had been close, but now there was a world between them — the world of duty, of retribution, of law. It troubled him more than he wanted to admit, but he knew that even if it meant a breach between them for the rest of their lives he could do nothing other than what he had already sworn to do.

He studied the Bible that night, but he hardly saw the words, for he was concerned with something far more important: the impact of the hanging on the criminals who were still free or on those who would be tempted to commit criminal acts in the future. To that end the entire mechanism of the hanging must be handled like a stage play; it must be built up to a great dramatic pitch, and full advantage must be taken of every chance to make this event one that never would be wiped from the memory of any man living in Indian Territory. He did not go to bed until daylight was breaking over the Arkansas hills to the east.

He consulted with Malone, and they pulled in four deputies from the Territory, including Will Sunshine, to set up a special guard for the prisoners; there must be no jailbreak now.

Excitement began to build up in Fort Smith, and everywhere Parker went people discussed the coming event. Even Lousy MacDonald, said Henry Fillmore, was planning to come to town with his nine children and stay all day. "An' it's the first time in Fort Smith's history that Lousy has ever done anything like that. He always said it was too hard on the mules to pull the whole family, but this time his wife is packin' a lunch and bringin' them all, because Lousy says this will be the best free show he's ever seen in his life. And if you know Lousy, that means somethin', for Lousy knows more about free shows than any man in Arkansas."

Parker nodded and went into the bank. Even the assistant cashier was full of questions, to all of which Parker answered: "Be there on Friday and you will see."

The next issue of *The Western Independent*

had two columns of description of the gallows and the probable procedure.

From all of this Parker held aloof, as was consistent with the dignity of the court, but he saw with secret approval the rapid buildup of interest.

On Monday, August 30, Parker opened court on the first day of the fatal week. Soon the first four months of his judgeship would come to a tremendous climax. Already he was known as the hanging judge; before the week was out, the outlaws and criminals would know it was well applied, and they would tremble in their tracks and would think twice before they went on with their murderous careers.

James Moore announced his desire to join the Catholic church before he died, and he was taken, with two guards in attendance, to holy communion. Daniel Evans softened and went also to the Catholic church. The Negro, Edmund Campbell, joined a Protestant church.

George Maledon now was carrying home a basket every night with his six selected ropes coiled in it, and an atmosphere of awe and silence preceded and followed him wherever he went. Maledon was oblivious; he went his own way and kept his own counsel, and if he was aware of the feeling that surrounded him, he did not reveal it. In the meantime, his four journeys a day to and from his home were watched by increasing numbers until, along toward the last, they lined the sidewalks along his route, shrinking back silently as he approached. Still Maledon gave no indication that he was aware of this interest. He was a man, Parker thought admiringly, with an iron nerve.

On Thursday the town was full of people, and it had the air of a holiday. Parker frowned at the drunks and at the boisterousness, but nevertheless the entire affair was having the effect he wanted. He spoke to Maledon one last time that day. "Are you all ready, George?"

"All ready, your honor." Maledon never smiled. "What time will the hanging start?"

"Ten o'clock."

"Very good. Ten o'clock it is."

Parker visited Malone at noon. "Do you have any reason to expect trouble?"

"None," said Malone. "We've got control of everything. The only way anybody could get out is to tear down the courthouse."

"Don't relax vigilance," said Parker.

He went into the jail to see that all was well, and was met by silence and hatred. He noted fresh garden flowers in the cells but pretended not to see them.

At noon Thursday Fort Smith resemble
tent town. Farm families from all over
area had come to town in their wagons an
had made camp wherever they could fin
space. It was like a great Fourth of July cele
bration, with children running and playing
games, men smoking and visiting, women
gossiping in groups. The town proper and
the saloons were filled with cowboys, blanket
Indians, railroad men and river men.

Clayton said during a recess, "There are
going to be thousands here, your honor."

"Yes."

"I'll hand it to you, your honor. You sure
engineered a whale of a show."

Parker announced as he adjourned court
on Thursday: "We will resume at two
o'clock tomorrow."

Colonel Boudinot was on his foot. "Your
honor, I had hoped for a recess for tomorrow, to give me a chance to catch up on
my work. I have several cases coming up
here next week."

Hickok jumped to his feet, but Parker
motioned him back. "Gentlemen, we have a
crowded docket. Two o'clock tomorrow."

He read the Bible that night, and finally
put it aside, completely satisfied.

He was at the courthouse at seven-thirty
the next morning, and made certain the

prisoners were secure. He saw Maledon come in with his rope-basket. A little while later, Parker, pacing the courtroom, watched him go over the gallows inch by inch, oiling the hinges, oiling the bolt and the trigger arrangement, testing the ropes with sandbags. At nine-fifteen Parker looked around the yard and saw that the grounds were almost filled. A man in the rear was selling lemonade and balloons. Parker stiffened. He had not bargained for that, but there wasn't much he could do.

And still people came by the hundreds and walked among the earlier arrivals, looking for advantageous places to sit. Many had blankets. Fifteen or twenty over-dressed girls came in in single file, led by the youthful Indian Rose. Some men called to them, and the girls waved and returned the calls. Indian Rose led them to an open place almost at the edge of the great gallows, and motioned them to sit down.

Parker raised his eyebrows; there would be repercussions from the spectators, but secretly he was not displeased.

Will Sunshine came up behind him. Sunshine wore moccasins, and walked very silently. "Chief Deputy Malone says he's ready, youah honah."

Parker turned. "Tell him to proceed with

the hanging," he said.

Sunshine left, and Parker went to his chambers, where he could watch without being conspicuous. He stood there, grim and silent, waiting. The prison door opened and the prisoners came out, two abreast, with wrists handcuffed together, and each fastened by a leg-iron. Malone led them, and behind him on each side were two armed deputies. Malone led them up the twelve steps. Maledon was already there. The men sat on a low bench at the back of the gallows, and again Parker was aware of that tremendous pressure building up inside of him; for a moment he thought he would be ill, but he clamped his jaws tighter and put the feeling down.

Man-Killer's mother and wife and baby found a way through the dense crowd which numbered several thousand, and took their places near Indian Rose's girls.

Maledon motioned. The six men walked forward in a ragged line, their handcuffs unfastened now. Armed deputies stood guard on all sides of the gallows.

The Rev. H. M. Granade, Methodist minister, said: "I have a final message written and signed by John Whittington, which he requests I read aloud."

Malone nodded.

Parker turned away in some annoyance. He did not care for an orgy of sentimental self-pity. He stood back until he heard the final words: "God save us all. Farewell."

Then, to Parker's further annoyance, Reverend Granade announced a hymn and began to sing; a few of the spectators joined, but none of the condemned men.

When it was over, Malone said, "Has anyone anything to say?"

Daniel Evans nodded. He gazed out over the crowd and muttered, "There are worse men here than me."

James Moore called, "Goodbye, Sandy," and tried to wave, but his hands were bound.

Malone nodded to Maledon. The little man with the big beard stepped forward. Carefully he moved each man onto the long double-hinged trapdoor and stood him on the line where the two halves came together. One by one, he drew a black cap over each man's head. Then, without hesitation or fluster, he went swiftly to the bolt. He put his finger in the eye and pulled, and the six men plunged downward together.

There was a collective gasp from the great crowd, and then the six men reached the end of the ropes and became inanimate bodies. They hung at the ends of their

ropes, some turning a little this way or that, none twitching.

Parker stood straight and tall; presently he looked again at the crowd, which was not breaking up.

Colonel DuVal was below the platform, feeling the men's wrists for pulses. He passed the sixth man and nodded, George Maledon stepped forward again, pulled a jerk-knot in the first rope, and lowered the body of Daniel Evans to the ground.

God is not mocked: for whatsoever a man soweth, that shall he also reap.

Parker turned slowly and went to his desk. He wished he had not announced court for that afternoon.

Chapter 14

Half an hour later, drawn by an inexplicable fascination for the gallows, he went again to the window and looked down. With some astonishment he noted that the vast crowd still filled the grounds. They were no longer sitting tense and expectant, but they seemed reluctant to leave, and hundreds of families had spread tablecloths and now were gathered in little clusters eating lunch.

He turned from the window at a footstep outside the door. There was a quiet knock. He went across the bare floor slowly. He opened the door and saw Malone, his big hat on the back of his head.

"Come in, Brett."

"Thanks, Mr. Parker."

Parker closed the door. "You look older."

"Yeah." Malone exhaled a deep breath. "Six men sent to meet their Maker. A fellow just jerks a bolt, and six men die."

Parker paced the floor with long strides. "I know," he said. "I'm thinking about that."

Malone looked at him and changed immediately. He came over and put a hand on

Parker's shoulder. "It isn't your responsibility, Mr. Parker. You only carried out the law."

"Thanks, Brett."

Parker felt a great surge of warmth for this boy-man deputy of his. There had not been many persons in his life who had been understanding or had tried to be, and Parker was appreciative. More and more, he thought, Brett was getting to seem like a son to him, and he appreciated this attempt at consolation.

But Parker felt no remorse for the hanging. "Now the people know," he said, "that this court will no longer tolerate lawbreaking. Bring in all the violators you can find. Bring in witnesses. You and your deputies will get extra pay for each team, and a food allowance for the prisoners. But bring them; keep the jail full."

"It's full now, sir," said Brett.

"Put more in each cell; chain them to the bars if necessary — but bring in more." He hit the top of the desk with his clenched fist. "The next time that trap drops, there must be twelve men standing on it! That is the only way to convince them."

"Yes, sir."

"What about the Kiamichi Kid? I'd like to see him be one of the twelve."

"We get news, all right. He's committed a couple of robberies, but nothing serious. He's been moving around a lot."

"Keep looking for him." Parker nodded toward the gallows. "We want him out there."

He was not very brilliant that afternoon, for he still had that feeling of vacuity, but he kept court in session until dark.

On the way home he encountered still another attitude of the townspeople. Again they drew away from him, but this time not as much in revulsion as in wonderment. That suited him: as a judge he wanted to be held in awe; as a citizen he would show them later he was not a man who had to be avoided.

Weaver carried several columns in the *Independent* about the hanging, but made no editorial comment. He seemed to be waiting.

The next Sunday Parker went to Mass with Mary, and made a special effort to speak to everyone and to smile and to be as pleasant as possible. He noted Mary's long absorption with her prayers and somehow this seemed to widen the breach between them, although he was sure it was not serious. After services at the Catholic church, Mary took little Charlie home while Parker

went on to the Methodist church.

It was not until several Sundays later, when they had been out walking in the afternoon and had returned to the hotel, avoiding the saloons on Garrison, that Parker brought up a subject he had tried to put out of his mind.

They had visited the "new" house, and Mary had studied the floor layout and the room sizes and had speculated on what they would be able to do with their furniture and rugs and curtains, and had developed ideas about new wallpaper and fresh paint and varnish. Mr. Hoffman had dropped in to visit, and as they left he had said earnestly, "Mrs. Parker, I don't suppose you can possibly appreciate what a Godsend your husband is to this country."

She had murmured something, and Hoffman had gone on. "It needed a man with backbone and courage, somebody who wasn't afraid of anyone, to put the fear of God into the lawbreakers of this country."

Mary had not answered immediately, and Parker had seen that odd, defiant look in her eyes. He had gone into the breach immediately. "It's nothing but a man's duty, really. Being a federal judge is a job, like being president of the bank."

Mr. Hoffman, who was a small, thin-

chested man, nodded. "It takes more back-bone to hang six men at once than it takes to turn down a big loan."

Parker, who was holding Charlie's hand, glanced at Mary and said quickly, "Thank you, Mr. Hoffman, for your approbation. I'll do my best to deserve it."

That night Mary put Charlie to bed and poured a glass of wine. Parker declined. He settled himself near the lamp and waited until Mary was seated. Then he began, "Mary, I think there is more to be said about your taking cake and flowers to the condemned men."

She looked at him from beyond the lamp. "Did you want some wine?"

"No. And I do not want to be turned from the subject. This is something that must be settled between us."

"There is nothing to settle," she said, looking away from him.

"I'm afraid there is. You must realize, Mary, that this is my life work."

"I understand that."

"But — you have deliberately made a fool of me, Mary." He allowed his voice to rise. "What must people have thought to see the judge's own wife consoling the condemned men?"

"You are taking it too seriously, Isaac."

But he would not be talked down. "Not only has it been a shock to my pride, but it has also been a terrible blow to my standing as a husband. Mary, you are practically saying to the world that you do not approve my judgment. It is a hard thing for a man to take — insubordination from his own wife."

He did not know what she was thinking, but he knew she was not really listening to him.

"They were to be killed by the state," she said. "I felt sorry for them."

"They needed no sympathy."

"The hangman took six human lives. Those lives can never be restored — no matter what develops later."

"Nothing can develop," he said. "They were guilty."

She avoided his eyes. "I was sorry for them."

"They were not entitled to sympathy. They were murderers. James Moore confessed to the murder of at least eight persons, not including Indians and Negroes. Samuel Fooy boasted that he had broken all the Ten Commandments," Parker said fiercely.

She looked up but did not answer.

"Remember the widows and the fatherless children and the bereaved parents who

are left," he admonished her. He added sternly, "Murderers need no sympathy and they will get none in my court."

"The people are saying it is because you are a Republican."

"That is not true and the thinking citizens know it. I am not concerned with politics in any way. I am above politics — and I promise you that no politics shall enter my court."

"I have not believed in capital punishment since I read *Eugene Aram*," she said slowly.

He was exasperated. "You are not in a position to make such a decision. You read something in a book that was written by a person patently biased. I sit in a courtroom through whose doors come the most degraded criminals of all time. I deal with realities — and I can tell you one thing: hanging is too good for many of them."

But his lowered voice and attempt at intimacy was lost on her. "There are times," she said, looking him in the eye for the first time that evening, "when I am inclined to believe your Protestant upbringing has made you cruel and heartless."

He stared at her. His arguments had been lost, because she had but one idea, one

thought, and she had heard nothing that he had said.

"I'm tired." She finished her wine. "I have to go to bed, Isaac."

"It's early yet, Mary."

"I'm going to Mass in the morning. I'm going to pray for your soul. . . ."

The next morning Parker received a notice that their furniture had been shipped by riverboat *via* New Orleans and would arrive on the eighteenth. He realized that this was the morning of the eighteenth, and knew he would have to get somebody with a dray wagon to transport the stuff to their new house. Probably Bentley Garth was the only one equipped for a job of that size. Too, a visit to Garth's freight office would give Parker a chance to size up the man.

So, after a rather slow morning trying a farm woman for adultery on a complaint signed by the guilty man's wife, he put on his coat and hat and made his way to the Garth Freight Lines office at the opposite end of the street the Row was on.

He was glad he did not have to walk past the houses of infamy, and he breathed a sigh of relief as he turned the corner and followed the well-beaten path in the drying mud in the opposite direction.

He was carefully picking his way when

he became aware of a flowered dress within his vision. He raised his head and looked into the very pretty face of Indian Rose. He opened his mouth but didn't say anything.

She seemed amused at something, for he saw little crinkles around her eyes.

His hand was halfway to his hat before he remembered who she was. As she waited open-eyed for him to speak, he hesitated for an instant. Then it occurred to him that she would be doubly embarrassed at any slight he might now deliver. If she had been the ordinary painted woman he would not have cared, but somehow this girl did not seem like the others. She wore no paint at all, and her skin was clear and smooth and her oval face was very attractive and showed no ravages. His hand had wavered; now it went on to his hat, and, to make up for this momentary indecision, he not only tipped his hat to her but bowed elaborately.

She smiled, and he liked the genuineness of it. She was about five feet three inches tall and rather slender, with full red lips, now slightly parted.

"Good day, madam," he said formally.

"Good day, sir."

He liked the rhythmic, low tones of her

voice; he could not understand how she could be what she was said to be. Then it struck him that he had expected her possibly to grunt like an Indian squaw, or perhaps to say nothing at all, whereas he realized with a shock that both her words and her tones were quite cultured. He said, "It seems there is room for only one of us on the path at a time."

"Yes," she said, her eyes on his.

"Well —" He laughed self-consciously.

She regarded him from under lowered lids. There was a disconcerting quality about her steady gaze. For a moment it threw him off-balance and he had a juvenile notion to pick her up and carry her back to the next wide place in the path, but he recognized that impulse for what it was — a temptation to surrender to a carnal delight, and he put it out of his mind. Hastily he turned around and went back to the corner, and took a step to one side to allow her to pass on the way to the Row, which she did quite circumspectly, pausing only long enough to murmur, "Thank you."

He watched her for a moment as she crossed the street. He saw that she wore moccasins, but they were white buckskin and very clean, ornamented with red and blue and green glass beads. She was very light on her feet as she picked her way across the rough clods, now half-baked by the Arkansas sun.

Chapter 15

He turned and resumed his way toward the freight office, a small, box-like building with a sign across the front: "Garth Freight." Once it had been painted white, but the boards were now well weathered and gray, and in some places had warped badly and curled away from the studdings. A small, dirty window on the front faced a large platform, at one side of which was a scale. At this moment a Pittsburgh wagon, with a 'paulin lashed over its load, was pulled up on the platform. Ann Garth, bareheaded and with her pigtails still in evidence, but now somehow looking quite mature, shifted the weights and wrote the figures on a pad. Parker stopped to watch, but she did not look up. Finally she said, "All right, Lousy. Take it away."

A very pleasant-faced, black-haired, bullet-headed young man got up from where he had been hunkered at the head of the eight-ox team. "Thank you, Miss Garth." There was a broad Scottish accent in his voice. "How many pounds do we have, ma'am?"

"Fifty-one hundred," she told him,

writing on the pad. She turned, shading her eyes with her hand. "Hello, Judge Parker."

"Good morning, Miss Ann."

MacDonald walked up toward the lead yoke of oxen and began to talk to them. "On your feet, you lazy bulls. Ye canna earn yer feed lying down. On your feet, I say. Put your big muscles into the bows." He cracked a bullwhip over their backs. "On your feet, I say. On your feet."

The oxen began to get up. The lead yoke slowly tested its strength against the long chain, and MacDonald kept up his talk while the whip rolled constantly over the animals' backs in a series of unbelievably rapid explosions. In a moment the big wagon creaked and the wood groaned as it moved off the scale into the street of deeply cut, half-hardened mud ruts.

"That's Lousy MacDonald, I take it," said Parker.

"Yes, he's one of Bentley's best drivers."

"Nice-looking fellow."

"He's one of the best. He'd take his shirt off of his back for you."

Parker stared at the receding wagon. "Why do they call him 'Lousy'?"

"It doesn't really mean anything. He got saddled with that name when he first came over from Scotland, because they didn't understand him. They still call him that, but there's nothing bad about it, and he doesn't mind."

"Young Malone seemed to think he was stingy."

" 'Frugal' is a better word. I guess he has to be, with eight small children to feed."

He smiled at her. "The sun is flattering to you, Miss Ann."

"That's probably because I've lived in it all my life."

"You were born here, I take it."

"No." She looked sober. "I was born in London, but father and mother emigrated here just before the war."

"And you and your brother?"

"Father and mother both died of consumption, about two months apart. That's when I was three. Bentley and I were raised by neighbors. Mrs. Hoffman bought our clothes — and when Bentley was old enough to work he insisted on paying board for me so they wouldn't separate us."

"It is understandable that you would have a very close attachment to him."

She looked at Parker. "Whether Bentley is right or wrong," she said, "I will defend him until I die."

He touched her upper arm. "I'm sure, with such a brother, that you will never have to defend him in anything you would not be proud of."

She watched Lousy MacDonald turn the corner to circle back toward the ferry, and then asked, "Is there something, Mr. Parker?"

"I wanted to see your brother about some hauling."

"Brett is in there right now talking to him. You know, Mr. Parker, there's a man who thinks you are a regular god."

He tried to pass it off. "Oh, I'm sure he doesn't —"

"He thinks the world of you. He's always telling me about things you do and the way he thinks you would handle certain things."

"Well — that's gratifying, to be sure."

"We might as well go inside," she said. "The sun is warm today." She opened the small door to a tiny room, half filled with a tall desk and a high stool. The desk was covered with ledgers, and half a dozen spindles bore slips of paper with penciled notes.

Ann sat on the high stool and motioned Parker to the scratched-up caboose chair padded with a wolfskin. "I don't know what they're talking about in there. Brett came in a few minutes ago and told Bentley he wanted to see him in private."

It was private only by sufferance, Parker

noted, for the other room must have been still more tiny, and the partition between was nothing but planks nailed onto two-by-four studdings.

"Bentley sleeps in there," said Ann.

"Does he cook his own meals?"

"No, he eats downtown."

"How about you?"

"I live with the Wilkersons."

Parker became aware of voices beyond the thin partition, and made conversation. "You do all the bookkeeping, I take it."

"Yes," she said. "Sometimes there isn't much, and sometimes, like when the *Maiden* comes in with a big shipment, or a wagon train comes from Little Rock — times like that I work until late at night getting everything entered and the bills of lading checked and new bills made out. Most of the goods that comes in here is from the wholesalers, and we have to sort it out and re-route it."

"You haven't room to do that here."

"There's a warehouse down at the river and another one behind the bakery next to the barn where we keep the stock. The empty wagons — when there are any — are left on the prairie behind the office here."

He thought the voices were rising beyond the partition, and he tried to cover them.

"I'd think you'd have the office near one of the warehouses."

"It was originally, but the warehouse burned down and Bentley bought another one cheap. He'd just as soon move this place but it would cost more to move the scale than it would to build another —"

A sudden loud voice came from beyond the partition. "I tell you I'm not going to unload and re-load my wagons!"

Parker glanced at Ann; she was staring at the door.

Malone's voice was lower but it too was raised and very distinct. "I didn't ask you to unload every wagon. I wanted to see what was in that load hauled by Mac-Donald."

Bentley sounded angry. "I would lose half a day letting you satisfy your curiosity — and meantime I'm paying MacDonald; I'm feeding bulls; and I'm running a risk not getting the goods to Tahlequah on time."

Malone's voice rose. "You've got plenty of time."

"Sure — while it's dry. But if it rains he'll have trouble."

"Listen," said Malone, "I'm as anxious to clear you as anything else."

"No, you're not! You haven't been able to

lay it on to anybody else and you've got to make a showing, so you come in here to tear things apart."

"All I know," said Malone, "is we've got forty-two men in jail now for whisky running, and I want to find out where they're getting it."

"They're getting it from Texas!"

"Maybe so. I just want to be sure it isn't going out from Fort Smith."

"Listen," said Garth, and he must have gotten to his feet. "I've torn a dozen loads apart for you in the last year, but I'm through — absolutely through!"

"All right." Malone got up too. "But I'll tell you this, Bentley. You've been a friend of mine and you're a brother of Ann's, but that won't stop me. If you *are* hauling whisky, I'll find out."

"You won't look in another one of my wagons without a search warrant!"

Malone's voice was cold. "If you make it hard on me now, I'll make it hard on you when I catch you with the goods."

"You've got absolutely no reason for suspecting me," insisted Garth, "except that I run wagons into the Territory."

"Don't be too sure." The doorknob turned, and Parker guessed that Malone was about to leave. The door opened an

217

inch or two as Garth demanded: "If you've got any evidence, what is it?"

There was a pause. Then Malone said in a lower voice: "What about Indian Rose?"

"What about her?"

"I've had a man keeping an eye on her because she's a sister to the Kiamichi Kid. I know that she comes down here at least once a day. She was here twenty minutes ago — just before I came in."

"You've got no right to persecute her. She sticks to the rules."

"I'm not after her," said Malone, "unless she's delivering messages from the Kid."

"Rose is none of your business," Garth said harshly. "Now get out of here before I throw you out!"

Malone said quietly, "You ain't throwing me out, Bentley. In the first place, you ain't big enough. In the second place, you don't have to. I'll be glad to get out if I rile you so much you can't speak decent."

The door opened and Malone stalked out, looking grim. He glanced at Parker but hardly seemed to recognize him. He did not look at Ann but stamped outside.

The man who came out behind him looked very much like Ann. He had tawny brown hair and moustache. He was about five feet seven but quite a bit heavier than

Malone — and none of the heaviness was fat. At this moment his tan face was red.

Ann stared at both of them, seemingly stunned for a moment. Then she leaped from the high stool, darted to the outer door, and pulled it open with a slam that rattled the small building.

"Brett Malone, you come back here!"

Malone stopped. "I'll see you later when I've cooled off," he called back.

She stamped her foot. "You come back here right now or I'll never speak to you again."

He took a few steps back toward the door. "I don't threaten very good," he said.

She waited for him to get closer. "What do you mean, insulting my brother?"

"I didn't mean anything harmful, Ann."

Garth went outside, bareheaded. "I —"

"You keep still," Ann told him. "I'll handle this."

"There's nothing to handle," said Malone.

"There's a lot more than you figgered," she told him. "You can't come in here and accuse my brother of whisky-running every time you turn around."

"My job —"

"That's the trouble with you," she told him. "Your job! Since you got to be chief deputy you got a swelled head over your responsibilities."

"I don't think that's fair, Ann."

"Don't try to tell me what's fair. Just because you can hang six men is no sign you can run over my brother."

Malone looked pleadingly at her. "I never —"

Garth started forward. "Let me —"

"Shut up!" For the first time Malone sounded dangerous. "Stay in your tracks unless you want to fight."

Ann seemed almost beside herself now — probably, thought Parker, torn by her affection for both of these men. "Just because you wear that badge —"

Malone began to unpin the five-pointed silver star. "I don't want to fight your brother," he said, "but don't never get the idea I'm afraid to." He put the badge in his pocket and looked up. "Now I want to tell you both something. I'm going to keep looking for whisky in them wagons, Bentley. If I have to get search warrants I'll do it — but I'll keep looking. And if I find it, you're going to prison for a long time."

"And I'll tell *you* something, Brett Malone! I would never marry a man who suspects my own brother of whisky-running." Ann's voice started to break. "If this keeps up, one of you will shoot the other one, and I don't want —" She stopped.

Malone said, "All right, Ann. Whatever you say. I reckon I can stand it if you can." He turned and walked swiftly away.

Garth took her arm. "Ann, you —"

"Don't touch me!" she screamed. She flung herself back inside, and burst into tears.

Garth turned to Parker. "I'm sorry, judge, you had to get here at such a time. We're usually pretty peaceful."

"Sometimes," Parker observed, "an understanding has to be reached."

"I'm sorry about the whole thing. I think Brett was a little high-handed, demanding to inspect my load when he never had any real evidence against me. But I never wanted it to end up this way. I been pushed a little too much, I guess. I took on some new contracts and had to buy more wagons and more stock, and it's been a tight squeeze." He took a deep breath. "Judge, what can I do for you?"

"If it isn't too much trouble," said Parker, "I'd like to engage you to move my furniture from the dock to my new house."

Chapter 16

They moved into their house, and Mary seemed quite pleased; she still thought George Maledon's house was too close, but she guessed they would get along all right.

After buying new things for the house, Mary faced up to the fact, with Parker, that thirty-five hundred dollars a year, while it was an extremely good salary, would not go as far as what they had been used to, and economy would be necessary if they were to give Charlie the advantages they would like to give him. Parker was determined that Charlie should read law and set up a practice, and Mary agreed. About that time too it became evident that Charlie would have a brother or sister, and some thought had to be given to that child's welfare, although they both agreed that Charlie, being the older, was entitled to the first consideration.

The *Independent* commented editorially on the happy effect of the sextuple hanging; it looked with no small degree of concern on such wholesale legal killing, but it considered the conditions that had led to it and it believed the end justified the means. It quoted two long columns of clippings from newspapers all over the Southwest, and from Washington, Atlanta, New York, and Boston. Some looked with alarm at such a precedent: hanging a man without giving him the benefit of appeal; others, notably those closer to Fort Smith, approved whole-heartedly.

The attitude of the people of Fort Smith changed. Parker walked down the street in his double-breasted coat and his high silk hat, and people went out of their way to speak to him. Certainly, he told Mary pointedly, thinking of her own attitude, it was a compliment and a vote of confidence.

Malone said that over in the Territory they talked of nothing else but the hanging, and for a while capital crimes were extremely scarce.

"That's what we want," said Parker. "When the next outbreak comes, we'll give them even more to talk about."

He found that Malone and Ann were still keeping company, but Ann would not talk marriage until Brett ceased to hound Bentley and his wagons. Perhaps, thought Parker, "hound" was a strong word, but it was the word Ann used.

Parker figuratively rolled up his sleeves and went to work. Now that the people had begun to approve his course, he felt fired with enthusiasm. He knew he was right and he was determined to let nothing interfere. The lawyers showed considerable dissatisfaction, but it was his court and he was running it. He had no intention of turning soft.

The next capital crime concerned a double killing. One Isham Seely and his uncle, Gibson Ishonubbee, both Chickasaw Indians, were proved to have killed a man and a colored woman who was the man's cook. The colored woman had been hit on the head with a gun barrel, while the man had been struck down with an axe after which his throat had been cut.

As far as Parker was concerned, there was no question of their guilt, and he instructed the jury to that end at some length.

There were others in a long and grim procession, but the result was always the same. And on a raw day in February he brought the second set of six men before him and pronounced the words of death. Again he experienced the overwhelming feeling of vacuum within him, and again he wept. This time, however, the members of the courtroom audience did not squirm uncomfortably until he recovered himself, but rather waited in respectful silence. This he noted with satisfaction.

He set the execution date for April 21.

As before, Mary started carrying cake and flowers to the prisoners. This time, since it followed his talk to her, and was done in obvious and open defiance, he was nonplused. Since he did not know what else to do, he pretended to ignore it. Intentionally or not, she was undermining his authority, but he would show her he was strong enough to overcome it.

The time for the hanging approached, and again Parker announced that it would be a public hanging. He consulted George Maledon a few days ahead, and made sure Maledon would be ready. He need not have worried. Parker sensed Maledon's unswerving, almost mechanical devotion to his job, and his pride in the perfection of its accomplishment.

Malone came in a few days before. "There's talk that you haven't allowed enough time for appeals to be made to the President," he said.

Parker said implacably, "The lawyers are merely trying to interpose delays in the hope that something will turn up. I am not moved by such criticism. These men were found guilty and they must pay the penalty. There is no excuse for weak-heartedness or sentimentalism in connection with murder." He looked down at the gallows. "We shall go right ahead with the execution as planned. My only regret is that we have only six. By the way, I've seen you and Ann walking together recently. Have you gotten things straightened out with her?"

Malone shook his head bleakly. "She says she won't do a thing until I give Bentley a clean bill of health."

"Maybe you can do that now."

"No." Malone was serious. "I've got a feeling if we could bring in the Kid, a lot of our trouble would be over, and one way or another I could let Bentley Garth alone. But as long as whisky pours into the Territory, and a lot of it through the Kid's country, and as long as I don't know definitely where it comes from, I've got to keep Bentley on the suspect list. The main trouble is that now, with him being rambunctious about me examining his loads, I can't clear him at all. The only thing I can do is get the goods on him."

"Doesn't Ann understand all this?"

"She understands — too much. She says she will not have her husband and her brother fighting each other, and she'd rather be an old maid."

"She's still — fond of you, though?"

Malone nodded morosely. "She says she

likes me — and nobody else, but —" He shrugged.

"I think I understand," Parker said softly. "I hope you don't mind my prying into your personal affairs, Brett. I'm really very much interested."

Malone looked up. "It's all right. I sort of look on you as taking the place of my father."

Parker felt very warm toward Malone. It was the closest personal thing anyone had said to him in a long time. At home there was now that wall between him and Mary on certain subjects, but with this young man he felt completely at ease. Between Malone and him there was no subterfuge, no animosity, nothing but mutual understanding. Not, of course, he remembered hastily, that there was anything unpleasant between Mary and him — but Mary was a woman and had her little ways of insistence. Of course Mary was his wife and he could afford to be indulgent.

The next day he watched George Maledon go over the big gallows. Malone pulled in four deputies from the field to guard against a possible jail break, and once again the town of Fort Smith put on a holiday atmosphere and began to fill up with sightseers, and the saloons and hotels did a rushing business. Newspaper correspondents came from St. Louis, Kansas City, Columbus, New Orleans, Dallas and Houston, and even New York, and this time there was a different air about the whole thing. Where before they had looked on it as a freakish sort of thing, sensational and startling, now they seemed to consider it in a more serious light as an aspect of law and order.

Parker was patient with the newspapermen, giving out the history of the condemned men, expounding his theory of law in the Territory, and explaining why it was that there was no appeal for a man condemned in his court. He rather thought, as Friday approached, that he had handled the whole thing very well and had struck a blow for justice.

On Thursday he found Malone waiting at the door of his chambers with a piece of paper in his hand. "Judge — Mr. Parker, you better look at this."

Parker took the paper and read the words handwritten in black ink:

"Washington City, D.C., April 19, 1876. To Brett Malone: I have this day granted a reprieve to Osee Sanders, sentenced to be hanged on the 21st instant. Suspend his execution. Acknowledge receipt. U. S. Grant."

Parker stared at the telegram, trying to ward off the sudden impact of the words.

"I don't know what the President was thinking of," he said slowly. "Sanders is guilty of murder. He killed Tom Carlyle for his wife's Cherokee warrants. He left a widow and a fatherless child."

"Mr. Parker," said Malone anxiously, "does this mean we can't hang Sanders?"

Parker looked up slowly. "I'm afraid so."

"That will ruin the whole thing, won't it?"

"Ruin?" Parker repeated absently.

"Sure. Six the first time, six the second. Couldn't we pretend we didn't get this, or that it came too late?"

At last Parker smiled tolerantly. "You're young, Brett, too young perhaps to realize that to all of us come great disappointments." He stared at the telegram without seeing the words. "This is an order from the President, Brett. If we were to disobey it, we would be guilty of murder ourselves."

"But —"

"There are no 'buts.' This order must be obeyed." He looked impersonally at Malone. "Notify Sanders."

"Yes, sir."

For a while afterward Parker walked the floor of his chambers. It was a great disappointment and not calculated to improve respect for the law. He had announced a hanging for six men; it would look like weakness to hang five, but he saw no alternative. For a moment he had the wild thought of wiring the President himself, but at once thought better of it. It might be considered petulant.

He did wish, though, that the President would consult with him before interfering with his plans. They had very little conception in Washington of conditions in Arkansas, and they could not know how carefully he had arranged this execution, building toward a dramatic climax calculated to accomplish a specific purpose.

He realized presently that it was after eight o'clock, hastily put on his robe and marched into the courtroom with his Bible. He laid his watch on the desk, saw that it was four minutes after eight. He nodded to the clerk.

"The United States of America versus Encephalus Towson, charged with illegally selling whisky in the Indian Territory. . . ."

He went through the morning mechanically; something nagged at the back of his mind, and he could not put his finger on it until Rudolph Clyman began his summation to the jury: "Gentlemen of the jury, this defendant has been, I think you will agree, more than hounded by the minions of the law. He was arrested twice under Judge Caldwell and both times acquitted; once under Judge Story and also —"

Caldwell! Yes, of course. Caldwell had sentenced a man to be hanged but had not hanged him. What was the name? He beckoned the clerk and whispered to him. The clerk nodded and hurried out.

Clyman glanced around at the bench with an expression of puzzlement and some displeasure.

"The court apologizes for the interruption, counselor. Will you proceed?"

"Thank you." Clyman continued to sketch Encephalus Towson's career, emphasizing his many narrow escapes from the relentless minions of the law, and completely ignoring the obvious fact that Towson at best had made a lifelong habit of skirting the thin edge of criminal acts. It didn't matter; Parker would take care of that in his charge.

In a couple of minutes Holbrook hurried back in and laid a sheet of paper on Parker's desk.

Clyman looked around again in annoyance, and Parker said with satisfaction, "The court suggests that counsel postpone the remainder of his address to the jury until a matter of pressing urgency has been disposed of." He wrote out a few words and handed them to the clerk who hurried out again. "The court might say, counselor, that it does not at all agree with your distorted version of the life of the defendant, and will undertake to correct the same before the case goes to the jury."

"But, your honor —"

"Yes, counselor?" Parker said coldly.

Clyman looked baffled, and finally said, "Very well, your honor, but I wish the record to show that I have entered an objection to prejudicial remarks of the court."

Parker nodded. So far he had tolerated Clyman and his sophisticated ideas of the practice of law, but some day he would crack down on him. Clyman sat down, looking frustrated. Then Malone came in with a prisoner — a small man with the straight black hair of the Indian. He was handcuffed, and Malone led him to a spot in front of Parker's desk.

"Does he understand English?" asked Parker.

"No, your honor," said Malone. "I don't think he knows any English at all."

"Get High Wind Blows."

"Yes, sir."

The man stood there while Parker ignored him, reading papers on his desk. Clyman, plainly displeased because he had been stopped in the middle of his speech, sat with compressed lips, while all others in the courtroom waited expectantly.

Malone came back with the interpreter, and the stench from both him and the man already there was overpowering, but Parker did not deign to notice it.

He stood up. "McClish Impson, you have been found guilty of the crime of murder and you have been sentenced to die by hanging. For nearly three years you have been in jail while your attorneys sought to get a presidential commutation, but this has not been successful. Therefore I now fix the date of your execution as April 21, 1876 — tomorrow, at which time you will be hanged with the others about to face their Maker."

Colonel Boudinot bounced to his feet. "Your honor, this setting of the date, I am sure, would come as a surprise to my colleague, Mr. Barnes, and since he is not in court I would like, on his behalf, to request a few days' delay in order that the defendant may have time to prepare himself for death."

"Counsel's voluntary appearance for the defendant is duly noted," Parker said dryly, "and his request denied. This man has known for three years that he was going to die. If he is not prepared by now, he never will be."

"Your honor, this is most unprecedented."

"Possibly," Parker admitted. "But I am concerned only with justice."

McClish Impson, hardly seeming to comprehend the words of the interpreter, was led back to his cell, and Parker instructed Clyman to proceed. But the entire momentum of Clyman's plea to the jury had been disrupted, and Clyman finished with no very distinguished effort, which was as well, for it saved Parker considerable thought.

The case went to the jury; the jury retired, and Parker started the next case. The jury returned in twenty minutes with a verdict of guilty, and Parker dismissed it.

At the close of court that afternoon he announced that court would be adjourned until Saturday morning, and Colonel Boudinot stood up and said, "Thank you, your honor."

Parker looked sharply at him to see if there was any sarcasm in Boudinot's manner, but decided there was not — which was good, for he respected Boudinot more than any attorney in his court.

He stopped outside the building in some astonishment at the large number of persons camping on the grounds of the fort — some within the very shadow of the gallows.

Malone came up with only that slight gritting of his moccasins and Parker said, "It seems that we shall have a bigger crowd than before."

"There are ten thousand people in and around Fort Smith — all come to see the hanging."

"It should have a salutary effect on crime," said Parker.

"Yes, sir. It was very quick thinking on your part to remember McClish Impson."

"One way or another," Parker said, "we shall cause justice to prevail."

"Maledon said for you to be sure to write out the order for execution."

"I'll do that."

"And since the grounds are going to be packed, the newspaper correspondents have asked me to find out if they may have seats in the windows of the courtroom so they can see better."

"I see no reason why not. Tell the janitor to admit them tomorrow."

"Thank you."

Parker watched him walk away, very proud of his chief deputy. The boy had already grown into a man. He wasn't old enough to be marshal yet, but he had every attribute of a good one. Some day . . .

Parker went home and read his Bible. He did not speak of the execution to Mary, who went to bed early. He stayed up until dawn reading his Bible and he was up early.

Again he watched from his chambers as George Maledon made his test drops with the sandbags. Again he observed the rigamarole of last words, prayers, and hymns. Again the tension built up pressure inside of him which seemed about to explode long before the six men marched out and lined up their feet along the crack in the trapdoor.

The grounds were jammed with human beings of every type — blanket Indians, farmers, cowhands, and a few men in silk hats like his own. He looked for Indian Rose and her girls, and was secretly pleased to see them sitting near the gallows. He saw men and boys perched on the broken stone wall and filling the branches of every nearby tree.

Outside the immediate grounds men were selling balloons and souvenirs, and almost in the moment of dropping the trap a whiskered man in a derby was making his way through the crowd with a bucket of lemonade and a tin dipper.

Parker watched the ropes tighten on the necks, the black caps drop over the heads. The sights and sounds and smells of the crowd below ceased to exist. He found it hard to breathe as the pressure in his chest became almost intolerable. Maledon, unflustered, efficient, pulled the bolt. The men dropped suddenly and swung a little. One man's legs pulled up in a spasmodic jerk and then slowly relaxed as women screamed. The rusty trapdoor hinge squeaked once and then was silent.

Parker saw DuVal walk beneath the gallows with his watch in his hand. And so the awful ceremony was finished, and six men had gone to their well-deserved deaths, and once again Parker wept. . . .

Chapter 17

The grim journey went on and on. The next time there were four, one of whom was Osee Sanders, whose reprieve expired without saving his life. At the fourth hanging there were three, and Parker's hopes rose with six scheduled for the succeeding execution, but again one man was reprieved, and this time there was no available substitute. Then it dropped down to two and then three. Then for the fourth time six were scheduled to die but once again a man was reprieved. It almost seemed that Washington was in a conspiracy against him, to keep him from hanging six again.

But capital crimes lessened. The next hanging was of only one man, and the time following that, one more.

He began to be filled with a great satisfaction. He had not brought the Kiamichi Kid up for trial yet but he had made the Kid walk softly. The criminals in the Territory had learned to be careful. There was increasing interference from Washington — some direct, from the attorney general; some indirect, from congressmen and government officials, but they did not know the conditions Parker faced, and so he went serenely on, secure in the rightness of his course.

One night after supper Mary approached him with that air of dogged defiance that he had come to know so well in connection with every execution. "Isaac, I do not think Charlie should play with the Maledon girl."

"I have told you many times that George Maledon is an upstanding citizen."

"He's a hangman," she said, "and you cannot get around it. But that isn't why I say that, Isaac. They are getting too big for each other."

"I don't know what you mean."

"They're too interested in each other." She blushed and added, "As boy and girl."

Parker laughed. "They're only children."

"Charlie's twelve," she said. "Annie is only eleven, but she's quite big for her age."

"I'm sure they would never do anything wrong."

"No matter what you think," she told him, "I am going to stop their playing together."

"Very well, very well." He tried to keep the impatience out of his voice. "You're his mother, and I'm sure you can handle him without any trouble."

"Charlie will come to a bad end," she predicted, "if this kind of thing is not stopped."

"You're imagining things," he told her, well aware that in the last few years it had not taken much to arouse her belligerence.

By this time Jimmie was six years old, and he was much quieter than Charlie and easier to handle; he obeyed better and was not as demanding. Parker excused this by saying that Charlie had "too much spirit." Jimmie was a good boy, he went on, but he probably never would make much of a mark in the world, whereas Parker felt that Charlie had unusual intelligence. He was accustomed to add fondly that Charlie was destined to "make his mark in the world. No question about that."

So Isaac Charles Parker strode up and down the streets of Fort Smith, feeling a great power and a great expansiveness, for it was he who was bringing law and order to this land. The banker and the postmaster and all the leading men of Fort Smith were very careful to greet him on all occasions, and he and Mary were invited to social affairs at the best homes.

It was true that his salary, with the coming of inflation after the panic, had remained at $3,500, and he had found that barely enough to cover their needs. He was still wearing the same coat and hat, and he had noticed that Mary did not often get a new dress or hat, but he assured her that all such inequities would be taken care of eventually. In the meantime they were respected citizens; they went to church on Sunday; they got along well together; sometimes at a gathering he could not resist chiding her good-naturedly for her sentimentality toward condemned prisoners, but it was done in fun, and he did it mostly because Mary's defiance was so obvious he dared not overlook it. By treating it as a joke before others, he thought to hide the seriousness of the rift it had caused between them.

No longer was he looked on as the "hanging judge" but rather as the man who had brought law and order, and children smiled at him and said, "Good morning, Judge Parker," and waited for him to smile in return.

He did not slow up in his work. Brett Malone was still his chief deputy. Jim Wilkerson, who now had eight children, was still with him; so were George Isha-harjo and Will Sunshine. The others came and went pretty rapidly; some of them became outlaws after they turned in their badges, and many of those turned up in the court at Fort Smith and stood trial like anybody else.

In 1884 a man named Frank Dalton was a deputy for a brief time; he was killed by whisky runners, and for a very short time three of his brothers — Grat, Bob, and Emmett — wore badges.

Frank Dalton had not been the only deputy killed. In the first two years of Parker's rule he had lost no deputies at all, and then, as the outlaws began to realize that a trip to Fort Smith meant a 50-50 chance of conviction, they began to fight arrest when the crime was a major one. In those eight years, thirty-three deputies had been killed.

Still Parker had no trouble getting more deputies. Either due to their respect for Parker or the persuasiveness of Brett Malone — or possibly both — there were always men ready to wear the star.

One event in those years made Parker sad. A man named Jacob Yoes was appointed U.S. marshal. He was a good man, but Parker had fancied that position for Brett Malone. Yoes, however, had friends, and there was nothing to be done but accept it.

"I kinda hoped," said Brett himself, "I'd get the full job this time."

Parker looked at him fondly. Brett had filled out and broadened, and had the lean, tough look of a wind-whipped persimmon tree. "I'm sorry," Parker said, "terribly sorry. I wanted you to have the appointment, but I guess I don't have as much weight in Washington as some of these professional politicians."

"No regrets," he said. "I'm more sorry they went around you than about anything else." He put a strong hand on Parker's shoulder. "Don't feel bad about it," he said. "There's a next time coming."

It was considerably different from Mary's attitude toward him. This was exemplified the following Sunday night, when Parker, home from church, paced the floor and recounted some of the good results of his tenure of office. "Eight years ago," he said, "this was a savage country where a man's life was likely to be forfeit at any time to the whims of outlaws and murderers. Today, due to the unceasing work of my court, a man and his wife and children are relatively safe in the Territory. Vast strides have been made."

Mary looked up from her wine, and that old, strange antagonism was in her eyes. She said implacably, "You sleep at night with the burden of thirty-six dead men on your soul."

"I don't consider that fair, Mary. There is nothing on my conscience. I have only done my duty."

"The sixth commandment says, 'Thou shalt not kill.' "

He stopped his pacing to look at her. He wished she wouldn't drink so much. "True," he said, "but you are implying that it is I who kill."

"You pronounce the sentences."

"As a judge of the federal court — not as an individual."

She got up and walked unsteadily to the kitchen for more wine. He never had been able to talk her out of her fixed idea that he personally was responsible for the hangings. She still took flowers and cake to the jail before every execution, and she never offered an excuse or asked him to understand. He wondered exactly what was behind her defiance. He had come to doubt that it was based solely on her strong feeling about capital punishment, for he had never heard her mention it before coming to Fort Smith. There were times when he wondered if it was an inherent antagonism toward him, but he dismissed that possibility as not worthy of thought. Sometimes he suspected it was rebellion against the primitiveness and inconveniences of living in the frontier country of Arkansas after enjoying a luxurious life as the wife of a congressman in Washington, but this too hardly seemed worthy.

She came back and sat down unsteadily. "They say you are a hanging judge — that you know no law but the rope."

"I can tell you one thing," Parker said sternly. "The men who come before the bar of justice in my court are hardened criminals. Talking would do no good whatever. The rope is the only language they understand." He said with complete assurance, " 'The murderer shall be put to death by the mouth of witnesses. . . . Blood it defileth the land: and the land cannot be cleansed of the blood that is shed therein, but by the blood of him that shed it.' "

"And yet," she said stubbornly, "they still come."

"Of course they do." He was little short of exasperation. "There are three times as many persons in the Territory as there used to be. Furthermore, I do not say that *any* method of handling crime would ever completely eliminate criminal acts. I say that the gallows at Fort Smith has reduced it by at least ninety per cent when all factors are taken into account."

She said almost defiantly, "You are forgetting the law. This has become a personal crusade with you."

At last he exploded. "I am tired of opposition from you. You know nothing of crime, nothing of the courts, nothing of punishment." He got to his feet and glared down at her. "I want you to know one thing: in spite of all opposition — yours and all others' — I am going ahead with my work. I am going to clean murderers and rapists out of the Indian Territory if I have to do it with my own hands. I shall be as Joshua. I shall smite the wicked from the face of the earth and I shall have no mercy nor shall I be swayed from my duty by the interference of politicians or the maudlin sympathies of those who know naught of the criminal mind. I shall be a scourge to murderers and rapists until the Indian Territory is as clean as the driven snow. Men shall hang!" he cried. "And the only review of my judgments will come when their depraved souls go to meet their Maker!"

But it was the next day that Parker received his first hard jolt. He got his usual copy of *The New York Tribune* in his mailbox, and opened it at breakfast. The first item to catch his eye was on the front page under the heading INDIAN TERRITORY: "Hanging Judge Gets Jurisdiction Whittled Down. Yesterday Congress, by passing the Act of Jan. 6, 1883, by a good majority, made the first move by that body to reduce the jurisdiction of the

Federal Court for the Western District of Arkansas, presided over by Judge Isaac C. Parker, the famous Hanging Judge. A move like this has been expected for a long time, since for eight years now Judge Parker's decision has been supreme, even in matters of life and death. He has hanged between 35 and 40 men, all without benefit of appeal.

"By the Act aforesaid, all land in Indian Territory north of the Canadian River, and not occupied by any of the Indian Nations, is attached to the District of Kansas; while all land south of that river and not occupied by Cherokee, Choctaw, Creek, Chickasaw, or Seminole Nations, is attached to the northern District of Texas. This has the effect of cutting the Fort Smith court's jurisdiction in half.

"It has been suggested that, to restore true democratic processes to the United States of America, Congress look next to reducing Parker's absolute authority."

He read it again, hardly believing. He half-rose and then sat down. He drank his water and read the item still again. The waiter came with his breakfast, and took the glass, saying, "You like the water this morning, Mr. Parker? It's a new well we got, deeper than the old one, and harder. They say this water is the hardest water in the Southwest."

"Uh — yes," said Parker. He got up, fumbling for his hat.

"Mr. Parker, you didn't eat anything!"

"No." Automatically he laid a half-dollar on the table.

"Something wrong, sir?" asked the waiter. "Maybe it's that new water. Maybe it's harder than anybody realized."

Parker went out without answering. He walked almost blindly down the street. His jurisdiction cut in half! This was a political move; no doubt about it. Men who had not been able to reach him any other way, now were determined to do it by whittling his jurisdiction.

He went into the courthouse and started for his chambers. Malone came out of the marshal's office and hurried after him. "I saw the paper, Mr. Parker," he said. "It wasn't fair."

He got into his chambers before he trusted himself to answer. "It certainly wasn't."

"I reckon we stepped too hard on somebody's toes."

"Apparently." Parker sat down, staring at the floor.

"This will change things for a lot of us,"

said Malone. "We won't need as many deputies when this goes into effect."

Parker looked at him. "No. It will not mean that to us. We shall keep the same number of deputies. There is plenty of work to be done. We'll comb the eastern half of the Territory more intensively, that's all. We can give more attention to a smaller area — and we'll make that area the cleanest spot in North America."

"All right, sir. We'll keep on bringing them in as long as you say so."

"I very definitely say so." Parker's head sank back on his chest. "Bring them in. We'll yet hang twelve from that crossbeam."

Even Mary was sympathetic that night. She met him at the door and put her arms around his neck and told him that she too thought it was unfair, that in spite of the way he had done it, he had brought respect for law to the Territory and she did not think it properly appreciative on the part of Congress to cut the ground from under him.

Parker began to feel better. "Thank you, Mary," he said gently.

Parker gathered himself and buckled down harder to the task before him. His territory was still a tremendous one, he realized as he went over the map with Brett, and there was, as he had already said, much work to be done. "Let's scour it clean," he said. "The Kiamichi Kid is still at large. Let's bring him in and put him on trial."

A woman named Belle Starr came before him for horse-theft, and he gave her a year in the penitentiary.

He was incredulous at some of the newspaper reports that described her as a "winsome girl," for privately and honestly nobody could deny that Belle Starr was a horse-faced old battleaxe. How she ever kept a man around her was a mystery to Parker — and yet she was said to have had a great many men.

He hanged three men in June, and then, suddenly and without any warning, came the news by telegraph:

"Fauntleroy Butterfield taken captive last night we are proceeding to Fort Smith Malone Deputy."

Chapter 18

The Kiamichi Kid arrived by train, handcuffed at both ankle and wrist to Brett Malone, who wore no weapon of any kind. George Isha-harjo sat in the seat behind them with a rifle, while Will Sunshine held down a seat across the aisle.

The entire town of Fort Smith, including Indian Rose and her girls, was down at the station to meet the train. Jim Wilkerson had to make way for Parker, and finally boosted him up to stand on a baggage truck to watch the unloading.

The Kid was older and heavier, more surly — a dangerous man if Parker ever had seen one. But Parker took a second look at Brett Malone and felt very proud, for the deputy was now a big and very capable-looking man. He gave the feeling that if he chose to do so he could break in two with his hands any criminal who should be rash enough to oppose him. And his courage in being the one handcuffed to the Kid, without a weapon, was a thrill even to Parker, for being close to the Kid was like being tied to a rattlesnake. You never knew when he might strike. A hidden knife, a smuggled pistol — anything of that nature or something even more diabolical, that only the Kid could dream up, would mean death to the man fastened to him. No man in the Southwest knew that better than Brett Malone, and yet he had done it, and Parker felt a great warmth of feeling for him.

They put the Kid on trial for a previous murder — the one he was charged with at the time of Parker's arrival in Fort Smith. Parker watched grimly every move of Colonel Boudinot and Thomas Barnes, and overruled them at every turn.

"Your honor," Colonel Boudinot said on the second afternoon, "I respectfully suggest that the court seems to have its mind pretty well made up as to the guilt or lack of guilt of the defendant."

Parker stared at him. "Colonel Boudinot, the court has had long and pleasant associations with you, but the court feels compelled to say that it not only has definite opinions on the guilt of the accused, but actually *knows* whereof it speaks. The court has with its own eyes seen the crime of kidnaping committed by this defendant, for which the defendant might well be imprisoned for the rest of his life. Surely, Colonel Boudinot, you are not presuming to say this defendant is not guilty in every sense of the word and deserving of whatever fate the law may apportion him."

"Your honor may have reason to dislike the defendant, but according to the law the defendant is on trial for one specific crime: the murder of T. H. Judkins. May I suggest, your honor, that if the defendant is acquitted on the present charge, there is nothing in the law to prevent his being held on any other charge that may legally be brought against him?"

"You may suggest all you please, colonel. The court has no doubt about this man's guilt — and neither does any other intelligent, thinking human being who has lived in Fort Smith since 'seventy-five."

"But, your honor —"

Parker said icily, "Does counsel wish to subject himself to a charge of contempt?"

"No, your honor." Boudinot drew a deep breath. He turned to glance at the audience; his black hair was beginning to show gray, but it still brushed his shoulders. "No, your honor, I do not." He sat down heavily.

Parker glared at the Kid, who sat stolidly, as usual. "Proceed with the examination," he ordered, and Clayton stood up again and began his questions.

It was a very hot day in July, and the judge's robe was stifling. The bailiff had gone around to open all the windows, including two immediately behind Parker. Parker ran his finger inside of his collar with a handkerchief, and wondered if this was not the hottest July they had had in Fort Smith.

"Now," said Clayton, looking up from his notes, "did you see the defendant, Fauntleroy Butterfield, come out of the house of his sister, Indian Rose, with a rifle that had been fired?"

"Your honor —" Barnes was struggling to his feet. "I object to that question."

"On what ground?" Parker asked impatiently.

"The witness is not competent to answer the question, your honor. How could he possibly know the rifle had been fired recently?"

"It is possible," Parker answered, "that he saw smoke curling from the muzzle."

"But, your honor, that is evidence for the prosecution to develop — not for your honor to read into the testimony."

Parker snapped at him. "That is your opinion?"

"It is, your honor."

"Mr. Barnes." Parker drew himself up straight; his voice was uncompromising. "Mr. Barnes, you will report at eight o'clock in the morning, on a charge of contempt of court."

"Your honor —"

"The court is ill disposed to argue the point at this time."

Barnes sat down slowly, and Parker turned again to Clayton. Clayton's desk was directly in front of his own and about three feet lower. The Kid sat slumped down in the defendant's chair, some ten feet from Clayton's desk. His handcuffs had not been put on today because of the weather, but Jim Wilkerson sat immediately behind him; Will Sunshine, towering almost to the top of the door-frame, guarded the door, and George Isha-harjo with two other deputies, Marsh Andrews and H. D. Fannin, watched the open windows around the courtroom.

"Now, I asked you —"

"I forgot the question," said the witness.

"We were talking about Indian Rose's home in Choctaw Country."

Parker became aware of movement at the big door, and looked up to see Indian Rose, older but certainly no less attractive, come into the courtroom and take a seat in the front row.

Without warning the Kid leaped to his feet, hit the floor in a running jump, vaulted to the top of Clayton's desk, took one crashing step there, and leaped to Parker's big desk.

He had moved as quickly as a cat, and Parker hardly realized what was happening before the Kid's moccasined foot thumped down before him.

In that instant Parker realized the Kid was heading for the open window behind him. Parker thrust out his right arm and caused the man to stumble. Then Parker was out of his big chair and clamped his long arms around the Kid, and they both fell to the floor.

The Kid was clawing, gouging, twisting, but Parker held him with all his strength, partly smothering his movements with the heavy robe. Then Jim Wilkerson came around the desk at a run and put his pistol muzzle into the Kid's side. "Cut it out!" he ordered.

The Kid grew quiet. George Isha-harjo snapped handcuffs on both his feet and his ankles, and they made him hobble back to the defendant's chair. Parker resumed his seat immediately, arranging his robe. He pounded the gavel and said loudly, "Mr. Clayton, proceed with the examination."

There was trouble developing a case, because the killing was ten years in the past and most of the witnesses had disappeared, but Clayton did his best.

Then Parker took over and gave the jury its instructions. He said, "I do not want any untoward incident that has happened in this courtroom to influence the jury. An attempt to escape has no bearing on the defendant's guilt. However, it is very difficult for this court to see how any jury, with the long record of defendant's criminal activities before it, can possibly find any verdict but that of guilty."

"Your honor," cried Colonel Boudinot, "surely this is an abuse of judicial discretion."

Parker was impatient. He glanced at Indian Rose, sitting inscrutable, and wondered what part she had played in the escape attempt. "Does counsel wish to examine the merits of his position?"

Boudinot sighed. "No, your honor. Not at this time."

Fifty-five minutes later the jury found Fauntleroy Butterfield guilty of murder. Parker turned self-righteously to Barnes and Boudinot and said, "If counsel will appear in court tomorrow, counsel will hear sentence passed on the defendant."

"Your honor," said Boudinot, "I was about to ask the court for a re-trial for errors committed in the taking of testimony, errors committed in the charge, and —"

"Denied!" Parker snapped.

Other cases came up in the following two weeks; four more men were found guilty of murder, and all of them were sentenced to hang. Then came the case of Matthew Allen.

Allen had been a respectable white farmer near Paul's Valley in the Chickasaw Nation. He was accused of robbing a Katy express train of $18,000 in gold, and of killing a guard during the holdup. The charge was murder, and the principal witness against him was Texas Jack Omohundro, a man who confessed to being an outlaw and who admitted having been in the same holdup, but who denied having fired the shot that killed the guard, and denied having the money, which had disappeared. Texas Jack had received a severe body wound and had lain out in the brush for weeks before getting back on his feet. Then he had been captured and brought to Fort Smith, and had offered to turn state's evidence against Allen, who he said was the real leader of the holdup gang, if he himself could have a clean bill.

Parker had made the deal with Texas Jack, unknown to anybody but Brett Malone, and the trial was one of the most hotly contested he had ever presided over. Allen was represented by Barnes, Boudinot, and Clyman, and Clayton as usual was prosecuting. The defense attorneys picked hole after hole in Texas Jack's testimony, and Parker many times had to assert the weight of his authority to make the testimony point toward Allen's guilt.

There had been two sidekicks of Texas Jack — Bruno Strong and Reuben Ashcroft — and they both supported Texas Jack's testimony.

Parker refused to admit Allen's wife's evidence that he had been home the night of the holdup, and before the trial was over he fired all three of the defense attorneys for contempt. The case went to the jury, and Parker instructed it specifically. The verdict was guilty, and Parker sentenced Allen to hang.

Clayton stopped in at his chambers after the sentencing. "Your honor," he said, "I can't say that I am fully satisfied as to Allen's real guilt in this matter."

"There's nothing to be uncertain about," Parker said, leaning back. "Three men testified that he was the leader of the gang, that he planned it."

"And yet," said Clayton, "the man denied it. I can hardly believe he would make a flat denial if he had been as active as they claim.

It seems more likely that he would try to shift the blame for the bigger crime — the murder."

"He's a very clever man," Parker said positively. "That is just what he would not do. He deliberately chose this course with that very reasoning in mind."

"You believe Texas Jack completely, then?"

"He impresses me as a very honest man, trying to make amends to society."

"He has a long record of felonies behind him."

"He has decided to go straight. I'm convinced of that."

"And yet," said Clayton thoughtfully, "if he really found himself in the shadow of the gallows, and if he had something against Allen, as they tried to show —"

"I would not allow that testimony to be given."

"I know, your honor. But suppose there had been bad blood between the two. What more clever way for Texas Jack to get out from under the murder charge, and at the same time take vengeance on Allen for a real or imaginary wrong?"

"And the other two witnesses?"

"They are both admitted lawbreakers of long standing. Is there any reason to believe they would balk at telling a lie under oath?"

Parker said impatiently, "Mr. Clayton, I have studied those men in my court for a day and a half, and I assure you I am a good enough judge of men to tell when a man is lying and when he is telling the truth."

"Well — I just wanted to make sure you were satisfied."

Parker stood up and put on his hat. "Mr. Clayton, I will stake my reputation as a judge on Matthew Allen's guilt. Let's walk up the street, and I'll buy you a soda."

He went over the prospects that night for another hanging. He had nine candidates for the gallows, but he was not ready to set the date. Two more trials scheduled for murder and one for rape, and those three, if convicted, would make an even dozen. He advanced the three cases on the calendar.

But Boudinot and Barnes had brought pressure in Washington. There were rumors of presidential clemency, and on Sunday Colonel Boudinot met him at church with a telegram. "The President has granted a full pardon to the Kiamichi Kid," he told Parker, his eyes on Parker's.

Parker frowned incredulously. "The Kid — a full pardon?"

"That's the word from the attorney general."

"But — the Kiamichi Kid — he's as guilty as he could possibly be. You know that yourself."

"I only know," Boudinot said guardedly, "what it says in this telegram."

A week later came the next blow: a presidential commutation of Allen's sentence to life imprisonment.

Parker adjourned court early that afternoon and went to his chambers, where Brett Malone found him. "We took the Kid over into the Territory to turn him loose, as you suggested."

"I don't suppose he liked that."

"No, sir. He wanted to stay in Fort Smith and go on a spree, but I convinced him that it would be mighty easy for me to shoot him if he got into trouble." Malone grinned.

Parker handed him the telegram commuting Allen's sentence. "What do you make of this?"

Malone read it slowly and looked up. "Maybe it's a good thing. I always wondered if Texas Jack made up that story to get out of it himself."

"I tell you," Parker almost shouted, "the man is guilty! I studied him. I know."

"At any rate," said Malone, "it isn't as

bad as if the President turned him loose like he did the Kid."

"It's bad enough. The discipline of the court is being destroyed."

The next morning he brought all the remaining men sentenced to death into court, and set the date of execution for six weeks in the future. But within the next week two more sentences were commuted and one man was pardoned, and in a moment of uneasiness Parker granted a fourth a new trial.

Nevertheless he had three candidates for George Maledon's ropes on July 11, 1884: Thomas Thompson, John Davis, and Jack Woman-Killer. Those three were duly dropped to eternity, and as always Parker watched from his chambers, and, as always, he wept after the execution.

By now the deputies, with their smaller territory, were bringing in more and more prisoners. Parker started night court sessions. He held court on Thanksgiving and on the Fourth of July. Negro, white, Mexican, Indian, halfbreed — they all came before him and they all, without bias for their race or color, heard the dreadful words; they stood on the long, narrow platform and felt it drop from under them as they were launched into eternity.

The Kid spread a new trail of robbery,

and Parker was grim when he gave Malone orders to go after him and to bring him in.

Six days later they brought the body of Marsh Andrews into Fort Smith in an express car. He had a bullet hole in his chest.

Malone said grimly. "We'll get the Kid. And when we do, he'll pay for this. Nobody can go around killing my deputies."

"Just so you don't kill anybody unnecessarily," said Parker. "Do you have any plans?"

"Garth is sending out a train tonight — two wagons. There hasn't been a boat upriver for several days, and I got a feeling if we're ever going to catch him with the goods, this is the time."

"You still think Garth is working some way with the Kid?"

"I don't know what to think, but I'd sure like to know one way or another."

"What do you propose?"

"I've got a man watching Garth's wagons. When that train leaves, I'm going to wait about three hours and then go after it and have a look at the freight."

"Do you have a search warrant?"

Malone pushed his hat on the back of his head. "By the time I get a warrant from the U.S. Commissioner, everybody in Fort Smith will know about it, and if there is anything in those wagons, Garth will get rid of it."

"That isn't strictly legal," said Parker.

"It wasn't legal when they put a bullet through Marsh Andrews' lung, either — but he's dead. Would you refuse to consider evidence just because I didn't have a search warrant?"

Parker considered. "I don't like to commit myself in advance. Let's see the evidence first."

"You'll see it," Malone promised.

"There is one condition," said Parker. "I'm going with you."

The word came at four o'clock that afternoon: Garth's wagons were loading.

Malone sharpened his knife and saw to it that his six-shooters were loaded. Parker refused a weapon.

The wagons pulled out at 3 o'clock in the morning, and Malone and Parker crossed on the ferry at six. The trail of the heavy wagons was plain in the sand, but presently left the banks of the river and ascended the grassy slopes of the prairie country. Here the sky was a pastel blue curve meeting the golden hue of the grass, for it was July again and very hot.

They moved on at a trot, Malone scanning the horizon constantly in all directions.

Finally Malone pointed. Two wagons — both with heavy canvas lashed down over them, and no hoops. Freight wagons.

Malone kept going forward, now standing in his stirrups. The oxen, heavily loaded, were moving slowly.

The driver of the first wagon was slender, a young fellow probably just learning the business. The older man on the second wagon scowled and started to shout, but Malone warned him by holding up one hand.

Malone rode up the left, Parker on the right, and made for the first wagon. The driver of that wagon, walking on the left side of the lead yoke of oxen, saw Parker first and looked back quickly and stared at him. Then the driver turned as quickly to the left and stared at Malone for an instant.

On Parker's side the dust ground fine and lifted by the big iron tires, drifted across his path and obscured his vision, but not before he recognized something vaguely familiar about the driver. Then he heard Ann's voice: "Brett Malone, what are you doing out here?"

Parker rode in closer. Malone took his time answering. "This is part of my territory. What are *you* doing here?"

Parker rode out ahead of the lead yoke

and pulled back in on the near side.

"We're short of drivers," Ann told Malone. She wore a big-brimmed hat that shaded her head and face but hardly concealed her attractiveness at close range.

Malone swung down from his horse and walked alongside her as the oxen continued to move forward.

"It isn't very often," Ann said, smiling, "that we have an escort of the chief deputy and the judge of the federal court."

Malone glanced at Parker, plainly embarrassed. "I'm sorry to say this, Ann, but I'd like to see your bill of lading."

Her eyes narrowed. "Brett Malone, are you starting that again?"

"Ann," he said stubbornly, "I'm not wanting to start anything. I asked to see your list of freight."

"What if I refuse?"

"If you refuse," he said, "I am justified in assuming it is an act of evasion, and that you are disobeying the law. I don't advise you to refuse."

"I'll do as I please."

"Yes, ma'am, you can do that — but it only makes it harder in the long run."

She glared at him, then took a thick sheaf of papers from her shirt pocket and handed them to him.

He pushed his hat to the back of his head and scanned the papers. He studied each sheet, and finally put them all together and handed them back to her. "Regular trade goods on the bills," he said. "How about the wagons?"

She flared at him. "What do you mean — wagons?"

He said persistently, "Is the stuff in the wagons exactly the same as the stuff on these bills?"

"Of course it is!"

"Did you load it?" he asked.

"Of course not. It was loaded last night."

"Yes, ma'am, I know that. After dark. It would have been easy to slip in a few kegs of whisky."

"Brett Malone, you —"

"Can't help it, Ann!" He was plainly reluctant, but Parker's admiration for him went up. Even though this was the girl he wanted to marry, and although his feeling for her and his dislike for his present task was plain to see, still he showed no tendency to back down. "For that matter," he said, "there could be whisky in these wagons without your knowing it and without Bentley knowing it."

Her answer was icy. "Nevertheless, if it is found, Bentley will have to answer for it."

"Unless he can show it got there without his knowledge."

The big-shouldered driver of the second wagon now came up ahead of his team. "Ask him for a search warrant, Miss Ann," he said.

"No, ma'am," Malone said honestly. "I haven't got a search warrant — but I aim to have a look at your freight anyway."

She was white with fury. "Of all the dirty, low-down —"

Then from somewhere a six-shooter jumped into the big driver's hand, and he said with an ugly face: "This says you ain't lookin' in no wagon of ourn without a search warrant — deputy or no deputy."

Malone did not seem to be startled. "Put that thing away, Rio. You aren't in Texas now."

Rio backed a step. "You heard me, Malone. Keep your hands away from your belt. Back up. Now git on your horse and git out of here."

Ann was watching with her mouth open. Malone looked at Rio without fear, but he moved slowly toward his horse and gathered up the reins. The horse swung around suddenly, shielding Malone, and at the same time Rio moved around to keep him covered, and for a moment was almost beneath Parker.

Parker lunged out of the saddle. He came down on Rio and clamped his arms around Rio's upper arms. The impact of his two hundred pounds made Rio stagger, and Parker bore him to the ground. Malone had drawn a knife in the fraction of a second that he was covered by the horse, and now he ran across the dozen or fifteen feet and jammed the knife into Rio's side. "Drop that thing!" he said.

Rio quit struggling. His fingers loosened, and the six-shooter slid into the dust. Malone picked it up and slipped the cylinder to one side. He punched out the five cartridges, snapped the cylinder shut, and handed the gun back to Rio, who was getting up out of the dust.

"I wouldn't advise you to fire that thing before you get it cleaned up," said Malone. "But in case you take a sudden notion —" he tossed the five cartridges up and down in his big hand — "you'll have to get over it by the time you reload — if you're still alive." He turned to Ann. "I hate to keep sayin' this, ma'am, but I aim to search your wagons."

She said angrily, "If you touch my wagons I won't forgive you as long as I live."

He gave her a sad smile. "Ann, I might

take that as a threat to the law, but I figure it's only a mighty pretty girl gettin' her back up."

"If you touch my goods, you'll have to put everything back exactly the way you find it. Otherwise we will sue you for damages and for unlawful search. And if your search delays us and we lose the contract at Tahlequah, we'll sue you for the value of it."

"I know all that," Malone said. He started toward the back of the first wagon. The oxen had stopped and were grazing. "Give me a hand, judge?"

For the next three hours they worked hard in the hot sun. Malone untied the canvas and examined every box and bale and barrel. It was around nine-thirty when Malone pushed his hat back on his head, wiped the sweat from his forehead with a blue bandanna, and said resignedly, "Well, judge, I reckon we're skunked."

Parker had long before shed his coat, and now he unbuttoned his vest and conceded. "It looks that way."

Malone sat down. "We'll take a quick breather and then reload so these people can be on their way."

"A drink of water would go very well," said Parker.

Ann came from behind them with a tin dipper.

"Here's water," she said, trying hard to be ungracious. "I don't know if you can drink it. I'm sure it's the hardest water in the Territory."

Parker was very grateful. He drank half, and passed the rest of it on to Malone. "It's good water," he said. "Thank you, Miss Ann."

But she was moving back to the second wagon, under which Rio was sound asleep. "Rio! Rio!"

He grunted and rolled over. "Trouble?" he asked.

"See if you can gather up the bulls. If the chief deputy marshal gets our wagons reloaded, we'll move on." She said aciduously to Malone, "For your sake I hope we don't lose any of the bulls. We aimed to do our traveling before the heat of the day. Bulls don't stand up so well in this kind of weather, you know."

"I know." He smiled ruefully as he got up. "But I have great confidence in the ability of the drivers."

He went to the rear of the second wagon. "I'll lift them, judge, and you stow 'em away."

Parker got up into the wagon. It seemed

even hotter up there, and loading the goods was not an easy job. Finally they got the freight juggled back in place and the canvas lashed down to suit Malone. His coarse blue shirt was soaked with sweat. He wiped his forehead once more and went to where Ann sat in the shade of a wagon. "I reckon I owe you an apology, Ann," he began.

She jumped up, her wrath blazing. "I never want to see you again."

He grinned weakly. "Then I reckon you won't be goin' to the hangings any more, then."

"If you're trying to be funny," she said coldly, "you're wasting it on me."

"Yes, ma'am." He was thoroughly humbled now. He had his big hat in his hands and was turning it, trying to think of something to say.

Rio was hooking up the last yoke of oxen, and Ann said scathingly, "I hope you've been satisfied in your persecution of the Garth Freight Lines, Mr. Malone."

He could only look at the ground. He stood there until the wagons got under way and began to spread their long trail of heavy dust over the golden grass. He watched them out of sight over the top of the slope, and finally turned to Parker. "We better get back," he said.

"Are you satisfied now about Garth?"

"Not quite," said Malone. He swung into the saddle. "It may be he has no connection with whisky in the Territory, but why is he so secretive about things he does? Why is he always seeing Indian Rose?"

Parker kicked his horse alongside Malone's. "There could be a fairly simple reason for that."

Malone stared at him. "I reckon you put a finger on something then," he said finally, and looked back. A thin cloud of dust was drifting northeast across the slope. "Then maybe you can tell me why a man would want to marry a woman as easy riled as that one."

Parker considered the matter judiciously. "It might be," he said, "that he can see that she wouldn't get half as riled as she does if she didn't want to marry *him*."

Chapter 19

Malone continued to have something on his mind for several days, and finally he stopped in at Parker's chambers. "I'm not satisfied about Garth," he said.

Parker tried to ease it over. "It really isn't the most important thing you have to do. In the first place, Ann will never forgive you if you bother her brother any more. In the second place, your deputies have plenty to do in the Territory. We don't need Garth."

"Sure, I know that, but I don't like getting the run-around. For my own satisfaction I want to get this business straightened out."

"What do you propose?"

"I want to go down to the Row and talk to Indian Rose and some of her girls. They must know what's going on. Somebody would be bound to let it slip."

"Maybe."

"And I want you to go with me, Mr. Parker."

Parker frowned. "Me?"

Malone explained. "If I go down there by myself or with a deputy, they can make up any story they want and they'll all swear to it and we can be in trouble."

"Take three deputies."

Malone shook his head. "The whole town would be laughing at me. Brett Malone has to have three deputies to protect him from the women on the Row. No, sir, that's not the way to handle it."

"I don't see how my presence would help any."

"Because you're a judge and you're respected by everybody. Nobody would dare to accuse you of anything unless they could absolutely prove it — so if you and I go together, we can be witnesses for each other."

"I'll feel a little silly," said Parker. "I've never been in one of those places before. But all right, I'll go along. When?"

"About nine-thirty. The girls will be in then."

"How about tomorrow? I'll hold court tomorrow night, and we can go afterward."

Malone got up. "One thing — you better not tell Mary."

Parker laughed. "I rather think that will be a judicial secret."

It was very dark the next night when they walked down the side street to the three houses that made up the Row. Brett went up to the door of the first house and knocked loudly. The door opened. "Who's theah?" asked a Negro maid.

"Brett Malone and Judge Parker."

The door closed. Several minutes later it opened again. "Who do you-all want to see?"

"Rose," said Malone.

It closed again, but after a few more minutes it opened. The maid said, "Miss Rose'll see you-all."

They went into the parlor. Aside from the red-shaded lamp it was like any other — perhaps a little more luxuriously furnished than most. There was a good rug on the floor, black walnut chairs, a black walnut center table, heavy draperies, pillows on a leather divan.

"You-all jest have a seat. Miss Rose'll be right in."

Parker sat, ill at ease. Malone stood, twirling his big hat.

There was movement at the portieres at the back of the room. Indian Rose came in. She looked a few years older than when Parker had first seen her; she was slim but not thin, only firm but not heavy. The red light became her dusky coloring.

"You gentlemen wish to see me?" she asked.

It was the longest speech Parker had heard her make, and he was pleased with the sound of her voice — low and well controlled.

"This ain't exactly a professional call," Malone began.

She smiled. "I thought not when I saw Judge Parker."

"We thought maybe you would give us some information."

She crossed the room and sat down. "It would depend on what kind of information you want."

"About Bentley Garth."

Parker, watching her, saw a change in her eyes but he did not know what it indicated.

"What about Garth?"

"You see him a lot."

"Yes. Isn't that allowed, Mr. Deputy?"

"Certainly it's allowed — but why?"

"Is no secret," she said. "We're in love."

"In love!"

"That's a natural state of affairs, isn't it?"

"Well, yes, but —"

"Of course. You see me here and you assume such a thing is not to be. It's true, most of my girls do not know what love is, and perhaps I don't myself, but when you care so much for a man that you will go to his room every day and make his bed and clean up after him, then perhaps it is love, don't you think?"

"Well — yes."

"If you're in love," said Parker, "do you

think Garth is too?"

She said with her eyes down, "I think he is too."

"Have you thought of getting married?"

"Naturally."

"Would he marry you in spite of — this?"

"He says he would." She shrugged. "Perhaps he has the Choctaw feeling about it. Here, in this place, love is not involved. There is no pretense. Therefore no harm is done."

"If he wants to get married" — Parker was determined to pursue it to the end — "then why don't you?"

"No," she said slowly. "I cannot. I have work to do."

"What kind of work?" demanded Malone.

"You should know that, Mr. Deputy. My brother, the Kiamichi Kid, is somewhere in the mountains over in the Territory. He is a wild one, and it is only a matter of time until he commits a bad crime and you lead your deputies over there and capture him. I know you look for him now, but you don't look very hard because he hasn't done anything very bad. But some day he will kill somebody and you will take a big posse and you will smoke him out of his hiding place, and then he will be brought to Fort Smith and he will need the best lawyers to get him out." She smiled. "Lawyers cost more than judges who can be bribed."

Parker watched her. His first inclination was to bristle at that remark, but she was so disarmingly frank and without malice that he could not find it within him to take offense.

"The Kid and I are brother and sister. There is not one to help him but me when he gets in trouble, and so I must stay here and work and save money for him when he needs it. As long as that is so, I cannot get married, naturally."

"Naturally," said Malone. "But in the meantime, are you passing word from the Kid to Garth and vice versa about whisky?"

"That could not very well be, Mr. Deputy. I have not seen the Kid or heard from him since the night he tried to escape from your jail."

"I don't believe that," said Malone.

She put her head on one side. "It is your privilege to decide what you want to believe. The Kid cannot write a word."

"Men come here from all over. He could send you a message."

She studied the toes of her white moccasins. "He could — but he does not. The Kid is not thoughtful. He never considers anybody else. And there is another thing you do not understand about him."

"What's that?"

"He's not an organizer because he has no need for money. He does not look ahead to a time when he will have to hire lawyers, as I do. He has no desire for money. His lawbreaking occurs when the fancy seizes him, and that makes it unlikely that he would arrange with Bentley to ship him whisky, as you have been trying to prove for years."

Malone put on his hat. "Well, it looks like we've troubled you for nothing."

"Not for nothing if you've learned something."

"No'm, I guess not." He stood up.

"There's something I'd like to know," Parker said.

"Yes, Mr. Judge."

"You speak remarkably excellent English."

"That's true. I was educated in a fine school in the East."

"But why, if you learned civilized ways, did you then come back to this? Surely your education fitted you to live with the whites."

"Quite certainly it did," she said, "but nobody has educated the whites to live with the Indians. They don't trust us; they don't understand us. The minute anything happens, either through misunderstanding or through forgetfulness on the part of an Indian, the whites point the finger at him, and he is guilty. The facts are always unimportant. He is convicted before he goes on trial."

Parker frowned. "But you —"

"I wear nice clothes. I talk well. I know my place. But it makes no difference. I don't want to go back to Choctaw country to live in an Indian teepee. So what can I do?"

"With your education —"

"With my education," she said, a little bitterly, "I am well fitted to work as a servant and to empty bed pails for the mistress of a big house, and I will be expected to come running to the bed of the master whenever he beckons, because I am only an Indian squaw." Her black eyes flashed. "Here I am a prostitute and everyone knows it. There are no false colors, and I do not have to submit to a drunken Indian husband or a drunken white man who is somebody else's husband. Here I am what I am and there is no deception. Does that make it clear, Mr. Judge?"

He cleared his throat. "I am afraid it does. I'm sorry, Miss Rose."

She got up effortlessly, and looked at him.

"I am afraid I have made you uncomfortable."

"Possibly — but I don't regret it. I have known a good many things about the Indians, and I am sad to say that what you say has all the ring of truth."

Malone said, "We better go."

Parker followed him out and stopped to pull down his hat. "Do you think she was telling the truth?"

"What she said was the truth, all right, but that's only part of it. She can stand up on her hind legs and howl like the wildest Indian you ever saw."

"Perhaps that's to be expected."

"Maybe it is. Here, what's this? Man leaving Lou's place already. Must be getting out early tonight."

Malone stood, watching the slender young fellow come down the steps of the house next door and follow the path toward them. Parker waited, curious to see who it might be.

"Don't block the road, mister," said a familiar voice.

Parker gasped. "Charlie!"

Young Charlie stopped. His eyebrows lifted as he looked at his father. "You down here too?" he asked. "First time I ever ran into anybody wearin' a silk hat down here."

After a moment Malone said, "We better go, Mr. Parker."

"Yes — I —" Suddenly Parker felt unsteady on his legs.

Malone's big arm went across his shoulders. "It's all right, judge. I guess you done your best, but there's some things you can't help."

Parker walked along, shaking his head. "I wouldn't have believed it. He's only fourteen."

"That's old enough."

"He doesn't know what he's doing."

"He may know better than you think. I'll tell you one thing, judge. I don't make a habit of giving advice, but I figure if a boy is old enough to be down here he's old enough to go to work."

"Yes — but I wanted Charlie to read law. He has the makings of a good attorney."

"Whatever he's going to do, he'd better get started."

Parker went home wearily. He hung up his coat, and noticed Mary's best silk dress, and, to cover his annoyance at her drinking, he said, "Mary, your Sunday dress is way out of date. The dresses now have those big sleeves."

"I know that. But it takes money to buy new clothes."

He looked at his worn and shabby suit and he knew she was right. She had been very patient and uncomplaining, and he felt guilty at not having provided better. He was unutterably weary.

"We could go back to St. Louis and I could practice law and make a good deal more money," he said thoughtfully, "but I started this job and I'd like to finish it. I have a duty to discharge." In his mind's eye he saw the huge crossbeam that would hang twelve men at once. "I have not fulfilled my destiny here. Some day, perhaps. Not now."

Chapter 20

In the next several months Parker kept the deputies in the field day and night, but an increasing number of presidential commutations made his work difficult. Then this excessive presidential clemency had a reaction that inadvertently played into his hands. Crime became more rampant overnight, and it was not long before he had, in the terribly overcrowded basement jail, eleven men condemned to die.

Occasionally he had made a request for more commodious quarters for the jail, but he was not perturbed when these requests were declined, for his private opinion was that if the criminals had not disobeyed the law in the first place, they would not have to be confined.

He considered the eleven men waiting for Maledon's ropes, and he well knew that the Kiamichi Kid would make it an even dozen, but then he remembered the Kid had been pardoned, and for the time being he forgot the Kid and concentrated on whomever he could find. A body turned up in the Arkansas River, and Malone himself got to work on the case, but then one of the condemned men died and reduced the total to ten. Three days later two more received commutations, and Parker reluctantly gave up, for the moment, his goal of hanging twelve at once.

Congress took three Arkansas counties away from the Western District of Arkansas and attached them to the Eastern District, and again Parker felt it was a slap in the face. Clayton seemed concerned, and suggested Parker ease up on his sentences. "The only reason Congress is digging away at this court," Clayton said, "is that the severity of punishment causes people to put pressure on Washington. If you relaxed the sentences, the pressure would stop."

Parker sat very straight and uncompromising. "I will not bargain with the forces of murder and rape," he said. "I have not reached my goal. Until I do I shall continue to administer justice according to the law and the Word."

Twice again he got the number to be hanged up to six, but now it was a foregone conclusion that the entire number would never be hanged. One time George Maledon pulled the bolt on four, another time on two.

He had a small reaffirmation in 1887, when Congress decided that any Indian killing an Indian deputy would be triable in federal court; theretofore a crime by an Indian against an Indian had been in the sole jurisdiction of the tribal courts. But this victory was shortlived. Three minor acts followed reducing his power or his jurisdiction, and then in 1889 occurred the one thing he had not anticipated: a bill was introduced providing for direct appeal of his decisions to the Supreme Court of the United States.

He sat in his chambers a long time getting used to the idea. "It may not even pass," he told Malone.

"It doesn't keep you from passing sentence anyway."

"Of course it won't," Parker agreed, "but it will mean more red tape, more delay, cases sent back for re-trial after the witnesses have disappeared, witnesses murdered by the defendants' friends to keep them from testifying a second time. This means chaos!"

"You'd better not let the lawyers know how you feel about it."

Parker, sitting with his head down, looked up from under his eyebrows. "No, I suppose not. But I will make a prediction: it will be a long time before any lawyer in Fort Smith appeals a case from my court."

"I don't understand, sir."

"I can make it very difficult for them to try any case in my court — and they know that."

"You don't mean you would intentionally —"

Parker raised his head — a little heavily. "A judge has it in his discretion to do many things. If he believes a lawyer needful of discipline, he can see that he gets it. All strictly legal, of course. It's a matter of interpretation, and the line is very finely drawn."

But *The Western Independent* took a different view of the matter. "We make a prediction," it said, "that procedure in the court will undergo a considerable change. Fort Smith attorneys long have complained of the heavy hand of Judge Parker, but up to now there has been nothing a lawyer could do. If he became too insistent, the court wasted no time disciplining him, invariably to the detriment of the lawyer's client — sometimes, it is said, to the detriment of a client's health insofar as the same is affected by a rope around the neck."

But Parker went ahead full steam. He would show them who was running the court. He ignored any suggestion that he temper his trial conduct or his sentences. If a lawyer dared to murmur "Exception,"

Parker saw that he paid for it by overruling that lawyer's objections to the prosecutor's testimony. There was only one thing that mattered: was the defendant guilty? If he was guilty, then, Parker reasoned, he should be convicted without further ado.

And whenever any remote reference to the Supreme Court came out in open meeting, Parker glared at the suggester. This court, he was resolved, would not be intimidated by any threat of appeal. After a number of months he was well satisfied that he had adopted the right procedure, for no lawyer had appealed — not even Colonel Boudinot, who Parker had expected to be the first to try it. The jail was filled with nine candidates for the rope. There was, Parker believed, still a possibility of hanging that evasive dozen that would shock the outlaw element and hold them in check forever.

In January, 1890, a Mexican named William Alexander came up for trial, charged with murder. He had traveled from Arizona with a man named Steadman, driving a band of horses. Steadman had disappeared, and later the remains of his body were found after most of it had been devoured by hogs. Alexander was arrested with $350 in his pockets and brought to Fort Smith.

The case was called in mid-morning, and

when Parker asked who represented Alexander there was no answer. He asked again, and finally Colonel Boudinot got to his feet. "Your honor, I understand the defendant is represented by a new lawyer from California — J. Warren Reed."

Parker said sourly, "He can hardly expect to represent his client adequately when he is not even in court."

Boudinot sat down, looking uncomfortable. Parker said, "Mr. Clyman, you have waxed fat in this court since the day I first appointed you to defend a killer. I will appoint you —"

There was a stir in the courtroom, and Parker looked up. Just within the door stood a very stout, very broad man wearing a silk hat. The man reached up with an extravagantly graceful gesture and removed his hat with a flourish.

Parker glared at him. For fifteen years the silk hat had been Parker's own trademark, and now a man whom he did not know had the gall to enter his courtroom with a silk hat. It was a new hat, and it did not help Parker's feelings to know that his old one would look pretty shabby beside it.

"Your honor," said the man, "I am J. Warren Reed. I presented my credentials to the court clerk some time ago."

Parker drew a deep breath. "Do you represent the defendant in this case?"

"Yes, your honor."

"Then I suggest you take the chair of chief counsel. The trial is commencing."

"Thank you, your honor." Reed seated himself with a flourish and laid his new silk hat and a silver-headed cane on the table.

Parker saw at once that he would have trouble with the man. Reed had spent some time, it seemed, in gathering evidence in defense of Alexander. He had even gone over into the Territory and interviewed prospective witnesses — and his knowledge of the law was extensive. Perhaps, Parker admitted to himself, Reed knew more law than the court, but Reed did not know one thing: the conditions on the frontier.

The inevitable clash of wills came during the first afternoon. Clayton was conducting direct examination of a witness for the prosecution. "You did not hear the defendant himself say that he had more money than he needed?"

"No, sir."

"Who did hear it?"

Reed, toying with his cane, his eyes fixed on the table, glanced up.

"A Seminole farmer — Thomas Wildcat."

"Did you hear Thomas Wildcat make that statement?"

"Yes."

Reed looked puzzled.

"Will you repeat what he said?"

"Hearsay!" said Reed.

Parker ignored it.

"He says he was standing at this bar and had ordered a bottle of Wilson's bourbon, and the bartender didn't want to give him a whole bottle, and Alexander threw out a twenty-dollar gold piece and said, 'I've got plenty —' "

Reed was on his feet in a flash. "Your honor, this child's game has gone far enough. I had no idea my distinguished colleague" — he glanced at Clayton — "would go so far as actually to try to introduce this testimony, which is completely and unquestionably hearsay, incompetent, and not the best evidence. Where is Thomas Wildcat? Let's hear him give this testimony himself."

"Overruled," Parker snapped.

Reed, in the act of sitting down, jumped up again.

"Your honor — I beg the court's indulgence. This testimony is unquestionably hearsay and therefore inadmissible. I register my complete objection to it, and I request the court to strike all references to it from the record."

"Denied," said Parker promptly.

Once again Reed was in the act of sitting down. Now he got up more slowly. He looked around at the lawyers sitting in the courtroom and then he scrutinized Parker at length. Finally he said: "Once more, your honor, and for the third time, I wish the record to show that I have objected most vigorously to the admission of a hearsay statement. I respectfully urge the court to reconsider its ruling." He remained standing.

Parker stared at him. He breathed deeply and exhaled slowly. "Is counsel quite through admonishing the court?" he asked levelly.

Reed's eyes narrowed. "I have not admonished the court. I have complete respect for the courts of the United States and for the judges who preside over them, but, your honor, I am entrusted with the life of my client. I cannot in all conscience allow any such illegal testimony to go to the jury."

"Do you now object?" asked Parker.

"I do."

For the third time Parker snapped: "Overruled."

Reed sat down. "I wish the record to show

that I take an exception to the court's ruling."

Parker glared at him. "Counsel will note that there is no —" He checked himself. He had almost forgotten.

Reed was on his feet again. "Did the court wish to make a clarifying statement?" he asked.

"The court rules," Parker said imperturbably. "The court does not expound the law for the attorneys practicing before it."

Parker chafed at the delay, and threatened contempt, but Reed was not abashed. "If the court wishes to try me for contempt when I am courteously and legally defending the rights of my client, I will cheerfully submit to trial, but I will assure the court that this court's decision will not be the final word."

Parker, nettled, asked, "Did counsel come to Fort Smith for the purpose of intimidating the court?"

Reed considered his answer carefully. "Your honor, I came to Fort Smith as a practicing attorney to defend, to the best of my ability, men charged with crimes. In that capacity, your honor, I am bound to follow practices that I have found acceptable in other courts over the nation, especially when I know those practices to be soundly based in law."

"In that case," Parker said coldly, "perhaps you will not mind if we proceed with the trial."

"Your honor does me an injustice. I have no wish to delay the court's proceedings. However, I must insist that I would be subject to disbarment if I failed to protect the rights of my client."

Parker looked at him dourly. Finally he said to Clayton, "Proceed."

"What did Thomas Wildcat say as to the words of the defendant in regard to money?"

"Your honor," said Reed quickly, "I must enter an objection to any and all testimony of this nature."

"Overruled," Parker said, controlling his temper.

It went that way for three days, but finally the case went to the jury. Parker delivered his charge and was interrupted so many times by Reed's objections that he fined him $100 for contempt, and finished his charge after threatening to have Reed removed from the courtroom.

The jury brought in a verdict of guilty, and Reed promptly filed notice of appeal.

This was a strange feeling for Parker, who never had had his decisions questioned before. But he consoled himself with the thought that the Supreme Court undoubtedly would uphold him.

On the morning he was to pass sentence on Alexander, he was toying with the idea of giving the man life in prison as a concession to Reed, when a telegram came from Malone:

"Tahlequah, Cherokee Nation, Feb. 15, 1890. Regret report Will Sunshine shot by Kiamichi Kid in attempt to arrest him for shooting up saloon. Kid is still at large. Bringing Sunshine's body to Fort Smith for burial. Malone, Deputy."

Parker read the message twice. Presently he stalked into the courtroom and sentenced Alexander to be hanged. Then he wept.

Chapter 21

Charlie went to St. Louis to read law. It would cost considerable money, but Parker didn't mind. The boy needed to get away from the town and to fresh surroundings so he could buckle down to work. Parker went into his small savings and bought the boy new clothes and a ticket, handed him money for expenses, and gave him a fond blessing when he left on the *Maiden*. Charlie was not the driving type, but then he was young. And, as Parker told Mary, he had always been brilliant and would undoubtedly make an outstanding mark in St. Louis. It was only right, therefore, that his parents should give him a chance.

One John Thornton came before the court. Thornton's daughter had married, and a week later Thornton had killed her with a pistol while she cowered under the bed. Out of respect to the survivors, nothing was said of the motivation for the killing, but it was rumored that Thornton had maintained an incestuous relationship with his daughter, had demanded that she continue it after her marriage, and had killed her for refusing.

Parker told Thornton at the sentencing that he was sorry he had no more severe punishment than hanging to inflict on him, and promptly sentenced him to death.

Lewis Holder came up for trial for killing his partner in the Sans Bois Mountains in the Choctaw Nation for a team and wagon and some clothes. Holder was found guilty. His attorneys appealed, but the decision was affirmed, and five hundred spectators were in the courtroom to hear him sentenced.

Parker, his beard now turning white, give him a long lecture on his sin, and finally pronounced the words: ". . . to be hanged by the neck until dead, dead, dead."

For the first time in his years on the bench, Parker saw a man go to pieces when he was sentenced. Holder's face turned white and his entire body trembled. With a piercing scream he fell forward on his face, and for a moment Parker, pounding his gavel to bring order in the sudden confusion, thought the man had cheated the gallows. But Malone and Wilkerson picked him up and took him back to the jail.

The man put on quite a show in the ensuing days. He begged all who came near not to let him be hanged. Mary daily took him choice bits to eat, and he told her solemnly that if he should be hanged he would come back to haunt them all.

Nevertheless, Parker set the date, and Holder's appeal to the Supreme Court was denied. Holder issued a public statement through the *Independent*, requesting the judge and all of the jury that had convicted him to be present at the hanging.

On the fatal day, Holder stepped to the front of the gallows platform and asked all who had had a hand in his execution to step forward. None moved, and he read a statement.

Parker, watching from his chambers, was unaffected. It was to be expected that a man capable of murder might also be capable of highly emotional acts that verged on insanity, and Parker watched coldly as Holder finished his statement and then said in a loud, unsteady voice:

"I want you to know that I forgive you all — but as for Isaac Parker, the hanging judge, who has killed more men than anybody in Indian Territory, it is my earnest belief that he should resign his office and that he should go down on his knees and ask God to forgive him for his many crimes!"

It would have been better, Parker reflected, if Holder had had such a great rush of sentimentality at the time when he shot his victim in the back with a shotgun. And so he saw the man drop against the rope, and knew that his neck was snapped, and was filled with a great sense of rightness. And then he wept.

Mary got a letter from Charlie, who did not write often, asking for more money. Parker visited his savings account and reduced it still further.

Mr. Hoffman looked at him over his glasses and asked, "For the boy in St. Louie?"

"Yes," said Parker. "The expenses of preparing oneself for admission to the bar are much heavier than they used to be."

"It's none of my business," said Hoffman, "but you and I are old friends." Hoffman looked at him strangely. "Whyn't you show some of that backbone you show on the bench — tell him to get out and earn some of that money?"

"He's never had to work," Parker explained. "He wouldn't know how to go about it."

"Fine time to learn," said Hoffman.

Parker, counting the money, said absently, "Charlie's on the frail side, you know."

Hoffman snorted. "Bosh! A boy that can carouse around all day and all night —

there's nothin' frail about him!"

But Parker sent Charlie the money.

Thornton's execution was set, and shortly thereafter Washington interfered again. Brett Malone brought him the telegram: "Jacob Yoes, U.S. Marshal, Fort Smith, Arkansas. From this date, further hangings will not take place publicly by order of the attorney general."

Parker read it silently.

"What does this mean?" asked Malone.

"It means they are trying everything possible to destroy the functioning of this court. It means you will have to establish a cordon of deputies to keep spectators out of the grounds unless —" He struck the desk with his fist. "There's one thing we can do! We'll send out invitations."

"You can't send them to everybody, can you?"

"No — but we can issue them freely. The people shall see," he said doggedly, "that justice is done. They are scuttling the ship of order at every turn, but by the help of God we will keep it afloat. Yea, we will establish order in this country no matter how much interference arises."

For a while things went smoothly. Parker was elected president of the Social Reading Club, and it seemed the members were fond of him. Sometimes he sang with them after meeting, and there was only one sour note: Mary wrote poems, which she insisted on reading at the meetings. They were sickly sentimental bursts that reflected on death, and Parker knew they were subtly directed at him. He had no doubt that others knew it too — but there was nothing he could do.

Thornton was duly hanged, and the man's head was torn from his body when he dropped. It was a gruesome, bloody sight, but it was justice. Parker watched with satisfaction, and later wept.

On a sunny morning in February, Mrs. O'Rourke, district court clerk, brought him the stunning message:

"Case of William Alexander reversed. Supreme Court directs new trial."

He sat for a long time after that, immobilized in body, blank of mind. The Supreme Court had reversed him. Isaac Charles Parker, who had brought law and order to the Indian Territory, was no longer upheld even by the courts of the land. But this, he vowed presently, would be only a passing obstacle. He would put his shoulder to the wheel. He would demonstrate to J. Warren Reed as well as to Washington that he was not a man to be overridden with impunity.

He would work harder, longer, try more cases. He would yet bring order, he would — single-handed if necessary — wipe out murder and rape from the Territory.

There were more appeals, more reversals. Almost every case now was appealed, as he had feared, and on many of them he was reversed. The language of the Supreme Court sometimes varied from its usual judicial impersonality and almost, Parker thought, referred to him personally. But he did not retreat. He lowered his head and forged onward. They were wrong up there in Washington, and he would have to work the harder to offset their mistakes.

Brett Malone was, if possible, more irked by the situation than Parker. He pushed his big hat back on his head and said vehemently: "Those guys in Washington don't know what we're up against out here. They're making it harder on us. Do you know how many deputies I've had killed since you came here?"

Parker looked up. "No."

"Sixty-one," Malone said. "Sixty-one men murdered by outlaws. Men doing their duty under the law — and now the Supreme Court is cutting the law from under us!"

"There is nothing we can do," Parker said wearily.

Malone swore. "We better *find* something to do."

And then, in 1895, after his long years of evading the law, the Kiamichi Kid was finally cornered in his cabin in the Bidding Springs area of the Cherokee country. Malone came to tell Parker about it. "This time," he said, "I'm going to get him. He's been evading us for years. This time we'll bring him in, dead or alive."

On an impulse Parker said, "I'll go with you."

Malone looked at him. "It'll be rough going. You ain't thirty-eight any more," he warned.

But Parker went. They surrounded the Kid and one or more of his henchmen in a massive log cabin that had been built as a fort. Marshal Yoes had a small cannon sent in, but its three-pound balls had no effect on the building.

George Isha-harjo volunteered to dynamite one wall, and went up behind a heavy plank shield erected on a pair of wagon wheels. He placed the dynamite, lit a fuse, and backed away. At the last moment he stumbled over a rock, and for an instant the wheels swung around and exposed him. A rifle cracked, and George fell with a bullet through his jugular vein. Malone swore and ground his teeth. "He has always killed my best deputies," he said. "He'll pay for that."

"Who fired the shot?" asked Parker.

"John Duck fired it," said Yoes.

There were now eighteen or twenty deputies surrounding the cabin on all sides. The roar of dynamite filled the hills and rolled and reverberated. Malone surged to his feet, one arm in the air. He shouted, "Close in!" and ran forward.

Parker ran too, but he was slower than the deputies. Over Malone's shoulder he saw the Kid and John Duck appear in the smoke-filled hole in the shattered wall. They both had rifles, but before a shot was fired the smoke swirled in and hid them.

The deputies continued to close in.

The smoke lifted for an instant, and the Kiamichi Kid was only three feet from Parker. The Kid saw him, and, his face distorted with rage and hate, he fired his rifle from the hip.

The bullet should have struck Parker in the stomach, but Brett Malone launched himself on the Kid and took the bullet himself. They rolled in the smoke, and finally, when the deputies stopped the fight, Brett had his knife buried in the Kid's ribs.

Malone got up, breathing hard. "He ain't dead," he said regretfully, looking at the blood on the blade. "It wasn't high enough for a lung. Tie him up good and tight." He looked around as they brought up John Duck. "Tie that one up with bobwire," he ordered. "He killed George. If he makes any kind of a move, kill him. I don't want to lose any more deputies."

Marshal Yoes came up. "You got that bullet yourself, didn't you?"

"I haven't looked," said Malone. "I want to get these two murderers back to Fort Smith."

"Blood is dripping from your belt," said Yoes. "I think you'd better sit down."

Malone rode his horse back to Tahlequah, and then collapsed. The physician took a .58-caliber slug out of his spleen. "He's mighty lucky," the physician told Parker, "that he's still breathing. Generally a slug like that, anywhere in the intestinal area, is enough to kill a man on the spot."

"He's a good man," Parker said soberly, and sat by Malone's bed until he regained consciousness. "Brett," he said, "I owe you my life."

Malone grinned. "I'm gettin' paid for it, Mr. Parker," he said, and fainted.

The Kiamichi Kid was tried for the murder of Will Sunshine, and Parker wasted no time and no words. He saw to it that the Kid was convicted, and without leaving the courtroom he sentenced the Kid to hang. Reed — of the silk hat and silver-headed cane — appealed, but Parker was not moved. This time the Kid would hang. He would have hanged him within the week if he did not have to wait for the appeal to be acted on.

A long telegram came from Charlie the next day, asking for more money, and a clipping from the *St. Louis Republican*, sent by the senior partner of the law firm where Charlie was studying, explained the trouble:

"A young student of the legal art, Charles Parker, Saturday night became inebriated in a house of ill fame on Persimmon Hill and tried to strangle another customer for refusing to yield his place in line for the affections of a mulatto lady known as St. Louie Lou. Young Mr. Parker is now languishing in the county jail on a charge of assault with intent to kill. It is said the lady in question has enjoyed a substantial increase in business as a result of this proof of her charms."

Wearily Parker drew out the last of his savings and took the trail to St. Louis. He appeared at Charlie's arraignment and pled so earnestly for him that Charlie was released in his custody.

"I can't see why you would do a thing like this," he told Charlie when they got to his hotel.

Charlie said sullenly, "There's a lot of things *you* don't see."

Parker, tired, went out for a soda. While looking for a drug store he bought a paper and read the incredible headlines:

"Two Killers Break Jail at Fort Smith. Kiamichi Kid and John Duck Loose After Setting Fire to Jail. 73 Shots Exchanged. Jim Wilkerson, Father of 11, Killed Trying to Prevent Escape."

Parker pulled his old silk hat down harder and made his way back to the hotel, his steps heavy and faltering. The clerk gave him the key, and Parker was dimly aware that the clerk nodded to somebody else. Then two men were at Parker's side, demanding: "Are you Judge Parker, the hanging judge? What do you think of this? Does this prove your theory about preventing crime?"

Parker swept them away with his big-boned hand. "If you gentlemen will wait," he said, trying to control the bitterness that filled him, "I will give you a statement."

First he wrote out a telegram to Jim Wilkerson's wife, and then he faced the reporters and said:

"You ask what is the cause of such a deed as this? The cause lies in the fact that our jail is filled with murderers. They have been tried by an impartial jury; they have been convicted, and have been sentenced to hang. But they are awaiting a hearing before the Supreme Court. Murders in my jurisdiction are now on the increase, due to the reversals of the Supreme Court. The Court never touches the merits of the case. As far as I can see, the Court must be opposed to capital punishment, and therefore tries to reason the effect of the law away."

"Your honor," said the man from the *Globe-Democrat*, "this is strong language. No judge has ever openly criticized the Supreme Court before."

Parker said bitterly, "Is sympathy to be only for the criminal? What of Jim Wilkerson, a quiet, peaceable, law-abiding citizen who has given all his life to the upholding of the law. Is there no sympathy for him and for his wife and children? Is he not worth more than a hundred murderers?"

He went home. Mary was not at the train to meet him. He got the mail and saw that his interview was prominently displayed. He went home and found Mary under the influence of wine. He went on to the courthouse and found Brett Malone, who wept unashamed when he talked of Jim Wilkerson. "He raised me from a pup," he said. "He fed me when he didn't have enough to eat himself — and I swear I'll kill the dirty bastards who murdered him."

"That's strong language," Parker said, his arm around Brett's shoulders.

Tears formed in Brett's eyes. "I mean it," he said. "I'll kill them both. I won't see them go to trial and get their cases appealed and be turned loose. I promise you that I'll kill them."

"You must not let your emotions get the better of you," said Parker. "Remember, I warned you years ago that I would treat you like anybody else if you killed unnecessarily."

Parker went out to see Mrs. Wilkerson. The oldest child at home was sixteen and had a job; the second one swept out the church and filled the lamps. The third one carried washing for a widow who lived near. Parker went away feeling very bitter against the Supreme Court and J. Warren Reed and all those who had made this kind of thing possible.

Clayton was in to see him next day. "I'm resigning my position, your honor. I'm going into private practice."

"I don't understand." Parker frowned,

bewildered. "You've been with me from the beginning."

"I know that, your honor — but I can't win cases any more."

"Why not? Don't I help you?"

"Your honor, that's the trouble. You help me too much. By favoring the prosecution you assure that any case will be appealable and a great many will be reversed. You charge the juries, and Reed accuses you of leading the juries —"

"Of course I lead juries! They *need* to be led! These men are not equipped by training to judge a man's guilt — but a judge is!"

"I'm sorry, your honor. That's not the law."

"Reed is the cause of all the trouble," Parker said, as if to himself. "If it were not for Reed —"

"It has been a pleasure to serve under you, sir." Clayton was holding out his hand.

Parker shook it without enthusiasm.

Chapter 22

Fourteen deputies were out after John Duck and the Kid. Nobody could say which one had fired the shot that had killed Jim Wilkerson.

The case of Sam Hickory was reversed, and the Supreme Court used these words:

"It is undoubted that acts of concealment by an accused are competent to go to the jury as tending to establish guilt, yet they are not to be considered as alone conclusive, or as creating a legal presumption of guilt; they are mere circumstances to be considered and weighed in connection with other proof with that caution and circumspection which their inconclusiveness when standing alone require. The rule, on the subject, has had nowhere a clearer or more concise expression than that given by Chief Justice Shaw in the Webster case, to which the trial court adverted.

"The learned Chief Justice said: 'To the same head may be referred all attempts on the part of the accused to suppress evidence, to suggest false and deceptive explanations, and to cast suspicion without just cause on other persons; all or any of which tend somewhat to prove consciousness of guilt, and when proved exert an influence upon the accused. But this consideration is not to be pressed too urgently; because an innocent man, when placed by circumstances in a condition of suspicion and danger, may resort to deception in the hope of avoiding the force of such proofs. Such was the case often mentioned in the books and cited here yesterday, of a man convicted of the murder of his niece, who had suddenly disappeared under circumstances which created a strong suspicion that she was murdered. He attempted to impose on the court by presenting another girl as the niece. The deception was discovered and naturally operated against him, though the actual appearance of the niece alive afterwards proved conclusively that he was not guilty of the murder.' A person however conscious of innocence might not have courage to stand trial. Even a man who admitted cutting off the head and legs of a female and hiding them, was not presumed on that account to be guilty of her murder.

"As to Biblical references, there is the classic instance where Laban taxed Jacob, 'Wherefore didst thou flee away secretly without taking solemn leave?' And Jacob said to Laban, 'Because I was afraid.' So it happens that even honest men in fear, may try to hide.

"The charge of the trial court is now demonstrated to have been plainly erroneous. It practically instructed the jury that the facts of concealment were conclusive evidence of guilt. The epithets applied by the court to the acts of concealment, and the vituperation contained in the charge, acted to instruct the jury to return a verdict of guilty. The charge says there may be exceptions to the rule of concealment, but it does not call any of these exceptions to the attention of the jury.

"This charge crosses the line which separates the impartial exercise of the judicial function from the region where reason is disturbed, passions excited, and prejudices necessarily called into play.

"The judgment is reversed, and the case remanded with directions to grant a new trial."

Parker was dumbfounded. How could the Supreme Court possibly ignore the fact that he, the trial judge, had been present at every word of the trial and had been the one man on earth best able to judge the guilt of the defendant?

He took it doggedly. Perhaps it was only a passing phase. Perhaps the next time they would understand what he was up against in this violent country. He tried a man named Alberty, and this time in his mind he was more convinced than ever before of the man's guilt. Again he charged the jury so there could be only one verdict.

Alberty was convicted and sentenced to hang.

Matthew Allen came back for his retrial, and Parker was determined he should be convicted, but this time it was hard to find witnesses, and no longer did the prosecution have the services of Clayton, for Clayton was on the other side, defending. This time Parker's charge to the jury seemed to be without effect. Allen was acquitted.

Then came the break. Brett Malone and his deputies brought in the Kiamichi Kid. Once again Parker felt lifted. This time, for good and for all, the Kid would swing. They had caught him and John Duck on Chippy Hill in South McAlester. John Duck, Malone reported, had been killed in a gunfight, but the Kid was in jail, and this time he would not escape.

Then the new prosecuting attorney, J. B. McDonough, a tall, cadaverous man with long black sideburns and a high collar, came to see the judge in his chambers. "Your honor," he said, "I have very unpleasant news for you."

Parker stared at him. "Most news lately is unpleasant, save for the capture of the Kiamichi Kid."

"It is something in connection with the Kid," said McDonough.

"All right, all right," Parker said impatiently. "Let's have it. Don't keep me waiting all day."

"The Kiamichi Kid," McDonough said slowly, "swears that Brett Malone murdered John Duck!"

Parker stared at him. "You're joking."

"I wish I were, your honor."

"John Duck was a refugee from justice."

"He is nevertheless entitled to a fair trial, and as you yourself have often said, not even a deputy marshal has a right to shoot a refugee unless it is necessary."

"Brett wouldn't do that. He's been a deputy for twenty years."

"I know, sir — but Malone had been heard to say he would kill them for shooting Jim Wilkerson. Everybody knows what he thought of Jim."

Parker pressed his eyes with his hands. "Brett has been like a son to me."

"I know. I have told you the facts, your honor. The rest is up to you."

Parker read the Bible that night for a long time. He went to bed at daylight but he did not sleep. When he got up that morning he was haggard. He reached his office and sent for McDonough.

"Does the Kiamichi Kid say he will swear that Brett killed John Duck unnecessarily?"

"That's what he says, your honor."

"Were there any other witnesses?"

"Not at that time. The Kid and Duck were both hiding in a room at this woman's place, and the deputies had it surrounded. Brett Malone insisted on going in first, alone, and he found the two. The Kid says they were both unarmed, and Brett himself didn't find any weapons on them. He says Duck made a motion toward his hip pocket, and Brett fired. It's a plausible story, and yet the Kid says Duck made no motion of any kind but started to raise his hands, and Brett shot him between the eyes."

Parker put his face in his hands. "Have Malone arrested and held for the grand jury," he said. "It is not a question for me to decide."

The grand jury indicted Brett Malone for the murder of John Duck. In succeeding days Isaac Charles Parker walked as in a cloud. He knew that people avoided him, but it was not a thing he could help. He was doing his duty. Under the law, Brett Malone as a murderer had no more rights than the Kiamichi Kid. He, Parker, had sworn to bring order, and he could not with good grace condone *any* murder, even by one of his own deputies.

The Kiamichi Kid was tried for the murder of Wilkerson, and Parker grimly saw to it that the Kid was convicted.

Reed appeared in court. He set a brand new silk hat carefully on the table and laid his silver-headed cane beside it. "Your honor," he said, without seeming to look at Parker, "defendant gives notice of appeal."

Parker, looking down at Reed, had never hated anyone as much as he did the lawyer. Reed had waxed fat and wealthy in his years in Parker's court. It was said that he sometimes made as much in one defense as Parker made in a year. And now he showed his contempt for Parker by refusing to look at him. Parker's lips were tight for a moment. Then he said, "Notice of appeal noted."

He immediately pronounced the death sentence on the Kid, and called the next case: The United States of America versus Brett Malone.

The courtroom was jammed, for Malone was well liked everywhere. McDonough built up his case, almost entirely on the evidence of the Kiamichi Kid, who was brought from jail in irons, and the witnesses who had heard Malone say he would kill the two outlaws.

It was strange to see Brett there in the defendant's chair after so many years. And yet if he had pulled the trigger without necessity, he belonged there. Justice was impartial.

Brett himself seemed not to have any deep feelings about the trial. He testified as to what had happened; he swore that the Kid had lied. He had no supporting witnesses but he did not seem worried.

Parker's charge to the jury for once was brief. "Gentlemen of the jury, in deciding the guilt or innocence of this man you are not to consider that he has been a deputy marshal. The charge is murder — the unnecessary taking of a human being's life, and I — I do not know what to say to you." He had almost broken. "Search your consciences. Do not bring in a verdict of not guilty because he has been a deputy marshal or because he has been close to the court, for the court is not a man but an instrument of law. In this respect you will give equal weight to the testimony of the Kiamichi Kid, and judge his honesty for yourself. The fact that he has been an outlaw does not mean that his testimony is discredited. If you believe in fact that Brett Malone did shoot John Duck without absolute necessity, then you must bring in a verdict of guilty."

He paused, then got control of himself and held his head up straight. He motioned to the bailiff.

The jury was out three and a half hours, and when they filed in there were traces of tears on some of the weathered faces. The foreman handed the verdict to Glen Holbrook, who was bald now and more roly-poly than ever, and he read it in his deep voice:

"We the jury find the defendant Brett Malone guilty of murder."

Parker raised his head slightly. He took a breath and turned to the jury: "Is this your verdict?"

Twelve heads nodded, most of them slowly.

Parker turned to Malone. "You will appear here one week from today for sentencing."

Brett's eyes were a little narrow, but he did not answer. He followed Jacob Yoes back to the jail.

Parker moved the next week in a vacuum.

His only real contact with those around him was through *The Western Independent*, which said:

"There is much speculation in Fort Smith as to the sentence Brett Malone will get. In view of his long and distinguished service, and considering the fact that the only testimony against him is the word of a convicted murderer, many persons are saying Judge Parker will give him a suspended sentence or a very light sentence, and rightly so. In Judge Parker's own words, a man like Brett Malone is worth a hundred like the Kiamichi Kid or John Duck. But others are pointing out Judge Parker's zealous attitude toward the punishment of murderers, and his fear of being called partial, and predicting that he will give Malone the usual sentence.

"There are those who point out that Parker's reign as a judge is waning, that he is losing his grip. His charge to the jury is cited as an example of this, for in that charge he reversed himself in respect to his usual stand regarding outlaws. What is behind this?

"Some think that Parker, believing that Malone will not fight him, will lean over backward to prove to the Indian Territory that he still does not condone murder. In spite of the unquestioned great value of Brett Malone to this country in the last twenty years, they believe Parker, in one last attempt to show that he has not softened, will maintain severity in the one case where he would be forgiven for relaxing it. It is hard to estimate the extent of an old man's frustration.

"There is another potent fact that no one has mentioned: *there are at present eleven men, including the Kiamichi Kid, awaiting the hangman's rope. Brett Malone would make the twelfth!* And it is no secret that Parker's ambition for twenty years has been to test the great gallows of Fort Smith to its full capacity."

Parker, of course, paid no attention to such scurrilous speculation. He would not be influenced by any such factor as that. However, he was still judge of the Western District of Arkansas, and it was in that capacity that he would have to sentence Brett Malone — not as an individual who had considered himself a father to Malone for those many years. It was, he saw, an unusual opportunity to prove to the doubters and skeptics, to men like J. Warren Reed who had no respect for right and justice, that the conduct of his court had always been based on the law and the Word. Surely none —

not even J. Warren Reed — could argue prejudice when they heard him sentence Brett Malone the same as all the rest.

Again he was awake all night, reading the Bible. Again he was haggard in the morning. He was heavier, much heavier, and now his beard was pure white and covered his chest. He was getting old — but not soft. Sentiment would have no part in his handling of Brett Malone.

At eight o'clock the bailiff knocked on the door of his chambers.

"Court is ready, your honor."

Slowly Parker put on his robe. He clutched his big Bible under one arm and walked into the courtroom and took his place behind the big desk.

The spectators sat down. Parker glanced at the papers on the desk, and finally looked up at Brett Malone, who was standing, without handcuffs, beside Jacob Yoes. It occurred to Parker that Clayton, now in private practice, had put up a very weak defense for Malone, but then it was difficult to do anything else. Malone was guilty; that had been quite apparent.

The courtroom was very still. Parker said, "The defendant will come forward for sentencing."

Brett moved forward, and, for the first

time, thought Parker, he looked uncertain. Well, it was time he realized that Parker had not been fooling when he had warned Brett against hasty killing.

Parker stood up and cleared his throat. He heard a sob, and saw Ann Garth sitting in the front row with a wet handkerchief to her face. Beside her was Mary, and he stared for a moment. Mary, who was older and a little heavier but still strong and graceful, was sitting in his court for the first time; Mary who was still wearing her out-of-date dress; Mary who always took cake and flowers to the men to be hanged. On the other side of the aisle was Indian Rose, who seemed not to have aged, but whose black eyes were fixed on Parker as if she would will him to say what she wanted.

He cleared his throat again. "Brett Malone —"

He looked at Brett. Brett, without his hat, seemed somehow naked. He still wore the same old blue cotton shirt, the sleeves were ragged at the elbows. He was tall and broad-shouldered and still lean of body, and he still wore moccasins, with the pants' legs in strings above them. Actually, thought Parker, he didn't look different from years before, when he had been sixteen, going on seventeen, and filling a man's job.

"Brett Malone," he began, "an impartial jury of your peers has found you guilty of murder, and it now becomes my unpleasant duty to pass sentence upon you for your crime. Let it always be said, and never forgotten, that no prejudice enters into this court. No sentiment, either for or against any man, shall avail against the principles and concepts of almighty justice. And no man, regardless of his closeness to the man who rules this court, shall have any claim upon this court's leniency when he stands before the bar of justice convicted of the heinous crime of murder!"

Ann began to sob, and Mary tried to comfort her. Indian Rose had a hard look such as Parker had not seen before. Colonel Boudinot stared as if he did not believe his ears. Marshal Yoes was staring at the floor, shaking his head either in disbelief or in hope that the inevitable would not occur.

The courtroom was still very silent. Parker looked at Malone and saw that he was white in the face.

"It is not for us," said Parker without emotion, "to look back and say that this is what we should have done, that we should not have pulled the trigger when we did. It is not for this court to give an opinion upon the moral aspects of the crime of murder.

This court upholds the law and the holy Word of God, and that is the only thing we are concerned with here today.

"It is thus that the harshest of all duties sometimes falls upon us — that of pronouncing just and deserved retribution upon someone whom we love very deeply. In such a case, all personal feelings must be thrown aside, all sentiment must be thoroughly banished. In such a case, the only prevailing influence must be the provisions of the law for the suppression of crime. Punishment of a criminal must be swift and certain. There is no other deterrent."

He looked down and saw incredulity and disbelief in Malone's face, and he was moved to a moment of softness. "Brett Malone, have you anything to say before I pass sentence upon you?"

Brett shook his head slightly as if trying to dispel a bad dream. He moistened his lips, then swallowed audibly. His eyes were fastened all the time on Parker's, and finally he shook his head, very slowly, and seemed to gather himself for a blow.

Parker said judiciously, "If the Lord in His great wisdom shall see fit to save you from the results of your crime, then this court will never question that action. But this court is mortal and as such is bound by mortal laws. Brett Malone!" Parker's voice rang out over the courtroom. "For the crime of murder, I sentence you to be hanged by the neck until you are *dead,* DEAD, *DEAD!*"

He stood with his head back, his eyes unseeing. For a moment the courtroom made no sound. Then Ann's sobbing burst out in a torrent. The courtroom, aside from her voice, was silent. Nobody moved. Brett stood where he was, his face reflecting his complete disbelief. Perhaps, Parker noted, that was what all condemned murderers thought.

Parker sat down and began to sign the papers. Jacob Yoes, with his eyes on the floor and his hand on Malone's arm, pulled him back and guided him away. They left through the big door and went toward the jail.

Parker went back to his chambers and took off his robe and hung it up. He put on his threadbare coat and his shabby hat and went to the drug store for a soda.

Gil Weaver came up the street with a copy of his paper in his coat pocket. "Your honor," he said jocularly, "you look like you need that drink."

Parker stared at him. Weaver hadn't been in court for the sentencing. Parker said slowly, heavily, "Yes, Gil, I reckon I do."

Chapter 23

His decision on Alberty was reversed the following week. Parker took it like a blow on the head. He sat in silence for a long time in his chambers, trying in vain to reconcile the higher court's judgment, from a distance of fifteen hundred miles, with his own verdict, formed on the very scene of the trial. He could not. Alberty was guilty, and no fact on earth could change that.

But the court had spoken. There was at the moment nothing he could do about Alberty.

It did upset his plans for the hanging. Alberty's reprieve left eleven to be hanged, and there were no more indictments on the docket. But even eleven would be better than six, providing the Kid should be one of the eleven. It was, he felt, vital that the Kid should be included.

A new deputy, Heck Thomas, who had served under Malone, came to see him at noon one day. "Malone wants to talk to you," he said.

"I have nothing to say to him," said Parker.

"Your honor, he requests you to see him.

He is not going to ask your lenience. He wants to talk to you for a minute."

Parker drew a deep breath. "Very well, I'll see him in jail — not up here. No special favors!"

"Yes, your honor."

They had a new jail by this time, but it was designed for eighty prisoners and already held two hundred and fifty, so that sanitary conditions were no better than before. The stench of filth and decay was a physical thing that made Parker recoil when he walked into it. He followed Thomas to Murderers' Row. Malone was on his feet, waiting.

"I hope," said Parker, "this is not going to be a plea for mercy. I would hardly expect that of you, Brett."

Brett said slowly, "I've learned a lot of things the last few weeks, Mr. Parker. A man might be excused for begging for his life — but that isn't why I wanted to see you." He took hold of the bars, and Parker noted how pale the backs of his hands were becoming. "I know why you did what you did, Mr. Parker. It was a thing you had to do because you're judge, and you wouldn't have been honest with yourself if you hadn't done it. I don't hold that against you, Mr. Parker, and I wanted to tell you not to feel bad because you had to do it, because I understand."

Parker stared at him. He had hardly expected anything like this.

"What I wanted to tell you, Mr. Parker — I hope you won't hold it against me. I know how you feel about Mr. Reed, and I'm sorry to do this to you, Mr. Parker."

Parker frowned. "What are you trying to tell me?"

Brett looked into his eyes. "I've hired Mr. Reed to appeal my case, sir."

Parker was stunned. "Not — not J. Warren Reed?"

"Yes, sir."

Parker was speechless for a moment. "I loathe the man!" he exclaimed.

"Yes, sir, I know. That's why I wanted to tell you myself."

"I don't see how you could do this to me, Brett. You know how Reed has ruined my court."

"Yes, sir, I know, but my life is at stake, Mr. Parker."

Parker left, shaking his big head. Reed! Reed again. The arch foe of justice in the Territory, the man who had done more than all others combined to destroy the edifice of justice that Parker had spent twenty years in building.

He adjourned court for the afternoon, pleading illness, and went home early, but there was small comfort at home. Mary refused to talk to him. She got a bottle of wine and retired to the bedroom and closed the door.

He went down to the Garth freight office to see Ann, thinking vaguely that she might be able to show Brett the wrongness of hiring a man like Reed, but she was home, Rio Grande said, with a headache.

There was, it seemed, no place to go, and he returned to his chambers, sitting there, slumped down in his big chair, staring at the floor.

He was still there when someone knocked. He called, "Come in!" and when the door opened he realized it was dark. "I'll light the lamp," he said, fumbling for a match.

"You don't need to," said the husky voice of Indian Rose. "I'd rather not look at you while I'm saying what I have to say."

"Are you speaking to me as a judge?"

"Any damn way you want it," she told him. "And afterwards you can do whatever you please about it. I don't care. I know what would fix you, but you're too old and too holy to take it. Otherwise I'd offer it to you. I'd let you sleep with me every night for ten years," she cried, "if you'd let that boy go!"

"Your offer is rejected," he said coldly.

"It wasn't an offer — because you aren't human. You're a fanatic, a Bible-crazy fool! You sentenced Brett to death for killing a man like John Duck who wasn't fit to wipe Brett Malone's moccasins."

"Your brother," Parker reminded her, "is in the same category."

"My brother!" she scoffed. "The Kid is worth just exactly the same as John Duck. He's no good to himself, no good to the world. If he hangs, the world is better off."

"You told me once you'd always defend him."

"So I will. He's my brother. Of course I'll defend him. Do you think I like running a whorehouse? Why else would I live down there on the Row and go through what I have to go through if it wasn't for my brother? Brett Malone isn't my brother at all, and he's worth a million of the Kid. And you sentenced him to die! You with your big, fancy words, and your white beard, and your hypocritical mouthings — you sentenced Brett Malone to die! And Brett Malone is the salt of the earth!"

"It is a duty of any judge —" Parker began pompously.

"God in heaven, what a monster you are!" she cried. "Every bastard baby I've ever smashed in the head with my fist the moment he was born was worth more than a thousand like you!"

She left sobbing, and he sat there in the dark for a long time. Then he went home. Mary was in the parlor, undeniably drunk.

"Eighty-eight men you've sent to their deaths on that horrible gallows. You are guilty of murder eighty-eight times!"

"I didn't hang them," he said righteously. "The law hanged them."

"You *hypocrite!* How can you walk down the street and smile at people and act pleasant when you know you have sentenced to death the boy who served you twenty years, who is practically your own son, who is a better man than your own son will ever be. How can you sit in church on a Sunday morning and sing hymns when you know in your heart you are as guilty of murder as any man who ever walked out on the gallows with a rope around his neck?"

He doubled the guard. He gave orders to watch the Kid every minute of the day and night. He knew that Brett would not try to escape, but he knew equally well that the Kid would. Two commutations came through, then a pardon, and three more commutations. There were only five condemned men left, and Parker hardened whatever weakness was in him.

The newspapers carried a story that Reuben Ashcroft, shot in an attempted bank holdup in Kansas, confessed on his death-bed that he had planned the train robbery that he and Texas Jack had tried to lay onto Matthew Allen.

"There's a case," said McDonough, "where maybe it's a good thing the Supreme Court did step in. Allen was innocent. Ashcroft says it was Texas Jack's idea to testify against him so that Texas Jack himself would be cleared." McDonough looked thoughtful. "It might be, your honor, that the Kiamichi Kid figured the same way about Brett Malone."

Parker said decisively, "I will not be moved by morbid sentiment. I have administered justice without fear or favor and I shall continue to do so. Brett must die." He looked at the floor. "I am sure," he said plaintively, "that no judge has ever had as much pressure as I have had over Brett Malone — but I am unmoved. My faith is in the Bible. I will not be swayed."

He announced the date of execution. There were only two condemned men left:

the Kid and Malone, and Parker was grimly determined that both of them would die.

In May, 1896, came the terrible headline: "Fort Smith Court Abolished. Congress Divides Jurisdiction. Judge Parker's 21-Year Rule Is Ended. The Great Gallows Will Be Silent. Blood Stains of 88 Men."

Again he sat a long time, trying to absorb this final blow. Was this a reprieve for the two condemned men? Then he reread the story, and found that the court was to be abolished as of Sept. 1, 1896. There would be time.

He sat again in the dark that night, his body unmoving, his brain reeling. Twenty-one years of service to law and order. Twenty-one years of his life, and now it was jerked from under him. The politicians, the attorney general who never had tried a case in his life, the President who acted from morbid sentimentality, the Supreme Court whose members conspired against him to negate the long and difficult work he had done — all these had finally prevailed.

In Washington they could not know how hard he had worked to stamp out murder and rape in the Territory; in Washington they did not care.

Two hundred deputies had ridden under Parker; sixty-five of them had been murdered in the line of duty. And now those sixty-five noble lives were tossed into the discard.

He was bitter when he went home that night. It was late, and the new arc lights showed him as an old man with a heavy head. He met men he knew coming out of the saloons but did not offer to speak to them, nor they to him.

He was not astonished when Brett Malone got a retrial. He knew the course. The second time was harder to get a conviction than the first, always. But Parker was grimly determined on one thing: his twenty-one years of work would not be wasted. Somebody would hang on July 30. It would be his last execution. . . .

Brett Malone was acquitted on his second trial. Parker could not understand it. The Kiamichi Kid testified against him the same as before, but Brett was acquitted.

Once again the brazen Reed with his always-new silk hat and his flourishing silver-headed cane had triumphed. It never mattered to Reed how he won, Parker thought bitterly. All that interested him was winning. Parker knew now that Reed had come to Fort Smith with the sole purpose of destroying his court.

Even reverses in court seemed not enough. Their well went dry at home, and Parker borrowed money to get a new one drilled.

He set his jaw and went ahead with the execution of the Kiamichi Kid. From his window he watched the preparations of George Maledon the morning of the hanging, but he hardly saw the careful, methodical work of the hangman, he hardly heard the squeak that had remained in one hinge for twenty years. For he knew that, no matter what happened today, he had been beaten. If in the very beginning he could have hanged twelve men at once, he would have whipped crime for good, but now he was beaten. The Kiamichi Kid, it might be said, had beaten him even on the gallows.

McDonough came up behind him and stood for a few moments. "Times have changed," he said quietly. "Things aren't like they used to be."

Parker looked down at the yard around the gallows. Once it would have been filled with spectators, but now, with guards at the gate, it was empty. No longer was the hanging a demonstration of the power of the law but merely a sort of brutal vengeance-taking. Parker turned away, shaking his big head.

McDonough started out.

"Don't go," Parker said. It was only nine o'clock, but he went over to the coat rack and began to put on his old coat and his worn hat.

McDonough looked at him questioningly.

"I'm going home," said Parker tonelessly.

"But, your honor, you've never missed a hanging since you've been here — and the Kid is the one man above all you wanted to see hanged."

Parker looked at him. Parker's lids dropped so as to half-cover his pupils. "I'm going home," he said. "I'm sick."

He went home and went to bed. The doctor said there was something wrong with his liver and that he would have him up in a few days, but Parker lay and stared at the ceiling and shook his head.

His well was finished, and Mary reported to him that the driller said proudly that it was the hardest water in Fort Smith.

Parker answered peevishly that he was interested only in water, not in its hardness. "I cannot see," he said, "why they persist in that childish boast. Here the world of justice and retribution that I have erected is falling about their ears, and they prate childishly of the hardness of the water!"

"Perhaps," Mary said, "it is their way of forgetting for a moment the hard realities of life." She added, "It would be better if you could do the same — not set your neck so hard against the things that are happening, but learn to submit to the inevitable. That's the only way they have learned to live with conditions out here."

But Parker didn't answer. He had sunk into a lethargy.

In September they carried him back to the courtroom wrapped with quilts, and he was placed by the side of the acting judge for the dissolution of his court. As he sat there in pain and looked out over the familiar room where he had presided for so long, he wondered fleetingly if it had been worth it, but he put aside that thought for more worthy ones. J. G. Hammersly, still small and slight but gray-headed now, got to his feet, and Parker remembered how they both had looked, and he glanced down at himself and was somewhat astonished to see how shrunken he was. His frame was still that of a big man but the flesh had wasted from his bones and his skin was wrinkled and parchment-like.

Hammersly gave the call: "Oyes, Oyes, the Honorable District and Circuit Courts for the

Western District of Arkansas, having criminal jurisdiction over the Indian Territory, are now adjourned forever. God bless the United States and these honorable courts."

His eyes sought Parker's for a moment, but Parker was tired and did not respond.

They came by to shake hands:

J. Warren Reed, with his silver-headed cane and a brand new silk hat, who laid aside his condescension long enough to say, "We shall all miss our beloved judge," but never once did he look straight into Parker's eyes.

W. W. H. Clayton, who had been appointed to a minor judgeship. "Your honor," he said, holding Parker's gaunt hand firmly, "it has been a pleasure to serve under you and an honor to appear in your court."

Colonel Boudinot, whose shoulder-length hair was quite gray. "Your honor," he said, "I am one who feels you did a great deal to bring order and justice to the Indian Territory, and I do not think you should feel discouraged. The country has changed, and a new theory of law has come in, but you should not feel that your own efforts have gone unheeded. Indeed, sir, you are one of the foremost Arkansawyers of us all, for you came when it was raw wilderness, and you have stayed until civilization is an accomplished fact."

"Thank you," Parker whispered.

Rudolph Clyman, older and stouter: "I shall never forget, your honor, the first day I appeared in your court, and you gave me a lesson in jurisdiction."

Parker nodded slowly.

There weren't many of them left. Barnes had died. Hickok and McClosky had moved to Muskogee to practice in the new court there. There were two or three new men but Parker didn't know them and didn't try to recall their names.

He went home and back to bed for the last time.

A woman reporter from the *St. Louis Republican* came to interview him. "Do you now believe in capital punishment?" she asked.

"Yes," he said slowly, his eyes closed. "There must be absolute certainty of punishment. It is certainty of punishment that prevents crime."

Mary had gone out of the room. The woman asked, "What about those who send cake and flowers to the condemned men?"

For a moment he felt a flash of the old belligerence, but he conquered it. "They are mistaken women," he said firmly, "moved by maudlin sentimentality. It is a mistake — a great mistake."

"Do you have any explanation as to why your wife did this?"

He closed his eyes. They were trying to pry into the recesses of his mind. But he would never tell what he had long suspected. Mary had done many other things in his favor, and he would not throw a cloud on her loyalty by any implication now. Finally he whispered, "She did not believe in capital punishment."

"You were born and raised a Methodist, Judge Parker. It is said that you guided your career by the teachings of your mother, who was a militant Methodist. Is this true?"

He shifted himself on the pillows. "It is true. I have gone by the Word," he said huskily.

Mary came and helped him with the pillows, and the lady reporter left.

The next few weeks were trying. His mind seemed to wander. His court was gone; Charlie was a disappointment. He would not think about Brett Malone, for Brett after all had not been his own flesh and blood, and Brett had turned on him by hiring J. Warren Reed.

Only one thing remained steady in his upset world: Mary's presence. Mary had opposed him persistently through the years over the one subject on which he could not yield, but she was still at his side and he could see her and feel her capable hands, and the knowledge of her presence was a great comfort. He forgave her in his mind for opposing him in the eyes of the community, because she had not the grasp of legal facts that would enable her to understand the vital importance of his work.

In November he knew he was near the end. Things no longer seemed black and white to him but were clouded with a grayish haze that every day grew thicker and more enveloping. He knew the great structure of logic and stern retribution he had built up over the years was slipping away, but it didn't matter. He tried to read the Bible but his eyes would not focus more than a few minutes, and he laid it aside.

The Methodist minister called, but Parker could not seem to make him understand what it was about the Book that had ruled his life. One evening when the haze was steadily growing thicker he told Mary: "Get Father Smith."

She said as from a distance: "Don't you want the Methodist minister?"

"I am going to die," he answered in a harsh whisper, "and the faith of my fathers has not sustained me. Get Father Smith."

He was vaguely aware that he was reversing himself, but Mary was his only hold on reality and he thought to draw her closer to him.

He confessed, was baptized, joined the Church, and received communion.

That night he had many callers. Some he spoke to; some he heard but did not try to answer for he could not seem to remember who they were. Then after a pause Mary bent low over him and said, "Isaac, can you hear me?"

"Yes."

"Isaac, here's Brett. Brett Malone."

Malone. Brett Malone. He struggled in his mind to remember, but could not. "Hello, Brett." His voice was feeble.

Brett took his thin fingers in a hard grip. "I suppose you heard, Mr. Parker. The Kid confessed on the gallows that he was lying about John Duck."

"No — no, I haven't heard," he said hoarsely.

"I just wanted you to know, Mr. Parker, it's all right. I hold nothing against you."

Parker's eyes closed. "The law is wrong in giving murderers a second chance," he whispered.

"Yes, sir."

Malone, the Kid, John Duck — he remembered none of these. Murderers — yes, he remembered about murderers. " 'I have pursued mine enemies, and overtaken them; neither did I turn again till they were consumed,' " he said.

As from a great distance he heard the man called Malone. "Let him rest, Mrs. Parker."

Who was Mrs. Parker? He tried to remember. " 'I have wounded them that were not able to rise: they are fallen under my feet,' " he said. " 'For thou hast girded me with strength unto the battle: thou hast subdued under me those that rose up against me. Thou hast also given me the necks of mine enemies, that I might destroy them that hate me. Then did I beat them small as the dust before the wind; I did cast them out as the dirt in the streets.' "

He lay back, tired, aware of comings and goings. Presently he looked up and saw McDonough with his tall collar. He remembered McDonough, and for a moment the haze seemed to lift. He saw Hank Fillmore come in on crutches, his feet dangling loose. If any man in Arkansas had reason to know what I had done for the Territory, it was Fillmore. Then he slipped back into the haze, and this time it was thicker and rolled closer and closer until it came over him and engulfed him, and he did not fight. . . .

★ ★ ★

The telegraph man came in. "Wire from Charlie," he said loudly. "Needs money. Must be in another scrape."

Brett took the message, and the telegraph man left, suddenly embarrassed when he realized Parker was dying.

"Water!" Parker whispered.

Mary went to the kitchen for a glass. She came back and helped him up. He slobbered a little, but when she laid him back down he said in a feeble voice: "New well. Hardest water in Arkansas."

The doctor felt his pulse, looked at his watch. It was 2:17 a.m., November 17, 1896. Quietly he rolled the judge's eyelids closed with the ball of his thumb, and Brett, watching, saw tears well in Mary's eyes. He comforted her for a moment, but she didn't break. He went outside with Ann to leave Mary with her grief. He and Ann stood on the porch, each with an arm around the other. The silvery moon was about to set beyond the blackjack across the Arkansas River.

Clayton came outside and said softly to no one in particular: "It's terrible to see what Arkansas did to him — but it was apparent for years what was going to happen." He stood for a moment, then stepped down and walked away on the path.

God is not mocked: for whatsoever a man soweth, that shall he also reap.

Brett began to talk in a low voice. "He was a hard man to understand in some ways. I don't reckon anybody will ever know just what made him do all the things he did. One thing he was determined on, though: to stamp out crime and lawlessness and bring law and order to the Territory." He quoted softly: " 'For he hath strengthened the bars of thy gates; he hath blessed thy children within thee. He maketh peace in thy borders, and filleth thee with the finest of the wheat.' "

Ann wept softly.

Brett said, "Let's not criticize him for the way he did it. He was probably the only man living who could have straightened things out right then." He paused. "Then the country changed but he didn't — and he never understood that. He did the best he knew, Ann. We can be thankful he was the man for the job."

"Whatever you say," Ann whispered, her face against his rough shirt. "I hold nothing against him if you don't, Brett."

His arm tightened. "We have a long life ahead of us. Let's be glad he helped to make the land safe for us and for our children."

Inside, Mary finally burst into great, racking sobs.

A Final Note

The story of the great court at Fort Smith, the only subordinate court of record in the world whose judgments were not subject to review by any court on earth, was not entirely ended with its abolishment by Congress. There were a few interesting developments subsequent to Sept. 1, 1896. But first let us look at some figures.

In twenty-one years Parker tried 13,940 criminal cases, and of this number there were 9,454 convictions. Some 344 of these were capital cases, and of these there were 174 convictions. Parker sentenced 174 to be hanged, and about half of this number actually died on the gallows. Two were pardoned; 43 received commutations of sentence.

From 1891 to 1896, there were 46 appeals. Parker was upheld 16 times, reversed or instructed to retry the defendant 30 times. During those five years the Supreme Court found itself writing decisions on points of law that had never been brought up before and that never would be brought up again, due to the unique jurisdiction of the court.

And lest Parker's judicial work be belittled, it should be recalled that there were many dissenting opinions handed down by the Supreme Court. In one instance — admission of character evidence against a government witness — he established a new principle of law which was upheld. In another, the famous case of Crain vs. U.S., 162 U.S. 625, the Supreme Court reversed him in strong language shortly before his death. Eighteen years later, however, in one of its very rare self-reversals, the Court overruled itself in Garland vs. Washington, 232 U.S. 642. And finally, in Greenleaf on Evidence, Vol. 1, p. 69, note 25, John Henry Wigmore calls Parker "one of the greatest of American trial judges."

In this fictionalized version of Parker's life at Fort Smith I have used facts. Very many of the characters, most of the events, and many of the long quotations presented are taken from the pages of history. Some manipulation of chronology has been used for dramatic purpose, but on the whole this is believed to be a fairly accurate and representative story.

The violence and brutality of those early-day criminals of the Territory is by no means overstated; actually it was widespread and was frequently more vicious and depraved than shown here.

The outlaw who personally caused Judge Parker so much difficulty will, of course, be recognized by historians as Crawford Goldsby, known as Cherokee Bill. Goldsby, however, was born the year after Parker went to Fort Smith and so was not a factor in Parker's life immediately. The man with whom Parker grappled in the courtroom was Mat Music, convicted of rape against a 6-year-old girl whom he infected with a venereal disease; he was convicted but later pardoned. The man blasted out with dynamite was Ned Christie.

George Maledon's later family life was unhappy; he went on the lecture platform with his ropes. Annie Maledon, accused of being more friendly than selective with men, was murdered in 1895 by Frank Carver, whom Maledon, to his great disappointment, did not get an opportunity to hang; Carver got life imprisonment.

J. Warren Reed died alone, unhappy, and broke, something of an alcoholic.

Also, it would seem that Parker, whose word was law in the Indian Territory for so many years, had many disappointments in his personal life — and would have had more if he had lived longer. Charlie Parker married Clayton's daughter but it didn't work; there is a suggestion of interference on the part of Mrs. Parker. Charlie died in 1925, having failed to make the mark his father had envisioned for him. Jimmie Parker committed suicide. Mrs. Parker herself died in 1926, after visiting Fort Smith and finding, to her astonishment, that she was hardly recognized.

The gallows was burned soon after Parker's death by the city of Fort Smith in a burst of civic self-consciousness, and a great tornado destroyed the Parker homestead in 1898.

The three best sources on Parker appear to be *Hell on The Border*, a contemporary account but badly organized and sometimes very difficult to follow; Fred Harvey Harrington's *The Hanging Judge*, a work of scholarship but possibly hampered by too much closeness to the subjects; and *He Hanged Them High*, by Homer Croy, which is well organized, thoroughly documented, and finely written by an understanding and gentle man who makes good use of perspective.

NOEL M. LOOMIS

Descanso, California,
The Land of Tranquillity.